THE MOROCCO AFFAIR

A Ronnie Sen thriller

by

Roy and Peter Misra

Copyright @ Roy and Peter Misra 2024

This book is dedicated to the memory of our parents,

Ron (Chota) and Mandie.

We are grateful to Rachel Misra for help with designing the cover and illustrations, and to Brian Holdsworth for going through the manuscript and providing useful edits and suggestions.

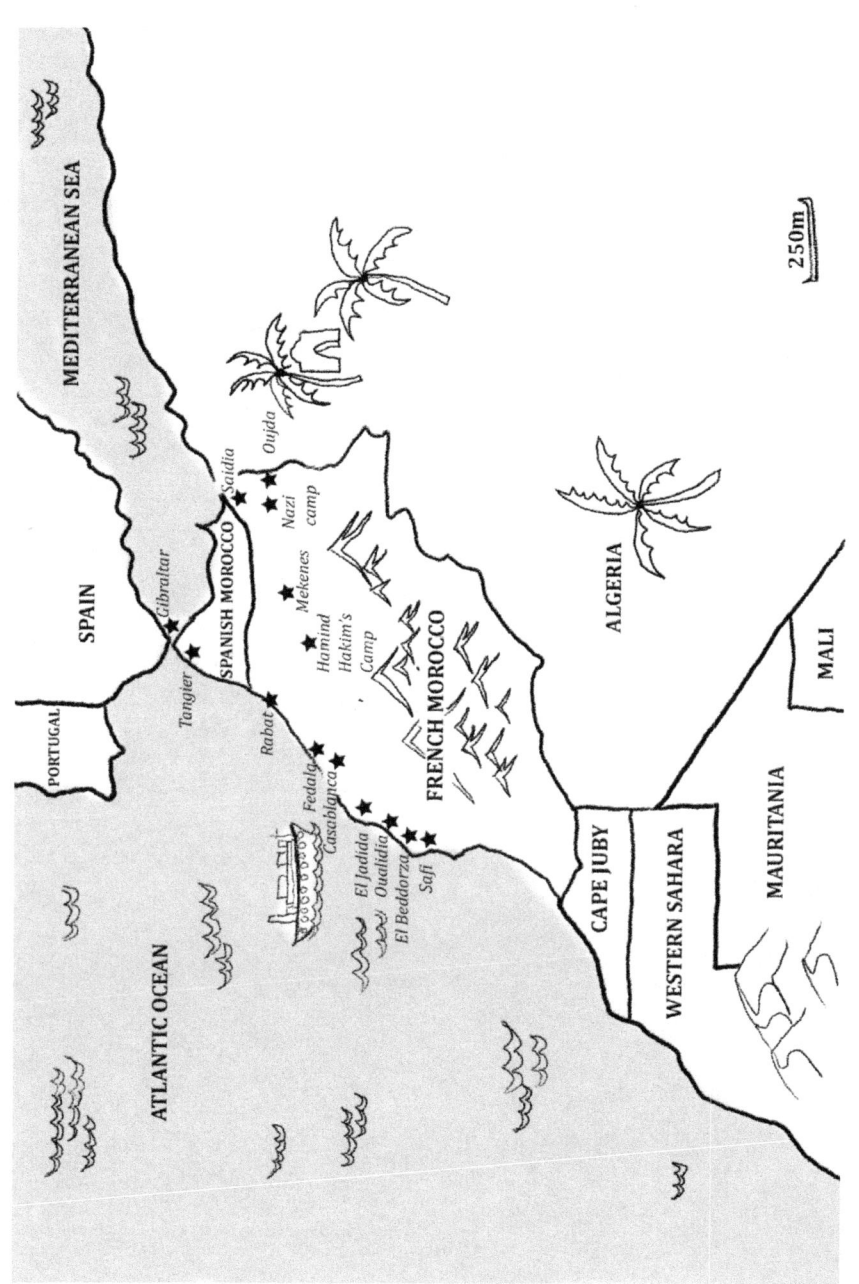

A pebbly inlet west of Fedala Beach, Thursday 13th November 1941

Two shadowy, hooded figures negotiated the elevated section of this tiny shingled curve of beach. It was a pitch black night and in the darkness the rocks could be treacherous and so they often had to feel their way forward on all fours. They knew how easy it would be to fall and twist an ankle!

Maggie, the shorter of the two, sweated freely under the coarse woollen fabric of her Berber gown and its oversize hood kept falling forward over her eyes. To add to her discomfort the sackcloth bag over her shoulder kept slipping forward, further hindering her progress. She stopped to mop sweat off her brow with her sleeve and she could hear Abbas, her rather bulky companion, huffing and puffing as he followed behind her. She pulled the hood of her baggy djellaba cloak off her head, adjusted her shoulder bag and lifted the cloak up above her knees before resuming her cautious way upwards.

From Fedala town, over in the next bay, she heard the call to prayer. "Allaaahu Akbar… Allaaahu Akbar…" Maggie knew that this call must be from the Al-Atik Mosque in the town's Kasbah. She checked her small wristwatch, its luminous hands pointed exactly to ten o'clock. Al-Atik's imam must have a pretty accurate watch, she thought.

Abbas had parked the Citroen C4 among a secluded clump of trees a short distance away and Maggie knew that from there Casablanca was only a short drive west along the coastal road. Let's hope we get this over and done with quickly and then we can head back home, Maggie thought to herself.

Maggie would have preferred to have come out here on her own, but she had conceded that if she had been stopped by the police it would have been difficult to explain what a woman was doing driving around on her own at this late hour. So, despite her initial reluctance she had agreed for Abbas to come with her.

They had now reached the highest point of the elevated rocky section and so they stopped and crouched down facing the dark sea. Reaching within a pocket of her baggy djellaba Maggie pulled out a small torch. She looked around in the darkness as if to reassure herself that they were completely alone.

"All clear?" she whispered to Abbas who nodded and replied "Yella," in response.

Maggie aimed her torch out to sea and pressed the button on and off three times. She counted to thirty and then repeated the same action again. In the darkness the light seemed extraordinarily bright. They scanned the dark sea before them. At first she thought that she may have imagined it, but she realised from Abbas's pointing finger that he had spotted it too. Then there it was again, from out at sea came three returning flashes of light. Maggie remembered her instructions and flashed her torch on and off three more times. The light from the sea flashed back again in response.

Now they were scrambling a way back down the rocks on to the pebbly beach and as they descended their feet loosened the smaller rocks in small showers below them. The tide was out and so it took them a minute to walk across the shingley beach to the water's edge where the tops of the small waves shimmered a faint white.

They spotted the small dinghy approaching from the phosphorescence that its oars stirred up every time they struck the water and then a rope was thrown out to them, Abbas tried to catch it but lost his footing on the shingle and dropped the rope. The rope was thrown again, and this time Maggie was prepared and managed to catch it cleanly. Hauling the dinghy in towards the beach was hard work as the shingle kept shifting under their feet. As the dinghy came closer they could see two indistinct figures onboard - one of whom jumped out into the ankle high water. He had a rucksack slung over one shoulder and used the rope as a guide to move in towards them. Once he was safely on the beach Maggie expertly coiled the rope between palm and elbow and then tossed it back into the boat in one fluid motion. The boat's oars splashed in the waves and the dinghy slowly backed away and headed back out to sea. The entire landing must have taken less than a few minutes.

Maggie spoke softly, "Let's get out of here quickly. The Goums sometimes patrol this area."

As the three of them made their way back from the inlet Maggie dug into her shoulder bag and pulled out a coarse coat just like the one she was wearing and offered it to the new arrival. "Here, put this on and pull the hood well over your head. We can talk later." They moved silently away from the sea and up towards the coastal road. The faint lights from Fedala town glowed off to their left and their cloaked and hooded shapes made them look like a small knot of mediaeval monks.

Soon they had reached the clump of trees under which Abbas had parked the Citroen with its high fronted mudguards. "Get in. It's not locked. You sit up front with Abbas," said Maggie as she pulled the djellaba off over her head revealing the incongruously smart cocktail dress which she wore under it. Abbas inserted the key and the engine turned over once but then caught and started. Abbas reached behind the steering wheel for the gear stick, engaged the gears and then released the clutch. The car crept forward, bouncing and swaying across the unlevelled muddy verge and then they were on the tarmacked road.

The new arrival turned in his seat, "Flight Lieutenant Sen, but you can call me Ron."

"I'm Flight Sergeant Maggie Yeomans. First things first, do you have your Moroccan identity papers on you?" asked Maggie.

Ron nodded and tapped his top pocket. "By the way, I presume we can speak freely in front of your local mate?" he asked.

"Yes, I trust him implicitly. Now, in case we are stopped, remember that Abbas here is my driver, and you are his trainee," said Maggie. "I presume you speak French and Arabic?"

"Yes, both fluently, almost like a native."

"Good. This road is not regularly patrolled and so It's very unlikely that we will be stopped on our way to Casablanca, but if we are then it will almost certainly be by the local police or by the Goumiers. Leave all the talking to me and Abbas. The story will be that I am on my way home from an official cocktail party in Rabat."

The Citroen cautiously made its way down the coastal road heading in the direction of the glow from Casablanca's lights.

Some thoughts while in a house in Casablanca, Friday 14th November 1941

The first rays of the strong Moroccan sun combined with the plaintive strains of the adhan, the morning call to prayer woke Ron from a deep sleep. Through the open shutter doors of the French balcony in front of him, he could look over the brown and red patchwork of tiled roofs and then on to the sparkling blue of the Atlantic Ocean beyond. Quite a different scene, he mused, from that dreary day in London that had changed so much in his life. Had it only been a month ago?

It had indeed been a grey and damp wet morning when Flight Lieutenant Ron Sen (Radio Officer 1st class) had arrived at his RAF base in High Wycombe to find a message waiting for him at his desk. It was from RAF High Command:

"Flt Lt Sen, requested to report to Mr. Greaves-Mortimer at his office in London without delay. This matter is to be treated as urgent and highly confidential." The message concluded with an address in Whitehall but did not provide any further detail.

When he informed his senior officer that he had been officially summoned to Whitehall, the officer seemed to already know all about it. So, rather intrigued, Ron gathered his peaked cap, briefcase and Mackintosh and ventured out into the fine autumn drizzle.

A couple of hours later he was ushered into the office of Mr Greaves-Mortimer who appeared to be some sort of a senior civil servant. Greaves-Mortimer had a ruddy complexion, a neatly trimmed beard and a rather portly figure. His pin striped suit and shiny brogues were immaculate.

"Flight Lieutenant Ron Sen reporting, sir," said Ron as he gave a smart salute.

"Excellent, excellent," came the response. "Do take a pew. Cup of cha? You know the muck they call coffee these days is rather dire."

The tea quickly arrived in dainty china cups and the two men settled down. Greaves-Mortimer stirred his tea carefully and then meticulously placed the teaspoon down onto the saucer.

"Tell me Sen, what do you know about Morocco? You know, the country?"

"Hmm.. Well, I know it's located in northwest Africa. Well known for its leather... belts and so forth. Run by a rather mixed bag I seem to recall - mainly the French, perhaps the Spanish in the north and some local rulers too. Not much else comes to mind, I'm afraid."

"That's broadly correct," agreed Greaves-Mortimer. "But the important point is that it's the bloody Vichy French who mainly run things there. You may have heard of that bunch, they are just puppets for the Nazis who pull the strings. You may not be aware but there is a large Jewish population over there in Morocco and so it's pretty ominous for them and they are getting increasingly oppressed. No telling what it may lead to... in fact, it's no secret that Churchill and Roosevelt have been mulling over the option for us to get involved over there. By the way, I hardly need to remind you that our conversation is strictly confidential. Official Secrets Act and all that..."

"Of course, sir. But regarding allied involvement in Morocco, with due respect, haven't we got enough on our plates fighting the Boche in the skies?"

"Ah Sen, you seem to forget that we are already heavily engaged in North Africa. Our Eighth army has had some considerable success in pushing west from Egypt into Libya but now the German Afrika Corps under Rommel are pushing back hard. A pincer movement from a western flank could be invaluable. But we are getting well ahead of ourselves. Let me tell you why you are here."

Greaves-Mortimer went on to explain that he was part of the Special Operations Executive (SOE) responsible for covert missions in enemy territory. He told Sen that the top brass in the war office needed more information about what was really going on in Morocco and had asked the SOE to send in operatives to reconnoitre the territory before any allied troop action was decided upon. They needed information on the strength of the Vichy French army, their armaments, combat skills, and most importantly their morale and stomach for battle. Greaves-Mortimer went on to explain that there was also an urgent need to somehow contact Sultan Mohammed V of Morocco - the Sultan was known to be sympathetic to the plight of the Moroccan Jews and the Sultan was a constant thorn in the side of the Vichy French and the Germans. It was hoped that perhaps the Sultan could be persuaded to support an allied invasion of Morocco.

"That's all very interesting to know, sir," responded Ron politely. He was slowly beginning to realise why he had been summoned over.

"Yes, Sen... and we know quite a bit about you too! Let me see....", Greaves-Mortimer picked up a slim file from a table by his side and scanned its contents. "Came over from India in 1938, joined the RAF volunteer reserve in 1939, quick promotion to officer ranks, qualified 1st class at the Marconi College of Telecommunications, fluent in English, Hindi, Bengali.... and most importantly Arabic and French!" Greaves-Mortimer paused, "So, to get to the point, how do you fancy the job, young man? You would be helping the war effort enormously and you're guaranteed an adventurous time in the bargain!"

"Well, this is all very sudden, sir," replied Ron. "Though I must admit I was getting a bit restless being desk bound at present..."

"Excellent!" said Greaves-Mortimer, "I thought you would be the right man for the job the moment you walked in! But tell me, how and why you ever managed to learn French and Arabic?"

"Well, sir, in India I went to a school to which all the diplomats sent their children. My two best school friends were from France and Egypt. I seemed to have a good ear for languages and so picked French and Arabic up quite easily," Ron explained.

"Your school sounds a bit like the Tower of Babel!" said Greaves-Mortimer while chuckling at his own joke. "Splendid... that's settled then!" he boomed, rising and pumping Ron's hand. "With the lingos and your dark skin, you'll blend in like a local. You see, there are actually some advantages of being brown and speaking native! Eh?"

Ron bristled internally at this backhanded compliment but said nothing. Greaves-Mortimer must have sensed this because he quickly added, "And you've also got skills in telecoms and a high IQ. Perfect! So, let's get the paperwork sorted and out and then we'll need to get you ready for what lies ahead." And with that Ron was ushered out of Greaves-Mortimer's office.

Later that afternoon as he crossed the Thames over Westminster bridge, he wondered about just what he had let himself in for. Despite some apprehension he felt a rising sense of excitement at the prospect of travelling to yet another new continent. He had already made the leap from Asia to Europe and now Africa beckoned!

The next day Ron was picked up and driven to an army facility in Salisbury where he had been told to report to a certain Major Bob Grimm. The Major was a tall, slim man with a firm handshake. His steely blue eyes, unsmiling mouth and a business-like demeanour seemed to indicate that he didn't suffer fools gladly.

"Right, Sen! All I know is that we need to get you ship-shape and do it fast. I'm not interested in why. But I can tell you that this is not going to be like the run-of-the-mill training you've had so far in the RAF."

Over the next few weeks Ron was put into a gruelling physical programme. There were long sessions in the gym building up muscle strength and stamina, personal instructions in hand-to-hand combat using Judo and Karate techniques and ten mile runs through the countryside wearing a heavy backpack.

Then there was intensive weapons training. Target practice in simulated battle conditions using a handgun and a rifle with a particular focus on using rifles with telescopic lenses at nighttime. There was also training in explosives and learning how to set timed fuses. Ron was taught how to kill... silently and swiftly, with a knife or just with his bare hands.

Finally he had been driven blind-folded and dropped off in the middle of Salisbury plain with just a knife and a box of matches. His instructions were that he was forbidden to speak or interact with anyone and get back to base under his own steam. Three days later Ron made it back, wet, tired and hungry. He had trekked for over a 100 miles, drunk water from streams, foraged for berries and any other edible vegetation. He had stolen a couple of eggs from under a hen at a farm, and when the clouds permitted he had navigated by the stars and eventually had found his way back to base.

By the end of all of this Ron was starting to feel that taking on this job had been a big mistake! But his hectic schedule ensured that there was really no time for either regrets nor rumination. And then one afternoon when he was in the mess, eating a hearty portion of Shepherd's Pie, a voice behind him said, "Well done, old chap. Didn't think you would have had the balls to stick out our training - but you did! And got through with flying colours I see. You Indians are made of sterner stuff than I had imagined."

"Just couldn't face going back to my squadron with my tail between my legs!" responded Ron with a grin.

"Ha ha... well said, old chap! That's the spirit!" A rare smile crossed Major Grimm's face. "Now eat up and then come over to my office!"

In his office Grimm opened a slim briefcase made of dark brown leather, "Now, down to business... I have a present for you; some err... 'tools of the trade'."

In neat, fitted compartments Ron saw a long-nosed pistol, a combat knife and a few other items that he could not identify.

"Right, Sen. Here we have a Welrod silenced pistol... a new development, 50 rounds of 19mm parabellum ammo, the latest night vision goggles, commando knife with eight-inch blade in non-reflecting stainless steel, various fake ID papers, some blank which can be filled in as needed, maps of the area and your radio transmission codes written on silk handkerchiefs. You should already be familiar with all these weapons here. Any questions?"

"Quite a collection," said Ron with a grim smile. "And what's that metal capsule on a neck chain?"

Without a smile Major Grimm responded, "Contains your suicide pill. You know, just in case!"

The Major snapped the case shut and handed it over to Ron, "Good luck, Flight Lieutenant. Godspeed. You leave this evening."

Ron nodded his thanks, shook hands and walked out of Major Grimm's office.

A platter of fruit and a bowl of couscous, Friday 14th November 1941

The sound of a cockerel crowing in the distance brought Ron out of his reverie. He stretched and looked out of his window over the rooftops of Casablanca. He remembered that Maggie had told him that she was going to collect him at 9 o'clock. Ron glanced at his wristwatch. It was twenty past eight already. I had better get cracking, he thought.

The shower in the bathroom was just a trickle but it was a relief to wash off some of the salt from his long and clandestine sea journey. He selected a white cotton shirt, comfortable grey trousers and a pair of tennis shoes. After a moment's thought he strapped on his shoulder holster and concealed it under a light linen jacket and then grabbing a straw Panama hat he headed out of the door.

As Ron waited for Maggie at the street corner he was taken aback by Casablanca's bustling multi-ethnic vibe. Local brown skinned Moroccans - Arabs, Berbers and Jews shared the busy streets with white skinned Europeans and black skinned Africans. Ron would soon discover that the majority of the well-heeled Europeans were from France and Spain while the shabbier looking ones were mainly refugees from all over Europe, many Jewish, desperately trying to escape the war and somehow get away to America. To add to the mix, the black skinned Africans from sub-Saharan Africa were here in Casablanca to seek employment and a better life.

Within this international milieu no one cast a second glance at Ron as he watched the world go by and softly sang a tune to himself. His right hand beat a light calypso rhythm on his thigh.

*"In Cuba, each merry maid wakes up with this serenade,
Peanuts! They're nice and hot.
Peanuts! I sell a lot.
If you haven't got bananas, don't be blue.
Peanuts in a little bag are calling you."*

Ever since Ron had been a young lad growing up in Simla, a town in the foothills of the Himalayas, he had been keen on music. He had been gifted with a fine tenor singing voice and had taught himself to play the Spanish guitar. When he was sixteen, he had been spotted by his father busking on the high street with a like-minded school friend. His father, who was a rather staid and respected member of the local community, was not amused and had ordered Ron to "Stop this nonsense immediately!" But this admonition did not deter Ron from learning new songs and at parties and outings he never lost an opportunity to produce his guitar and sing one of the latest songs.

The tooting of the Citroen C4's horn attracted Ron's attention. Maggie pulled up at the curb. "Jump aboard.

Couldn't get the Rolls today, so this will have to do!" she said with a smile.

The Citroen sped off down the street leaving behind a cloud of dust and exhaust smoke.

"How was your room? Sleep OK?" asked Maggie.

"All tickety boo! It does the job. No complaints," responded Ron. "Now, what's the plan for today?" Without waiting for a reply he continued. "I need to make contacts with the local community and make a start on getting some gen."

"Take things slowly. First things come first. To begin with remember that here I'm known as Magdalena… Magdalena Marion, and I'm supposed to be a Swiss national. Being able to speak French fluently lets me play the part. I work part time in a watchmaker's shop. It's owned by an old French Jewish chap called David who you may probably soon meet. He has an inkling that there's more to me than meets the eye, but he is very trustworthy and discrete. But now I first need to introduce you to some key people."

Ron looked over at Maggie and took in her pretty face, pageboy hairdo and full but athletic figure. She wore a lightly patterned floral dress that reached just below her knees, a short-brimmed sun hat and sensible shoes. Her round rimless wire glasses gave her a slightly academic look.

"Je suis entre vos mains, Mademoiselle!"

Maggie manoeuvred the Citroen expertly through the crowded streets of Casablanca weaving past vendors with baskets on their heads, horse drawn carts, food stalls on wheels and strolling camels. Ron had never seen anything like it before! Eventually they pulled up outside a house on a quiet backstreet.

As they alighted the car, Ron glanced furtively up and down the street, but no one appeared to be paying any attention to them. Maggie rapped on the front door with a coded knock.

The door swung open and a burly, tall man in a djellaba robe filled the opening. He had a swarthy complexion, a full beard and sharp eyes that narrowed slightly as he saw Ron.

"Greetings Magda… This is the guest you were expecting?" he asked in a deep baritone.

Maggie nodded and moving quickly into the house, she made the introductions "Good to see you. Yusuf, this is Ron. He arrived just last night from England. Abbas and I picked him up from the beach without incident."

Turning to Ron she added, "Meet Yusuf. He and I work closely together and along with Abbas, the driver who you met yesterday, we make a small tightly knit team."

Ron and Yusuf shook hands and eyed each other warily, assessing each other like boxers before the first-round bell.

Then Yusuf smiled broadly and spread his arms wide. His French was rather old fashioned, "Come, my friend. Where are my manners! Sit down, I beg you. You will take tea? Some fruit?"

Soon they were seated in the living room on low padded couches with cups of mint tea and a platter of fresh fruit in their midst.

Maggie began the conversation.

"Ron, I have known Yusuf for over a year now and we have worked together on quite a few hairy escapades. I trust him with my life. And Yusuf, Ron comes with the full backing of the English SOE. So, though you have just met, you must trust him too."

Ron and Yusuf looked at each other and nodded.

Maggie continued, 'Over the last year or so we have been sending London information back about what's going on here. Also Yusuf, Abbas and I have tried to hinder the Vichy French the best we can. Things like jamming their radio communications, shorting out electric power supplies, sabotaging their vehicles with nails in tyres or sand in the petrol tanks."

"It can be risky," rumbled Yusuf. "And though we have not been caught we have to be very careful in how far we go." He tossed a grape into the air and expertly caught it in his mouth.

After a moment's silence, Ron spoke. "Excellent work I'm sure, especially for such a small team! But I'm sure you must be wondering why I'm here at all. Well the intel, the intelligence back in England suggests that things may be getting progressively worse for the Jews here. In fact it may be getting to the point where the Allies need to take action. I can't say any more on that front. But with your help I need to find out the capabilities of the Vichy French over here. You know… how many combat personnel, vehicles, armament, state of readiness and so forth."

Yusuf tugged at his short beard thoughtfully. "Yes Ron, I think I will be able to assist you in some reconnoitre work. But it will be dangerous I fear."

"And, as you already may know, we have access to radio comms back to Blighty," added Maggie.

Ron nodded and flashed them both a thumbs up sign.

Maggie looked at Ron over the top of her rimless glasses. "But first our instructions were that we should get you to meet the Jewish elders here so that you can hear first hand from them about what's going on in their world."

Yusuf added, "Yes, and so it has already been arranged for you to meet the Jewish elders at the synagogue on the Jewish Sabbath. And now I will start to look into some reconnoitring possibilities."

With that, Maggie and Ron took their leave and headed out into the midday sun.

"Are you working in the shop today, Maggie?" asked Ron.

"I need to go in after siesta time, around four o'clock. I have time for a quick bite of lunch if you fancy it?"

"Best thing you've said all day, I'm famished. A couple of dates and a few grapes don't go very far!" said Ron.

As they drove along, Ron noticed that as the sun had climbed higher in the sky the streets had visibly become much less crowded than earlier. Maggie took them to a little restaurant where the shutters were closed against the hot sun and the interior was relatively cool.

They sat at a quiet table and once they had placed their food order and were sipping more mint tea, Ron leaned forward in his chair.

"What's it been like, being over here in Casablanca? The undercover bit and so on?"

"Quite an eye-opener!" responded Maggie. "A far cry from Blighty, and I don't mean just the distance and the weather. Casa is a real melting pot of a place. Whilst

Morocco is not in the thick of the war, there are quite a few Germans around; mainly troops taking a break from the battles further east in Libya and Egypt. Then you've got the Vichy French who are 'wolves in sheep's clothing'. They are almost completely controlled by the Germans."

Ron nodded while Maggie paused for a sip of tea. She continued, "And finally you will find that the place is awash with refugees from France and the rest of Europe all seeking visas for a safe haven in America, usually via Portugal. So, as you can imagine, the situation here is pretty chaotic - which is good for you. If you keep your head down the gendarme is not likely to stop you or question you."

"Hmm… What a potpourri! But from what I've been told it seems as if the situation could take a turn for the worse at any moment. I can see why the bigwigs think that our mission here is pretty urgent and critical."

Their food arrived, a bowl of couscous with small black olives, lamb chops and a large salad. It was simple but fresh fare and very tasty. They both tucked into the food in a companionable silence.

Later that afternoon, Maggie dropped Ron off at his room in town. The meal and the heat made him realise why an afternoon siesta was so popular in this part of the world.

"When in Rome…" he thought to himself as he stretched out on his bed.

A visit to Beth-El synagogue, Saturday 15th November 1941

"If you have any weapons on you, please place them in this box … you can collect them later," said the old doorman with a toothless smile. He wore a loosely knitted chachiya, the traditional Moroccan skull cap which was worn by nearly all Moroccan men, Muslims and Jews alike. The doorman was seated on a stool just inside the high arched imposing main entrance to Casablanca's Beth-El synagogue. A cup of mint tea was placed on a small table to his right and in his left hand he held a pipe attached to a tall glass shisha which stood by his side.

Ron looked over at Maggie who nodded a fraction. In response Ron rather sheepishly brought out his pistol from its shoulder holster and handed it to the old doorman who overly carefully placed it into an elaborately carved wooden box. With another toothless grin he waved them on into the building.

Ron and Maggie took their seats at the rear of the high-ceilinged chandeliered hall and watched the Torah service that was unfolding before them. The rabbi who chanted the Hebrew liturgy wore a hooded cloak with thin ropes hanging from its top and bottom. He took the Torah scrolls from the 'ark' and displayed them to the congregation before replacing them back in an ancient ceremony which had remained very much unchanged for thousands of years. But Ron and Maggie had not come to the synagogue to witness the ceremonies - they were here today as they had an appointment to meet with the elders of the local Jewish community.

After the service concluded, Ron and Maggie stood up and looked around expectantly. A slim young man approached them, bowed in greeting and addressed them in French.

"Greetings my friends. It is good to see you. We were informed that you would be visiting and are expecting you. I am Benjamin. Please follow me."

Benjamin ushered them out of the main hall and into a secluded inner tiled courtyard. A central marble fountain stood in a low stone enclosure which was set in a star of David pattern. To one side of the tinkling fountain, seated around a round table were five bearded older men. "The elders of our community," whispered Benjamin as they crossed the tiled courtyard.

The elders were all similarly dressed in long waistcoats worn above baggy trousers which were gathered tight below the knee. On their heads they all wore loosely knitted chachiyas.

One of them stood up as they approached.

"I am Avraham and on behalf of my fellow elders I welcome you to Casablanca." He paused and then added with a wry smile, "Though I wish it could have been under more favourable circumstances. But it is heartening to know that Britain is aware of our plight and appears willing to hear our woes and to help us."

Like the French which he had heard spoken on the streets of Casablanca, Avraham's French had a slight sing-song element to it. Ron realised that this must be the typical accent of French spoken in Morocco and so he made a mental note that he must try his best to mimic it when he spoke. He knew how important it would be to try and blend in unnoticed in the coming days.

"Glad to meet you all. May I present Magdalena Marion who some of you may have met in David the watchmaker's shop. Please don't think that I am being rude not to introduce myself other than to say that my name is Ron, I suspect that the less you know about me the better it may be for everyone. But now that I am here I hope I can be of some assistance. Let's crack on, do fill me in on the situation here as you see it."

With Avraham leading the conversation and the others chipping in, they painted a rather gloomy picture.

"Well sir, Ron…, here in Casablanca we have never been a very wealthy community. We mainly live simple lives in our mellahs, which are our humble dwellings in the Jewish quarter. And for as long as I can remember, we have never given the French authorities any trouble. Did you know that when the war broke out some of our young men even signed up to join the army!"

"But…. this new Vichy government does not even afford us the dignity of being allowed to fight," interjected Nathan, another one of the elders. "Nowadays we are only allowed to do unskilled labouring work in the factories or in the fields. Often our strong young men are treated worse than old women!"

Avraham shook his head in dismay and then continued, "Yes, some months ago laws were put in place by the Vichy administration which forbade us from working in our usual often prestigious jobs as doctors, lawyers or teachers."

An elder with the longest beard of them all and clad in a more elaborate traditional long waistcoat closed by a row of gleaming small silver buttons butted in, "In fact all our Jewish brothers and sisters living in the better neighbourhoods have now been ordered to leave their houses and to find accommodation within the mellahs."

"Ezra speaks the truth," said Avraham, nodding in agreement.

Maggie, who had been silent for a while interjected, "And just whilst I've been over here, I've heard that the Vichy Goums have been encouraging anti-semitic propaganda. Pamphlets against the Jews have been found pinned up on the front of Jewish shops, including the watch shop where I work. Things like that."

There was much nodding of heads and mutterings of agreement amongst the elders.

"True, true," said Avraham. Turning to face Ron he added "Sir, sadly I must tell you that even worse things than that have happened here. Only last month, over seven thousand of our people attempted to flee this oppression in the hope of a better life in America or Israel. However, word of their escape plans got out and they failed to succeed. The Gendarmerie somehow obtained a list of all those trying to escape and rounded them up and moved them to far away detention centres or labour camps run by the Vichy regime."

Ron ran a hand through his thick black hair. "All this sounds very painful. Tell me chaps, has anyone stood up to the Vichy? Tried to stop this injustice?"

The chachiya caps nodded vigorously and between them the elders spoke in glowing terms of their Sultan. Mohammed.

"Sultan Mohammad is the only one standing up for us"

"He has refused to enforce two key Vichy laws fully. You know, the one restricting us from certain professions and schools and the other one requiring us to live in mellahs.

Maggie interjected, "Yes. The word on the street is that your Sultan is no pushover."

Avraham nodded in agreement, "Yes indeed, madam. The Sultan is a force to be reckoned with and refuses to be intimidated by the treacherous Vichy French."

"Ah, that is interesting!" interjected Ron. "Right ho, let's put the gloom and doom aside for a moment and see what we may be able to do about it. I know that this might be tricky, but I have been instructed to somehow try and meet or at least make contact with your Sultan. Any ideas?"

Avraham looked questioningly at the others. No one spoke immediately.

Ezra, the elder with the long beard and the gleaming silver buttons then spoke hesitantly, "Well, I heard that next week the Sultan is holding his annual banquet in Rabat to celebrate the anniversary of his Sultanate. I believe that he has also invited some senior representatives of our community to attend… could a way be found for our friend here to be somehow included?"

"An excellent thought, Ezra!" exclaimed Avraham "Why didn't I think of that. And apart from being able to see his highness and meet his officials there will be many of the Vichy officials attending - so it will be an opportunity for our friend to see at first-hand what kind of beasts we are up against!"

Avraham turned to Ron, "Sir, err, Ron, we will move heaven and earth to try and find an invitation for you. But I fear the security will be tight at the palace. We will have to justify your presence and your papers will certainly be checked. Do you have suitable identification… something that would pass such scrutiny?"

Ron thought about Major Grimm and the briefcase full of tricks. He smiled faintly, "Don't worry Avraham, just tell me who I'm supposed to be and I should be able to provide the identification!"

"Excellent," replied Avraham. "If you can provide the appropriate identification we could try and take you along posing as a young community leader. Perhaps there is an invitee from the community who is unable to attend. We will look into it and let you know."

After some more discussion Maggie and Ron bid farewell to the elders and were ushered out of the building. As they left the building Maggie turned to Ron, "Are you not forgetting something?" she asked. Ron raised an inquiring eyebrow. "Your bandook, you know your little bang-bang?"

Ron turned back sheepishly and retrieved his pistol from the dozing doorman. "I would actually suggest that if you plan to blend in then it may be better for you not to carry that thing around - unless you really think that you may need to use it." advised Maggie.

Rather crestfallen Ron nodded in agreement.

Outside the afternoon heat enveloped them like a blanket and the bright sunlight was blinding.

"Fancy a spot of lunch, Maggie?" asked Ron, "And I could do with a cold beer!"

"Yes Sir!" replied Maggie with a teasing smile. "But over here, it's not as easy as walking down to the Dog and Duck for a pint! Never fear though, I think I know just the place."

Ten minutes later, they were seated in a small gloomy bar hidden in the back streets of Casablanca, each with a glass of lukewarm French beer. Their order of a lamb tagine for two was being prepared, and the spicy aroma was making Ron's mouth water.

"Glad we made some progress today, Maggie. You did a super job setting up that contact with the elders."

"Mmm.. Ta," responded Maggie taking a swig of her beer. "Yes, fingers crossed that it leads to something. Anyway, how are you finding the weather… bit of a change from Blighty… but I guess you Indians are used to the heat and the midday sun. First time I've met an Indian in the flesh by the way."

Ron smiled "Yes, I can handle the heat OK. Although Simla, my home town in India, is in the foothills of the Himalayas. Plenty of snow there in the winter. So, I'm the first Indian you've ever met, eh? Well, I hope I haven't let the subcontinent down so far!"

Maggie chuckled, looked Ron up and down, and took in his twinkling eyes, handsome face and strong physique. She nodded approvingly to herself.

A Goumier encampment near Rabat, Monday 17th November 1941

It was about one o'clock in the morning and a waning crescent moon did little to illuminate the bleak landscape some ten miles southwest of Rabat. Rocky outcrops dotted the sandy scrubland and in the weak moonlight the terrain took on the appearance of some remote alien planet. Behind one of the larger piles of rock two figures lay prone on the ground. They wore long black djellabas that blended well into the surrounding gloom and their dark skin helped the camouflage. They were virtually invisible from ten metres away.

There was a glint of reflected moonlight as the larger man lowered a pair of binoculars from his eyes.

"Have a look, Ron," said Yusuf softly as he handed the binoculars over. "The encampment is just five hundred metres ahead and about fifteen degrees to the left. Take a bearing from that brighter star over there," he said pointing forward and upward.

Ron adjusted the focus on the eye-glasses and scanned in the direction Yusuf had indicated. As his eyes grew accustomed to the low light, he could see the outlines of tents and closer to them there were shadows that moved slightly. A couple of pinpoints of light flickered, suggesting embers from campfires.

"Traditionally the Goumiers have always used horses to move around. You should see their herd between us and the tents," added Yusuf in a whisper. Ron nodded realising that the shadowy movements he had seen had been the horses.

Ron and Yusuf had come to reconnoitre this Goumier encampment. They had driven out in Maggie's Citroen as close as they dared and then had continued on foot into the desert scrub. On the way, Yusuf had explained that it was a complex political situation - the Goumiers were subjects of Morocco's sultan but at the same time they were also soldiers of the French Army of Africa which was controlled by the Vichy French who, of course, had sympathies with the Axis forces. Yusuf told Ron that the Goumiers, or Goums as they were commonly known, had a reputation for being fearless and skilled fighters. Many of them were recruited from wild Berber tribes.

Yusuf tapped Ron on the shoulder and signalled with his hand to indicate that they should move forward. Keeping a low profile, the two men padded silently towards the military camp.

"Beware my friend, they will have lookouts with eyes sharper than ours," whispered Yusuf. "We must hope that the guards have eaten well and drunk their fill of mahia."

Approaching closer to the encampment, they took shelter among the low bushes. The camp, which covered an area of many hundred square metres, loomed large ahead of them. They could now hear the herd of horses snuffling and moving slightly. Ron took a Kodak Vigilant folding camera out from beneath his djellaba and took some photos from various angles. He knew the boffins back in England should be able to extract much more info from the images than what he could see in the gloom.

"I need to get round the back to take some more snaps," whispered Ron. Yusuf let out a sharp sigh but nevertheless slowly arose and beckoned Ron to follow him. As they skirted the perimeter of the camp they had to pass by the horses.

Suddenly there was a whinny, a horse raised its head sniffing the air. Yusuf dropped to the ground and pulled Ron down. The men lay still for a few minutes and waited for the horses to settle.

But the horse's restlessness had caused one of the guards to saunter over to check on them. Yusuf's eyes grew wide at this danger.

"If they find us…." he mouthed, drawing a finger across his throat, "They are barbarians."

The guard strolled among the horses patting one here and there. Satisfied that there was nothing amiss, he returned to his post near a small campfire.

After spending five minutes lying flat on the ground, Ron and Yusuf cautiously rose and carefully continued their path around the camp's perimeter.

On reaching the far side of the encampment, row upon row of artillery came into sight. Through his binoculars Ron could see that the field cannon had large wheels and shafts designed to be towed by horses. Then behind the artillery he could see the outlines of at least a hundred light armoured vehicles. Large calibre machine guns atop the desert vehicles were silhouetted against the dark sky.

Ron's lips drew into a mirthless grin. "Bingo. So it's not just horses and swords these days," he said to himself. Drawing out his Kodak Vigilant again, he took several photos of the scene before them. He hoped that in spite of only the dim moonlight the photographic prints would bring out the details of the armaments.

Ron felt a hand on his shoulder. Yusuf whispered urgently, "Come on my friend, it is time we made our way back. We have been lucky thus far, but we should get back home before our eyes are gouged out or our tongues severed by a Berber dagger!"

The men retreated the way they had come and after a couple of hundred metres they reached the herd of horses up to their left. Ron and Yusuf moved with great care, half crouched and with their heads down.

"Neeeeigh!" The sound cut through the night air like a scimitar. The men flattened to the ground, but the horse let out another loud whiny causing some of the other horses to grow agitated as well. The guard at the campfire must have heard the commotion because he grabbed his rifle and strode purposefully towards the horses.

He passed through the horses and stopped at the edge of the encampment, peering into the darkness. He was now no more than half a dozen strides from where the two intruders were hiding.

Ron eased his commando knife out from his waistband and put a cautionary hand on Yusuf's shoulder. The Goum moved a couple of paces forward with his rifle at the ready. Ron knew that if the rifle was fired, it would alert the whole camp and the game would be up for them. Now the man was almost upon their hiding place and if he took more than a couple of paces forward it was clear that they would be discovered.

The guard half turned away from them and Ron, seizing the opportunity, rose out of the desert darkness like a silent shadow. In a couple of silent strides he came up behind the guard and clamped his left hand firmly over the guard's mouth. The knife in his right hand came down and struck twice. The man went down without a sound.

Yusuf meanwhile quickly crept over to the horses and murmuring some deep unintelligible sounds managed to quickly quieten them down.

Between them they dragged the dead guard's body behind a clump of rocks. This time Ron needed no encouragement from Yusuf to beat a careful and quick retreat away from the Goum encampment.

They found their way back to the Citroen without further incident and as Yusuf put the car into gear and pulled away Ron felt a delayed emotional reaction come over him. Not surprising because, after all, it was the first time that he had ever killed a man!

Outside the Dar-al-Makhzen Palace - Rabat, Tuesday 18th November 1941

Today was the anniversary of the coronation of Sultan Mohammed the fifth and the whole of Rabat was abuzz. All day the crowd had inched and jostled around the city's market squares and wound its way through covered souks on millipede legs. Harassed mothers had been simultaneously tugged in different directions by competing children - one towards the piles of meskouta orange cakes which were heaped high and another towards trays of honey and almond flavoured sellou. Meanwhile yet another energetic little boy had pulled in the direction of the fire eating magician with a monkey perched on his shoulder. It was a day of great celebration!

Then, in the evening, the crowds had gravitated towards the Mechour, a large open space which led up to the entrance of the Dar-el-Makhzen palace with its imposing high horseshoe-shaped entrance archways, intricately carved and artistically tiled in shades of blue. Once gathered in the Mechour, the crowd witnessed the royal procession. First came ranks of marching crimson capped palace guards decked out in long white muslin gowns belted tight across their waists and then following behind came lines of horse cavalry holding aloft long spears topped by fluttering pendants. The crowd enjoying the spectacle cheered and waved, but the loudest cheers went up when the Sultan made his grand entrance. Sultan Mohammed rode in on horseback. He was seated on a black stallion with a broad deep maroon umbrella canopy held above him. He wore a pure white and heavily embroidered gown and the fabric wrapped around his head and face left only his features exposed. Cheers and ululations filled the Mechour.

In the midst of this celebration Abbas, with much tooting of his horn, had managed to manoeuvre the Citroen through Rabat's busy streets and had dropped Ron off at a simple house in the mellah which was located within backstreets just behind the palace. Ron, wearing a nondescript white hooded djellaba and chahiya knocked at the door which was opened by Avraham, the Jewish elder he had previously met at the synagogue in Casablanca.

"Welcome, my friend," said Avraham patting Ron on his shoulder. He ushered Ron into a sparsely furnished room with heavy wooden shutters across its windows. The six other men gathered there did not seem surprised to see Ron. "This is our friend who I spoke to you of," explained Avraham to the others. "He will be taking the place of Ben Jarmon who is unable to attend the banquet." He turned to Ron, "No doubt you have the required identification?"

Ron tapped his upper pocket. "Just as you instructed, with my photograph on it too," he replied.

"Good," said Avraham. "Now in case you thought that we were all going to grandly present ourselves at the palace gate, then please think again. Although we have been officially invited by the Sultan it is very possible that the Vichy soldiers on guard at the main gate would turn us away. So we have planned to get in by another route."

"Tunnel our way in, perhaps?" asked Ron flippantly.

"Not exactly," replied Avraham without a smile. "We will enter through a side service entrance, concealed in the back of a covered cart carrying boxes of fruit. This entrance is guarded only by the Sultan's own palace guards, and they are expecting us to arrive in this way. Once we have entered we cannot be touched by the Vichy police as we will be under the protection of the Sultan and will be his guests."

Ten minutes later a horse-drawn covered cart pulled up and Ron and the six others jumped into the back and sat on the cart's floor surrounded by several wooden boxes filled with grapes and peaches. The cart set off, swaying as its wheels bumped over the cobblestones. Within a few minutes they reached one of the palace's side gates where they were stopped by a Moroccan palace guard with a black hat decorated by a diamond motif. He paused to adjust the strap of the long rifle slung over his shoulder and then carefully inspected their papers and invitations. He shone a torch at each passenger inside and in turn asked each to identify themselves. Then after a few courteous words he waved the cart with its passengers through.

"That was certainly much easier than tunnelling," thought Ron to himself.

The Sultan's banquet - Dar-al-Makhzen Palace, Tuesday 18th November 1941

Ron and the Jewish elders were then led through opulent marbled corridors and into a grand dining hall where long tables had been arranged around the four sides of the room in a rectangular fashion. As the guests arrived they milled about in the empty central space before being politely ushered to their places by one of the many finely liveried palace staff.

The guests were exclusively men. The Berber and Arab tribal elders were dressed in their traditional gowns while the European and American officials, diplomats and businessmen were dressed in tuxedos. Uniformed military officers with chestfuls of gleaming medals and colourful sashes were plentiful. A small delegation of Italian military officers who were even more elaborately uniformed than the rest wore thick black plumes in their hats. Not surprisingly though the majority of the Europeans were Vichy French officials - some in formal evening wear embellished with medals and others in dress uniform with their distinctive round and peaked kepi hats decorated with much brocade.

A couple of heavily bemedalled German Afrika Corp senior officers looked more sunburnt than the rest of the Europeans and Ron was interested to register that they seemed studiously to be avoiding any interaction with the two black clad and jackbooted SS Nazi Officers present.

The palace staff seemed to know exactly where everyone was to be seated and were individually showing the guests to their seats. As each took their place it became apparent that the seating arrangement had been designed such that the Sultan and his royal contingent were to be flanked on either side of the top table by Moroccan tribal and local religious leaders while the foreign guests were to occupy the other three sides of the rectangular seating arrangement.

Ron and the Jewish contingent found themselves seated to one end of the top table and extremely close to where some of the Vichy officials and French army officers had been placed. Ron could tell from the body language and the stern faces of some of the Vichy officials that they were not at all pleased to have been placed so close to the Jewish contingent!

Then a gong sounded and the guests fell silent. A pair of wide doors opened and Sultan Mohammed made his entrance. The Sultan was dressed in a long white satin gown heavily embroidered around the neck and shoulders by shimmering silver thread brocade and on his head wore a scarlet fez. Flanked by a small entourage of senior royals and palace guards he walked up to the top table and before sitting down on his throne-like high-backed chair he made a gesture of greeting to the assembled guests.

Ron examined the Sultan with interest. He was pleasant looking and quite young, early thirties perhaps Ron thought. Slim and of medium stature.

The Sultan then clapped his hands once and the banquet began. Attendants arrived bearing trays overloaded with dishes of all sorts - plates of falafels, tagines of various kinds, zaalouk, fish chermoula and mounds of couscous and flat bread. To drink there were juices of various kinds - pomegranate, apple, peach and more.

Avraham, seated to Ron's right, whispered quietly in Ron's ear, "The old man with the clipped moustache seated down on your left is General Charles Nogue, he is the Resident General, the Commander-in-chief of the Vichy French forces and is in overall charge of the Vichy military government here. He is a consummate politician and an able administrator." Ron nodded. "To Nogue's immediate left is Brigadier Anton Martin," continued Avraham. Ron observed a middle aged, very overweight officer with a red round face and a bushy moustache which curled up at the ends. "Martin is Nogue's fixer. Martin hates us Jews immensely and given any chance he strictly enacts anti-semitic laws whenever he sees an opportunity."

Ron nodded, "Do you know anything about those German officers?" he asked in a whisper.

"I have never seen those Afrika Corp officers before. As far as I am aware there are no Afrika Corp troops permanently stationed in Morocco and from the look of those two, they look as if they may have recently spent time out in the desert. I suspect that they may be stationed in Algeria or Libya and are here only for tonight's event. But I know the SS Officers though. The one closest to us is Major Wilhem Schmidt," Avraham dropped his whisper even lower, "He is truly a beast, notorious for taking delight in tormenting and arresting Jews whenever he gets the chance. With my own eyes I have witnessed him using extreme and unnecessary violence."

Ron cast a sideways glance at Major Schmidt. Schmidt was thin and had receding and thinning wispy blond hair. His rather cadaverous looking face was clean shaven, and he had incongruously blubbery lips which seemed to be perpetually set in a downward arc. Ron noticed how the silver death head and the metallic twin lightning bolts on Schmidt's jacket lapels caught the light from the overhead chandeliers.

Schmidt probably sensed that they had been talking about him because looking fixedly in their direction he casually drew a finger across his throat. "Charming!" whispered Ron, "He certainly looks like a monster! What about those Italians?"

"Err.. ah," said Avraham trying to regain his composure. He had been obviously flustered by Schmidt's unexpected gesture. "The man with the biggest plume in his hat is Captain Andretti. He is the Italian military attache. Whenever I have seen him he appears to be quite drunk, and he has a reputation of being a serious womaniser."

As if to confirm Avraham's observation that the Italian drank too much, Ron noticed that Captain Andretti was gesticulating over-vigorously and speaking inappropriately loudly to another Italian officer who sat by his side.

Then the gong sounded and the room fell silent. The Sultan got to his feet and began to address the gathering in a rather high-pitched voice. He began by speaking in Arabic and welcoming the assembled Moroccan Berbers and Arab tribal elders.

He then turned towards the Jewish contingent seated to his left and switched to speak in French. "I also welcome the Jewish members of our community. As you know I do not see my citizens as Muslim or Jewish and as I have said in the past, regardless of their religion all my citizens are equally Moroccan."

It was pretty obvious to everyone present that the Sultan had switched to French so that his remark relating to the Jews would be understood by all in attendance. The effect, especially on SS Major Schmidt and the Vichy Brigadier Martin, was immediately obvious. Martin went even redder in the face and looked as if he might explode while Schmidts lips curled even lower than before, and his eyes narrowed into slits.

There was some nervous shuffling and muttering among the various army officers and they looked towards General Nogue for a cue. But the old General's face was deadpan, and the uneasy shuffling subsided.

Ignoring the obvious disquiet that his words had caused, the Sultan then went on to welcome the French officials and then the other foreign delegations present. He spoke at some length about his kingdom and about his plans for the future before sitting down to a smattering of polite applause.

General Nogue then got to his feet and spoke briefly congratulating the Sultan on the anniversary of his enthronement and then raised his glass of pomegranate juice in a toast to the Sultan's health and long life.

The banquet then proceeded without incident until finally the sweetmeats were brought out and mint tea was served.

Once dinner was over the sultan and Royal contingent rose and moved to line up by the main door and the guests slowly filed out stopping to shake hands and congratulate the Sultan. It was obvious that some of the congratulations appeared less effusive than others.

Once the foreign guests had all filed out it was the turn of the tribal and religious elders. Here the greetings were warmer, there were kisses to the cheeks rather than handshakes and more words were exchanged.

Finally, it was the turn of the Jewish group to be presented and last of all Ron stepped forward. As he approached Ron noticed that one of the Sultan's officials leant over and murmured something into the Sultan's ear. Avraham introduced Ron to the Sultan, "May I present to you, Ben Jarmon from Casablanca."

The Sultan raised a quizzical eyebrow and a half a smile played on his lips. "Yes, I was told by a little bird that you, Ben Jarmon, would be visiting. Tell me, Ben Jarmon, do you know much about birds?"

Ron, taken aback by this line of conversation, stammered something back about indeed liking birds.

"That is good," continued the Sultan. "One of my favourite birds is the Peacock. It is dazzling in colour and flies freely in the forest but also walks in beautiful gardens."

Ron was completely taken aback at this reference to the Peacock.

"Yes, your Majesty," replied a confused Ron, pulling himself together and attempting to respond coherently, "The peacock is truly a remarkable and beautiful bird."

The Sultan nodded and his gaze now turned to the next guest in the line and so Ron bowed and left the room along with the rest of the Jewish contingent.

A safe house in the Casablanca Medina, Thursday 20th November 1941

"The Sultan appears to know who I am!" declared Ron. "Last night I worked it out. I suddenly remembered that the Peacock is India's national bird. I am sure that the Sultan was discretely letting me know that he knows who I am and he is even aware of my Indian heritage! But how can he know? And if he knows that, then who else knows about me?"

Yusuf nodded. "I believe that the Sultan has many links with the Jewish community and his network of informers is vast. I am not at all surprised that he would have been informed both of your arrival in Morocco and also that you would be attending the banquet."

"What I'm really concerned about is whether that SS thug, Schmidt, also knows who I am… if he does then that could be curtains for me!"

"I very much doubt it," said Maggie reassuringly, "If Schmidt knew about the activities of any one of us then we would all have been toast by now!"

Ron, Maggie and Yusuf were sitting around a battered kitchen table in a whitewashed house deep within Casablanca's medina. The floor was made of uneven flagstones and the small windows which looked out onto a narrow crooked lane were firmly shuttered making it quite dark within the room. Outside, in the lane, Abbas sat balanced on a small stool strategically placed in the shade. He sipped a cup of coffee while simultaneously passing the beads of his tasselled tasbih rhythmically between his fingers. From where he sat he could see all the way down the narrow lane which was terraced on both sides by whitewashed walls occasionally interrupted by low doors and small windows.

"Let's hope you're right about who knows what, Maggie," said Ron grimly. "Now, you told me that you have some radio comms with our chaps in Blighty."

Yusuf nodded. "Yes. This is why we are here today. Hidden away in this safe house we have a radio and London is expecting a transmission from us today. He paused to smile, "And we will be using Maggie's special delivery system to send your film roll back."

Ron raised an eyebrow in enquiry "You have a courier?"

"Sort of," replied Maggie, "A flying one though - homing pigeons. I managed to smuggle in quite a few when I first arrived here. You should have seen the state of my hat-boxes! The pigeons are now all housed in Yusuf's coops."

"But it's a long, long way from home. Have you tested your system? Have you tried sending any messages home by your pigeon post?" Ron enquired rather sceptically.

Maggie nodded, "Yes, several times. It has taken a couple of days, but nearly always the bird has got back home so far." Ron reached into his pocket and took out a roll of film and handed it to Maggie. "Please tell your flying friend that this is precious cargo. It came at quite a cost." "Alright, I'll use our sturdiest bird," responded Maggie.

Yusuf got up and opened the front door a crack. Outside, Abbas from his vantage place, nodded an all clear. Yusuf moved over to the kitchen fireplace from where he picked up a short iron poker, he walked over to a corner of the room and using the tip of the poker raised a loose flagstone. From the small cavity below he heaved out a small brown leather attache case which he placed onto the kitchen table. He snapped open its catches and displayed the radio snuggly set inside.

"Ah," said Ron, "I guessed that you would have a B2 transceiver radio. Very modern… and it's a beaut. So easy to use. You know, just before the war, when I was a student at the Marconi College, I did some work helping to design this."

Ron put his hand into his pocket and pulled out a silk handkerchief. On it, in small lettering was a whole series of numbers and letters. "It's my own special transmission code," he said by way of explanation. He spent a few minutes using his code sheet to write out his message on a sheet of paper. When he had finished he then turned to the others, "Right ho, I'm ready. Shall we crack on and let the big-wigs at home know what's going on here."

Maggie slung the aerial across the room while Ron powered up the machine and then quickly turned its various knobs and dials. Consulting his coded message sheet and with the radio's headphones placed over his ears his index finger began rapidly tapping out morse signals.

Fifteen minutes later the radio was back in its hiding place.

"Glad that we've got the first set of intel sent off, they now know I have arrived and made contact with you. So the next time we communicate we should be able to speak to them," said Ron rubbing his hands together. "Okay, let's put our heads together and think about what we do next."

Without waiting for an answer, he then added "Actually… since they know who I am, I wonder if there is any mileage in trying to make further contact with the palace? London seemed keen that I keep a finger on that pulse. Perhaps I'll follow up on that through Avraham."

Yusuf who had been scratching his beard thoughtfully spoke slowly, "My friends, there is something else which may be useful. There is this man, who goes by the name of Hamid Hakim. I know him from some past encounters. He is the local chieftain of a desert tribe who hold much sway in this area. A bit of a rogue and quite ruthless but very loyal to his friends as well - I can personally vouch for that. He despises the Germans and the Vichy French as much as we do and I think it may be worth for you to make his acquaintance. He could prove to be most beneficial to our cause."

Ron glanced at Maggie and she nodded imperceptibly.

"Good man, that sounds like a promising lead," Ron responded. "If you can set that up, I'll be happy to meet Hamid."

"That's another iron in the fire," said Ron thoughtfully. "Now Maggie, old girl, I have another idea." Maggie raised an eyebrow at Ron's familiarity of address but still smiled back, "Okay, what does the great man think?"

"Well…," said Ron, "at the Sultan's banquet there was this Italian officer, Captain Andretti. I was told by our Jewish friends that Andretti is very close to the Germans - after all, they are both very much part of the Axis. Now, the captain is known to be very partial to drink but also has the reputation of being a womaniser. This may make him vulnerable to the right approach."

Maggie could see where this was going but kept silent.

Ron continued, "This is where perhaps your female charms could come in, Maggie? Perhaps we could engineer a chance encounter with the captain and see where that leads to? What do you think, Maggie?"

"I suppose I could give it a go," responded Maggie with a slightly dubious expression. "But there's only so far I'm prepared to go for England, war or no war!"

"I believe that the captain you speak of is a regular at Rick's Bar," said Yusuf. "It is well known as a meeting place for the high society crowd. A magnificent mansion with a central courtyard. This may be the best place to find the man."

"Yes, I've been there a couple of times," responded Maggie. "Rather too opulent for my taste but it sounds like a good spot to try and snare a lecher. I'll sound out a girl I know, she works at the shop next to mine and see if she will go there with me," She paused, "But don't expect anything from it!"

Having agreed on these various courses of action they concluded the meeting. Yusuf left on the back of Abbas's motorcycle, his right hand raised in farewell as the motorbike pulled away. Ron and Maggie walked to the Citroen which they had left parked just outside the medina and they drove off slowly into the gathering dusk.

Sultan's private offices - Dar-al-Makhzen Palace, Saturday 22nd November 1941

Sultan Mohammed was discussing the events of his anniversary banquet with his vizier, Karim Halimi.

The Sultan's office was high-ceilinged and its walls were decorated in a geometrical style with mosaics of many different colours. The Sultan sat behind his large desk while his vizier, a tall and elderly man with a ramrod straight back, sat facing him in an armchair.

"And now, your highness, on to the matter of the Indian who the Jewish contingent brought with them to your banquet."

The Sultan brought his fingers together in a pyramid, "You tell me that he is some sort of a British agent."

The vizier nodded, "Yes, that is certain. We had already been slipped that information even before we were approached by the Jewish elders, your highness." He paused in thought for a second before continuing, "But I wonder why the British chose to send this particular man? They could have sent one of their own - a white Englishman. Many Englishmen are fluent in both Arabic and French and can easily be passed off as Europeans from neutral countries. Casablanca is awash with Swiss, Spanish and even Americans - and we know that many of them are actually spies and agents. But instead the British chose to send an Indian. I wonder if there was a reason?"

"I presume that they thought that with his brown skin he could blend in better with my people?" suggested the Sultan.

"Yes, you are very right, your Highness. That is very likely to be the case, but we must also consider if there is also a possibility that he has been sent here in order to make a statement to you? As you are aware in India there is a strong movement for independence and there is a rumour that the Indians have been assured independence should the Allies win the war."

The vizier paused, deep in thought, before he continued, "Also as you know the Americans have also clearly hinted that they would support our wish to break free of colonial rule should the Axis forces be defeated. The British are masters of subtle diplomacy so perhaps this Indian has been specially selected and sent here to make that promise on behalf of the British?"

The Sultan smiled, "Like a carrot before a donkey?"

The Sultan sighed before continuing, "But should the Allies be defeated. What then? My feeling is that we must continue to walk a very narrow path here while always being very careful not to tread on anyone's toes."

"Yes, you are absolutely right, your Highness. But if you are in agreement perhaps I can arrange for this Indian to be monitored closely. Also you may like me to arrange for him to meet one of our freedom fighters and see what he has to say? There would be no traceable connection to the palace of course."

The Sultan thought for a moment and then nodded in agreement, "Come, let us talk as we stretch our legs in the garden."

They rose and walked towards the wide open doors which led out onto a large walled courtyard which was open to the sky. The floor was tiled with white marble and the courtyard's high surrounding walls were decorated with fine mosaics. Fountains in four corners of the courtyard tinkled faintly and sent small cascades of water into low channels leading into a central rectangular clear pool. All around the pool orange trees grew from massive pots.

They strolled about the courtyard for a few more minutes and the Sultan made some observations about the condition of the blossoming orange trees.

He then pointed to the mosaics on the courtyard walls, "You know, I believe that Zellige tiles just like these ones were also used by India's Mughal emperors to decorate their palaces in Delhi and Agra." The Sultan obviously still had India on his mind as he continued, "No doubt you will also ensure that the freedom fighter you arrange for the

Indian to meet will immediately report everything back to us."

"Of course, your Highness."

Cocktails at Rick's Bar - Casablanca, Monday 24th November 1941

Maggie and her friend Dagma walked up to the elaborately carved wooden doors of Rick's Bar which was framed by tall, elegant palms. The bar's entrance left you in no doubt that you were about to enter a special venue.

"It will be a special night out," Maggie had assured Dagma while inviting her out the day before, "and it will be my treat."

Dagma, who was rather dowdy and shy, worked in the pharmacy store next door to Maggie's watch shop. She was somewhat in awe of Maggie's confidence and flair and had immediately accepted the invitation with a mixture of enthusiasm and concern.

"I've heard so much about Rick's Bar, but have never been. Oh my gosh, whatever will I wear? I hear that it's where all the posh people go! Will I fit in? Oh my, Magda, how wonderful! Thank you. Is it your birthday? Are we celebrating something?"

"No, just a girl's night out," replied Maggie with a shake of her head. "We work so hard that I feel that we both deserve it!"

Maggie wore a fitted dark blue knee length dress and a matching short-brimmed hat. She had chosen the outfit to match the colour of her eyes and as she entered Rick's Bar it was obvious that more than a few heads turned to size her up. Dagma, dressed in a rather ill-fitting black and white polka dotted frock, only helped to amplify Maggie's good looks, casual elegance and style.

The doorman at the entrance touched his gloved hand to his head in a salam and summoned a waiter to show them in.

"Good evening, Mesdames," said the waiter as he escorted them into a central courtyard and led them to one of the vacant small round tables.

The bar had an elegant and expensive feel. Highly polished black and white floor tiles set in a checkerboard fashion contrasted against the palms in highly polished brass pots dotted about the space. Along one side of the courtyard ran a long polished black marble bar counter behind which barmen dressed in smart white jackets embellished with black bow ties and red fezzes were busily shaking cocktail mixers above their shoulders and pouring drinks. Looking down on the courtyard was a covered gallery decorated with ornate arches.

Once they had settled down Maggie looked around. The courtyard bar area was about half full. The European male clientele mainly wore smart linen suits and ties although there were also a few tuxedos; the European women present were all well turned out in fashionable dresses and hats. There were a few Arab men, also dressed in suits and ties and most of them wore red fezzes on their heads. Maggie was not surprised that there were no Arab women to be seen at all.

Maggie took in the smattering of uniformed army officers, some of whom were standing at the bar counter. From their uniforms she could tell that they were mainly French.

Then seated at a side table she spied a rather red faced and moustached middle aged officer, his stomach straining against the restraining gold buttons of his light blue uniform jacket with cuffs, lapels and shoulders adorned with shiny gold insignia. He was seated with a couple of suited men and on the table in front of him rested a brimmed hat adorned with black plumes. He spoke excessively loudly.

"That has to be him, he fits the description Ron gave me," thought Maggie to herself, "That must be Captain Andretti."

"Oh, Magda," said Dagma, interrupting Maggie's thoughts. "This is so grand!" She looked around nervously, "Are you sure I look OK?"

"You look marvellous," replied Maggie reassuringly, "Now let's order ourselves some cocktails."

The steward responded to Maggie's raised finger and very soon they were both sipping dry Martinis from chilled Martini glasses.

"I must be very careful with this," said Dagma after her first sip. "It tastes awfully strong to me, and I am sure that it will go straight to my head!"

Maggie noticed that their presence had begun to attract some attention. Even in Rick's bar, for two young women to be out on their own was not the norm in Casablanca. Though Maggie studiously made sure not to not look in the direction of the Italian officer she could sense that he was taking some interest in them.

From her handbag Maggie drew out a slim silver cigarette case and offered Dagma a cigarette before extracting one for herself. She fished into her handbag for her lighter and knowing that the Italian's eyes were upon her she made out as if she was having difficulty finding it. A few seconds later she heard a lighter snap behind her.

"May I light your cigarettes, mesdames." Although the voice spoke in French it was very heavily accented with Italian.

Maggie turned her head and looked up at Captain Andretti. "He must have had to move pretty quickly across to get here," thought Maggie to herself. "Oh, thank you. That is very kind," she said aloud.

Andretti lit Maggie's and then Dagma's cigarettes and then bowed his head. "I am Capitano Anderetti and may I say that your presence here this evening has brightened up this dull bar!"

"Capitano Andretti, I think this bar is charming and not at all dull," replied Maggie with a smile.

"May I introduce my friend Dagma Fisher and I am Magdalene Marion," continued Maggie.

"It is a privilege to meet you," replied Andretti reaching for Maggie's outstretched hand. He lifted it up to brush his lips. He then accepted Dagma's hand but without adding a kiss to it. It was clear where Andretti's interest lay.

"Now that we are introduced, may I have the honour of buying you a drink?" asked Andretti, indicating their nearly empty Martini glasses.

"Nuh, very kind but…" stammered a rather flustered Dagma.

Maggie cut in quickly, "That would be very nice of you, Capitano, thank you. Dry Martinis, please."

Andretti headed off to the bar.

"Do you know what you're doing, Magda?" asked Dagma, slightly alarmed. "He seems very creepy to me and slightly drunk."

"Don't worry. We are only accepting a drink, Dagma. He appears perfectly harmless," replied Maggie reassuringly.

Andretti soon returned bearing two Martinis. "Why don't you bring your drink over and join us, Capitano?" asked Maggie.

Dagma shot Maggie a look - a look which Maggie studiously ignored

"Forgive me for being inquisitive, but may I enquire what brings you two beautiful French ladies to Casablanca?" asked Andretti once he was seated.

"Well, we are actually not French", replied Maggie, "My friend is American while I am Swiss and in good Swiss tradition I work in a watchshop."

"Ah," said Andretti, "All Swiss creations are works of art and things of beauty."

"This is going well," thought Maggie to herself, "Ron would be proud of me."

Andretti downed his Negroni and impatiently snapped his fingers for a refill which appeared almost immediately. By now Andretti words were more than just a little bit slurry.

"Tell me ladies, are you fond of Italian art?"

"Who is not?" replied Maggie.

"Well then," said Andretti, "May I invite you to visit my offices in the Italian Consulate where I am the military attache. We have a Caravaggio and a Bernini. They are exquisite." He only just about managed to get his tongue around the word "exquisite" on the second attempt.

An hour later, as they left the bar and walked back to where Maggie had parked, Dagma was obviously annoyed.

"Magda, you really did not need to lead on that drunk Italian. It was not at all like you to flirt with him the way you did. And are you seriously going to visit him at the Italian Consulate?"

"Oh, he is just harmless drunk and it will be a great opportunity to see a Caravaggio up close."

"Well, if you want to see that lecherous drunken Italian again, then I am afraid you will have to find someone else to go with you. Count me out. Caravaggio or no Caravaggio!" declared Dagma angrily.

"Oh, Dagma. Please don't be cross with me," replied Maggie. She smiled, "Do you remember how funny he was when we were leaving and how he bowed and made that elaborate gesture with his hat. His feathers went straight into his drink!"

Unable to stay annoyed with Maggie, Dagma relented and giggled aloud, "Oh, Magda. You're right - he was like a circus clown! But still, do be careful. I'm just worried for you."

An excursion into the desert near Meknes, Thursday 27th November 1941

The motorcycle roared along the desert road that stretched out ahead as far as the eye could see. The driver and his pillion passenger both wore goggles and the head scarves wrapped over their nose and mouth managed to keep out some of the fine sand that swirled freely around them. They passed a few groves of palm trees and isolated small clusters of stone dwellings. Behind them the sun, now a fiery red ball, sunk lower in the western sky as dusk approached.

"I hope you know the way well. This does not seem like a good place in which to get lost," shouted Ron from the pillion seat.

"Have no fear, Ron." Yusuf shouted back. "I know this area like the back of my hand. We should arrive at our destination soon. No more than a few minutes."

The men had left Casablanca an hour ago and were heading eastwards towards Meknes in the interior of the country. As they progressed Ron was beginning to feel rather sore from the bumpy ride along the un-tarmacked road.

A couple of minutes later the note of the engine changed as Yusuf dropped a gear and veered the motorbike off to the left. They left the main road and joined an even rougher and narrower secondary path. Now as the sun dropped below the horizon it rapidly became dark and the motorcycle's headlamp cut a cone of light through the twilight.

After bouncing along for a few more minutes, they rounded a bend and ahead of them saw a tree trunk which lay across the pathway. Yusuf braked and brought the bike to a halt. He cut the engine and glanced around. The sharp sound of a gunshot rang out close by, startling them. Clearly it was a warning shot.

Still astride the bike with his feet planted on the ground, Yusuf raised his arms into the air and called out in Arabic.

"Peace be with you. I am Yusuf Bensaid. We come to meet Hamid Hakim bearing important news."

From either side of the path, out of the deepening shadows emerged two figures wearing jellabas and turbans. They held rifles that were pointed squarely towards the men on the motorcycle.

"Get off the motorbike and uncover your faces. Now!" Ordered one of the guards. Ron and Yusuf swiftly lowered their goggles and unwrapped their headscarves.

One of the guards came over and patted down the two men for weapons while the other kept them covered with his rifle. Ron was relieved that he had heeded Yusuf's advice about not carrying a gun, Yusuf had warned him that it was very likely that they would be searched. After satisfying himself that they were unarmed the guard looked closely at Yusuf and gave a short nod, "Hmmm ... yes, maybe I do recognise you."

With one guard leading and the other bringing up the rear, the group marched off through the scrub land and soon they could see flickering lights a short distance ahead.

They entered a sprawling campsite and Ron could see that there were perhaps forty large tents, each probably capable of accommodating ten men or more. Several campfires burned brightly, some set over with metal tripods from which hung large cooking pots. The central area around which the tents were pitched was relatively well lit by the flaming torches placed on long poles.

They were led to a tent which was larger and better appointed than the rest and one of the guards indicated that Ron and Yusuf should wait while the other guard entered. After a few minutes he emerged and motioned Yusuf and Ron to enter. Inside, Ron's eyes widened as he took in the scene before him - it felt as if he had travelled back a few centuries through time and that he had been transported into the Arabian Nights!

A large man lay reclined against cushions placed upon ornate floor rugs. A curvaceous woman lounged at his side and although she was scantily clad her face was incongruously covered by a veil. The large man had just picked up a grape from a bunch on a platter set in front of him while his left hand casually stroked the woman's bare thigh.

As they entered Hamid Hakim put down his grape and looked up at the visitors with a slightly irritated air. He made a dismissive gesture to the woman beside him, and she silently slipped out of the tent.

"Ah Yusuf, welcome, it is good to see you again. But tell me, what brings you all this way from Casablanca to disturb me on this fine evening? And you bring a companion as well. God grant that you have considered this at length before taking such a liberty."

There were four other men in the tent, two to Hamid's left and two to his right. They eyed Ron and Yusuf suspiciously and Ron noticed that a couple of them had raised themselves off their cushions with their hands hovering over their dagger hilts. The hookah pipes by their sides lay abandoned for the moment. Ron surmised that a few of these men were probably Hamid's inner circle of advisers and that the ones with the hands hovering over daggers were bodyguards.

"A thousand apologies for this intrusion, Hamid," said Yusuf with a slight bow, placing his right hand over his heart. "I took the liberty of bringing my friend here because he has journeyed to our land from across the sea to the North. His country's enemies are our enemies too and he seeks your assistance in his quest to quell these evil forces that conspire against us all."

Ron took his cue from Yusuf and bowed too. He spoke in Arabic. "Monsieur Hamid, I am indeed honoured to meet you. I have travelled here from England and yes, I believe that we have a common interest in our struggle against the Axis powers which occupy your country."

"Be seated and rest after your journey," smiled Hamid waving to the rug in front of him. He seemed to have recovered from the irritation of being interrupted and his natural good humour had returned. Looking right and left at his henchmen he added briskly, "Go now. We will continue our discussion later. And send some refreshment for my guests."

In a short while, the woman that they had seen earlier reappeared with a tray bearing cups of mint tea and a bowl of fruit. As she bent over to place the tray on the ground, Ron was treated to a sight of full breasts that were barely contained by her scanty bodice. She looked briefly into Ron's eyes, her dark almond shaped eyes twinkling in amusement above the veil covering her lower face.

Once they had settled down comfortably against the cushions with cups of tea, Hamid laced his fingers together and looked at the men with a raised enquiring eyebrow.

"Yes, let me explain why we are here, Hamid," began Yusuf. "You are well aware of how the treacherous Vichy French grow more and more powerful, all the while making life miserable for our inhabitants, especially so for the Jewish community."

Hamid gave a brief nod "That is true but, but this is old news."

"Indeed. But of late, these actions have not gone unnoticed by the British. To cut to the nub of the matter, Ron has been sent here from England to learn more about the situation first hand and to report back."

Ron stepped into the conversation, "Monsieur Hamid, you will understand that it is best that I do not reveal too many details but suffice it to say my task here is to understand how the Germans are operating in this area. At the same time I need to evaluate the capabilities and control of the Vichy French. And finally the sentiments of Sultan Mohammed and the allegiances of the Goumier Tabors are also of interest to my superiors."

Hamid sipped his tea and tossed a date into his mouth. He took a while to respond.

"Hmm.. it would appear your masters have burdened you with many difficult tasks. But we may indeed have some similar goals. The question is if your country will actually do anything to help dispel these invaders." He paused to take a noisy sip of his tea, "But first, tell me a little more about yourself. You say you are from Britain, but I see your skin is even darker than mine. How can this be?"

Ron acknowledged this comment with a slight nod.

"As you know the British Empire spreads wide across the world. My homeland is in the mountains of India, which is also a part of the empire. When I reached adulthood my father allowed me to travel and I found myself in England and then soon after that the Germans invaded Europe. So there I was, a young man in a foreign land looking for adventure." He shrugged with a smile.

"OK, my adventurous Indian Englishman, let us assume that we have more in common than just our brown skin," responded Hamid. He seemed to mentally have come to a decision and continued in a business-like tone.

"You may have already noticed that there is some German presence in Casablanca. There they act as if they own the place, monopolising the bars, harassing the Jews and behaving like pigs with the women. I believe the Afrika Korps use this city as a place of respite, to give the war weary troops a break from the battles against the British and Australian forces in North Africa."

"I have seen a few German soldiers and even SS Officers both in Rabat and Casablanca," agreed Ron.

"Tribesmen like me try to keep a watchful eye on the comings and goings of the Germans over the land routes from Algeria into Morocco although of course it is not possible to monitor this very closely due to the danger involved. Several of my men have been shot for simply being in the wrong place at the wrong time."

"This is indeed something that we also are always aware of when we move around the country," added Yusuf. "We plan our routes carefully to avoid encounters with the Germans and the Vichy French."

"So Monsieur Hamid, may I ask you if there have been any current activities of note concerning the Germans?" asked Ron, trying to get the conversation back on track.

Hamid considered Ron's query for a moment and then raised his voice to call out to a henchman who must have been waiting outside. A very thin man with a bad squint entered and bowed his head in front of Hamid who fired off several questions in quick succession.

Addressing Hamid as 'Rayiys' or boss, the man replied, "The troop movements in and out of Morocco have continued for several months. Smiling soldiers coming away from the battlefields and gloomy faces going back to fight and lose their lives," the man paused to chuckle at his own joke." Hamid raised his hand, "This I know. Tell me something new," he asked. The man's squint became worse as he paused for thought, then he nodded, "Yes, rayiys. The latest news is that a week ago our lookouts near Oujda in the northeast reported an unusual convoy of about ten large, closed trucks that did not carry troops at all. It was strange as there were hardly any soldiers and even the trucks did not look like the normal traffic."

"Hmm… this is unusual. You have done your work well, Ali. So now you must inform our lookouts further south of Oujda to keep a watch out for these trucks and monitor where they are headed," said Hamid, dismissing the man with a wave of his hand.

Hamid then turned to Ron and Yusuf and said, "Let us wait and see if any more information about this emerges. But it will be a couple of days before I get a response from my men. In the meantime, it is late and dinnertime approaches. Tonight we have a special meal to celebrate the sighting of a new moon and so you must both join us as my guests."

Without waiting to see if they had accepted his invitation Hamid clapped his hands. When a man appeared Hamid barked out a few instructions and then turned to Ron and Yusuf, "My man will show you where you can wash before eating."

The attendant led them out to a tent where they were offered bowls of water with which to wash their hands and faces. A few minutes later feeling refreshed, they were then shown to the central area of the camp where rugs and cushions had been arranged in a wide circle around a blazing fire.

The intricately patterned rugs upon which they sat seemed incongruous in the surrounding sandy desert scrubland but after his long and bumpy journey Ron was thankful for the softness of the rugs and to rest back upon a pile of cushions. Hamid had insisted that Ron and Yusuf sit on either side of him and soon a tray of drinks arrived, mint tea, sharbat and mahia.

Hamid turned to Ron, "Try some mahia, I think you will like it," he said. "It is our traditional brandy distilled from fruits such as jujubes, figs and dates, and then flavoured with anise."

Declaring that it was against his faith Yusuf declined the alcoholic drink, but Ron gladly accepted a glass of mahia and sipped it appreciatively.

A large communal platter of food now appeared before them. It contained a tagine of steaming spicy lamb stew, bowls of chickpeas, couscous, various types of bread and a few further bowls that Ron could not identify.

"Come on my friends, let us eat," invited Hamid, breaking off a large chunk of bread and dipping it into the thick lamb stew. Ron and Yusuf did not need a second invitation, it had been a long day and by now they were quite hungry. Throwing aside any inhibitions that table manners may have imposed, Ron tucked into the food with gusto.

The tasty food washed down by a few glasses of Mahia proved to be a heady combination and Ron began to feel a warm glow spread through him. He leaned back on the cushions and looked up at the dark desert sky and the bright twinkling stars above. A far cry from the wet and overcast streets of London, he mused.

The sound of some plucked musical notes brought Ron out of his brief reverie. A man sat cross legged playing a strange guitar shaped instrument.

"Perhaps you have not heard an oud before," enquired Hamid. "It is a bit like the mandolin but has more strings. Its name refers to the wooden plectrum that is being used to pluck the strings."

Ron listened to the tune and watched the player's nimble fingers darting over the fingerboard. He was especially interested in the technique as he had learned to play the guitar as a young lad. Indeed Ron was quite used to standing up at a party or in a pub and belting out a few songs in his powerful tenor voice.

After a while, when the oud player paused to rest, Ron turned to Hamid and asked, "Monsieur Hamid, I play the guitar myself and find the oud fascinating. Would you mind if I tried playing it?"

Hamid vigorously nodded his assent and asked for the oud to be brought over to Ron. Bowing his head in thanks, Ron accepted the oud and explored its tuning. He quickly worked out that by playing just the bottom three pairs of strings, he could play it like a six-string guitar.

Raising himself to his feet, Ron looked around to the circle of men seated around the fire and with a broad smile launched into his favourite tune, 'The Peanut Vendor'.

Ron breathed deeply and sang,

"In Cuba each merry maid wakes up with this serenade
Peanuts (they're nice and hot)
Peanuts (he sells a lot)
Peanuts
If you haven't got bananas don't be blue
Peanuts in a little bag are calling you."

Ron had an engaging style and soon he had the men clapping along to the rumba rhythm. He concluded the song with flourish on the oud. There was a round of applause and shouts for him to play another song. "You must sing another one, my Indian Englishman friend!" said Hamid.

Without any further encouragement Ron gave a stirring rendition of 'Hear my song Violetta', his voice rolling out across the dark desert around them. He concluded with a bow to his audience and then handed the oud back to its owner who seemed at a bit of a loss of how to follow Ron's unusual but rollicking impromptu performance.

Ron sat down and finished his glass of Mahia.

Yusuf looked at Ron rather bewildered, possibly wondering how this Indian agent from England could also be such a showman.

"Most entertaining, you have hidden talents indeed!" exclaimed Hamid with a broad smile. "So, we must reward you for your performance." He clapped his hands and turned to an attendant standing nearby, "Go and bring Rachida."

In a short while a woman appeared and stood in front of them. Ron recognised her as the same woman who had earlier served them tea in the tent.

"Ron, this fine woman is Rachida," smiled Hamid. "Go with her now. I assure you that she will show you how to enjoy many delights that you have not even dreamed about."

Rachida wore a veil over the lower part of her face, but turning to look at Ron, her eyes were dark and inviting. "It will be my pleasure to entertain a man who makes the night echo with his songs," murmured Rachida.

Feeling relaxed after several glasses of mahia, it took all of Ron's willpower to remember why he was there and where he had better draw the line.

Holding Rachida's gaze he spoke "Mademoiselle, a thousand thanks for such a gracious and tempting invitation. I am honoured."

Turning to face Hamid he added "I am sorry my friend, but sadly I must decline your generous offer on this occasion. We have had a wonderful evening, and you are a fine host. But we cannot tarry here any longer as we have much to do in Casablanca early tomorrow morning."

Hamid and Rachida seemed to take Ron's rejection without rancour, though Rachida made sure that Ron had a clear sight of her long shapely legs as she turned and walked away with an exaggerated sway of her hips.

Farewells were exchanged and Hamid assured them that he would send word if any further news of the strange German convoy emerged. Yusuf kick-started his motorcycle which came to life with a roar and with Ron clinging on firmly they bounced their way along the rough desert road.

Observing a Caravaggio,
Saturday 29th November 1941

The Italian Consulate was located in a smart district of Casablanca. It was a well proportioned white building built in a neoclassical style. In the entrance foyer the receptionist seated behind an enormous desk had a completely shaved head. He wore a dark suit which seemed to be one size too big for him and although he could not have been much more than forty he had enormous bags under his eyes. The overall effect was to make him look like a cartoon caricature of the life-sized portrait of Mussolini which hung on the wall immediately above him.

"You have an appointment to see Capitano Andretti?"

"Yes. For eleven o'clock, I am Mademoiselle Marion and I am here to view your Consulate's art works," replied Maggie looking very chic in a grey pleated skirt and cream satin blouse topped off by a loosely tied blue silk scarf. "Especially the Caravaggio."

"Ah, yes, the Caravaggio. It is very popular, especially with the ladies," said the receptionist raising his eyebrows enigmatically. He looked down at the ledger in front of him. "Yes, I can see that you have an appointment with Capitano Andretti, at eleven o'clock."

Maggie nodded. "That is correct."

"But unfortunately, Mademoiselle Capitano Andretti is not here yet." said the receptionist looking down at his ledger again. He then looked up with a wry smile, "You see the Capitano is sometimes delayed in the mornings as he often has other duties to attend to."

"In that case I will wait," declared Maggie. "May I?" she asked, indicating a seat to one side of the room.

"Of course," replied the receptionist reluctantly. "But I warn you that it may be a long wait. Sometimes the Capitano only arrives after lunchtime."

Fifteen minutes later a car drew up outside the entrance and Maggie could hear the soldiers at the front gate snapping to attention. Captain Andretti strode into the building and although his uniform appeared crisply ironed and his cheeks freshly shaved, his eyes tellingly looked rather bloodshot and bleary.

The receptionist stood up respectfully. "Buongiorno, Capitano."

The captain completely ignored the receptionist and headed straight for the staircase while a uniformed aide carrying his briefcase trailed behind him. The receptionist caught up with the aide, whispered something in his ear and turned to indicate Maggie.

A couple of moments later Captain Andretti came rushing down the stairs with a broad smile on his face. He extended both arms out in front of him, "Mademoiselle Marion! How could I have not seen you when I entered. A million apologies for keeping you waiting!"

He turned towards the receptionist, "You should have informed me immediately that the lady was waiting," said Andretti.

The receptionist shook his head slightly with an expression of bemused bewilderment, the movement created some stirring in the bags under his eyes. "But, but, sir…"

"Enough! Incompetent!" exclaimed Andretti. He turned to Maggie and bowed. Just as had done in Rick's Bar when they had first met he took her extended hand and raised it to touch his lips. "Mademoiselle Marion, such a pleasure to see you again. I am so pleased that you could come. Please, accompany me up to my office."

Andretti's wood panelled office was on the Consulate's first floor. It had two windows which looked out to the road in front and another to one side facing onto the next building. A large photograph of Mussolini hung on the wall over a leather topped desk behind which was a high-backed chair while a few deep leather armchairs faced the desk in a semicircle. To one side of the room, by the windows, there was a round wooden table bearing large open maps, some notebooks and sheets of paper.

Andretti escorted Maggie to one of the armchairs. "Forgive the receptionist's lack of hospitality. An idiotic fellow! He did not even offer you a coffee!" He shook his head in disgust. "Tell me Mademoiselle Marion, what may I offer you? A coffee or perhaps it is now not too early for something stronger, a Prosecco perhaps?"

"Prosecco?" said Maggie with a bright smile, "You know I have not had a Prosecco for years! In Casablanca there is Champagne aplenty, but not Prosecco."

"We will have Prosecco then!" declared Andretti. He turned and gestured at his aide who stood at attention by the door. "Two Proseccos. Quickly!"

The Proseccos arrived and Andretti dismissed the aide with a wave of his hand. Maggie raised her fluted wine glass and looking straight into Andretti's eye declared "To Italian art!" Andretti raised his glass and replied, "To beauty!"

With her Prosecco in hand Maggie stood up and moved towards the front windows by the map table. "Your office has a lovely view," she said, peering out of the window.

Andretti came over behind her and placed his hand over Maggie's shoulder. Feigning surprise she jerked her shoulder up and abruptly turned around. In the process of this she dropped her glass and strategically spilled Prosecco over the maps on the map table.

"Oh" How clumsy of me!" she exclaimed. She extracted a lace handkerchief from her cuff and proceeded to delicately dab the Prosecco off the maps.

"Please don't worry Mademoiselle. Leave it, I will get someone to mop it up later," declared Andretti.

"I am so sorry, Capitano. But look, your papers are almost dry now," said Maggie, still dabbing at a map, "No damage done I think… except that my glass is now empty!"

"That will be remedied immediately, Mademoiselle," declared Andretti, lifting Maggie's fallen glass, "Give me a second!"

Andretti left the room and as soon as he did so Maggie rapidly rifled through maps laid out on the table. She could see that they were ordnance maps of North Africa and the Mediterranean and were lettered in Italian. But one map immediately caught her eye and stood out from the rest. The top of this map was prominently stamped in red with the word "VERBOTEN" and it bore the insignia of the German Afrika Corp and all the lettering was in German. It only took Maggie a second to note that it was a map of Morocco with grid coordinates and to see that various arrows and symbols had been inscribed upon the map. They all seemed to be centred around the northeast of the country. Maggie automatically made a mental note of the grid coordinates for the inscribed area.

By the time Andretti returned bearing two refilled glasses of Prosecco, Maggie was back seated in one of the armchairs and well away from the map table.

"It was so clumsy of me, Capitano," she said, accepting her refilled glass of Prosecco. "My apologies. Now, Capitano, perhaps we could visit the Caravaggio?"

"Of course, please follow me. Perhaps another glass of Prosecco?"

Maggie shook her head. "Thank you, but my glass is full."

"Very well then," said Andretti, draining his glass in one go, "But I will have a refill."

The Caravaggio was prominently hung in the Consulate's main dining room, a wood panelled room with a long dining table. A plush divan was placed just below the painting. The Caravaggio depicted David bearing the severed head of Goliath, and the characters in typical Caravaggio style were illuminated by a shaft of light emerging from an otherwise dense and dark background.

"It is quite exquisite!" exclaimed Maggie appreciatively. "I particularly admire the play of light and darkness. I believe it is called chiaroscuro if I am not mistaken?"

"You appear to know quite a lot about art," murmured Andretii, coming to stand by Maggie's side. She tensed slightly as she felt Andretti's hand brush against her bottom. She then felt his grip grow perceptibly slightly tighter.

In response Maggie, as if admiring the painting from another angle, moved to one side and then, with one eye on Andretti, took a step backward so that she could keep Andretti in front of her.

"Divine," murmured Andretti as he moved forward again towards Maggie.

"Yes, the brush strokes are so bold, and the effect is certainly divine," mused Maggie.

Then, when Andretti was only a few inches away from her she nimbly swayed backwards as if still studying the painting while Andretti lurched past her with a foolish expression on his face. He shook his head in disbelief and then turned, regrouped and this time came at her with both arms extended. She waited until he was almost on her and then sidestepped and swayed backwards like some limbo dancing boxer and watched an outstretched arm sail above her face. Andretti stumbled a few steps forward, lost his balance and almost fell over. He righted himself, panting slightly from all the unexpected exertion.

As if nothing was amiss Maggie chatted on, "Observe how the play of light and shadows create a three dimensional effect. One second you think that you see the subject near you and then you blink and when you look again it appears further away."

Andretti, now out of breath, changed tactics. He closed in more slowly and with purpose. But again when he was only an inch away Maggie made a lightning quick move and Andretti found his legs disappearing from under him. He was not quite sure what had happened but the next he knew was that he was lying flat on his back on the divan gazing up at the Caravaggio.

"Oh, Capitano. I did not realise that it was your resting time," said Maggie with false concern. "So, for today please let me not take up more of your time. Take a rest now and perhaps it would be best if we postpone viewing the Bernini another time."

She put her glass of Prosecco down on the table. "And truly, Capitano I would really love to visit again and drink some more Prosecco with you. But please don't bother to rise to show me out, Capitano. I am sure that I can find my own way."

With that Maggie left the room leaving a panting Andretti lying on the divan like a beached whale. From the wall above him David, bearing the severed head of Goliath, gazed down upon him.

A cold and wet morning in London, Monday 1st December 1941

Greaves-Mortimer had a faraway look on his face as he gazed out of his office window at the low grey winter skies that hung over London. He warmed his palms over the cast iron radiator mounted just below the window. His thoughts were interrupted by a knock on the door.

His chief-of-staff Major Smith entered the room and saluted. "Morning Sir, you wanted to see me?"

"Yes, yes do sit down, old man. Glass of sherry?" responded Greaves-Mortimer moving to his desk in the centre of the office.

Major Smith took a seat but declined the offer of a drink.

"No, well perhaps it's a bit too early after all, but still..." said Greaves-Mortimer pouring himself a generous measure from the decanter.

"Anyway, let's get down to business. Now you remember that Indian officer we recruited from the RAF and sent off to Morocco? Flt Lieutenant Sen...capital fellow, a good find. Well, the chap's only been away a couple of weeks but he seems to have been quite busy."

Greaves-Mortimer went on to describe Ron's mission in Morocco.

"Sen has made his base in Casablanca and linked up with one of our operatives there, Maggie Yeomans, a remarkable woman. Now, Casablanca is a real melting pot of politics and people, and whilst the war hasn't reached Morocco, there appear to be quite a few Germans around, taking a break from the action in Libya and Egypt."

Greaves-Mortimer paused to have a couple of sips from his glass of sherry.

"As you are aware the local gendarmes are Vichy French who tow the German line. You've probably heard how they have turned against their own people in France." Major Smith nodded as Greaves-Mortimer continued, "In Morocco there's also a fair presence of Italians but the main fighting force is made up of the Goumiers who are local troops recruited from fearsome tribal warriors. Then you've got Sultan Mohammed who is the nominal ruler. He is well respected by the entire local population and has the support of both the Muslims as well as the hundred thousand or so Moroccan Jews. The Sultan has the reputation of standing up for them all, regardless of their religion. Then there is a refugee European contingent, mainly Jewish, who are fleeing Europe, trying to escape the Germans and to find safe passage to America."

Major Smith nodded politely, thinking about the desk full of paper-work that awaited his attention downstairs.

Greaves-Mortimer ploughed on, "Well getting back to our man on the ground. Sen has been able to reconnoitre a couple of the groups I mentioned and has sent some useful gen. Let me show you something."

Greaves-Mortimer got up and led Smith to the large meeting table that ran along the far wall of the office. The table was covered with several 6"x 8" black and white photographs.

"This batch over here is a Goumier encampment. Looks like it was a night-time recce and the photos are dark, but clear nonetheless."

Major Smith looked at the photos with renewed interest, his desk-work forgotten for the moment. Picking up a magnifying glass his experienced eyes evaluated the armament and armoured vehicles in the grainy photographs.

"Yes, very good work," agreed Smith slowly. "I can get the lab boys to identify the equipment more precisely and get some idea of the strength of the position and so forth."

"Splendid, let's get cracking on that Smith," said Greaves-Mortimer.

When two worlds collide,
Wednesday 3rd December 1941

Dusk was falling as Maggie's Citroen rumbled along a back street leading to the Medina area of Casablanca. Ron sat beside her looking out with interest at the colourful shops and food stalls that lined the road. Soon the street narrowed so much that it allowed pedestrian access only.

Maggie parked the car in a little alley and they continued on foot into the Medina. Shopkeepers held out scarves, shawls and trinkets, calling out to tempt them inside to buy something. The smell of spices and roasting meat wafted through the warm air.

Maggie walked through the melee purposefully and Ron who followed behind was slightly bewildered by this full-on assault on his senses.

They stepped at an old wooden door with rusty but ornate metalwork. Maggie knocked firmly and after about half a minute, a little window in the door opened and a pair of eyes peered at them. The window closed and the bolts on the door were drawn back. An old man stood in the doorway. He slowly smiled at Maggie and beckoned them inside.

Once they were settled at a table Maggie explained, "This is a place that is safe from any eavesdroppers and enemy informants. Ahmed here is Yusuf's maternal uncle. And he makes an excellent goat tagine."

While their order of the tagine was being cooked, Ahmed produced platefulls of olives, bread and zaalouk, a dip made from aubergine. A couple of glasses and a carafe of mahia appeared.

Feeling more relaxed away from the hustle and bustle of the busy medina streets, Ron gave Maggie a brief account of his trip to visit Hamid's camp. He thought it prudent to gloss over the incident with the voluptuous Rachida, especially as he was growing increasingly taken by the attractive woman who sat in front of him right now.

"So, you see Maggie.. or maybe I should be calling you Magda!" he joked, "Hamid seems a very useful person to have on our side. Let's see what his scouts can find out about the German movements."

"I expect you'll be wanting me to call you 'Sir' next!" retorted Maggie with a smile. "OK, my turn. Let me tell you about my fun and games with the pompous Captain Andretti."

She went on to relate the highlights of her night out at Rick's bar and the subsequent visit to the Italian consulate. She told Ron about the Secret German map she had spotted and how it had shown activity out to the northeast of the country. She laughed as she went on to describe Andretti's amorous moves but then became serious as she outlined a plan she was mulling over inorder to get a better look at the maps.

"Goodness me, you are a bold operator!" exclaimed Ron with an admiring smile. Maggie grinned back at him cheekily. They held each other's gaze for a long moment and a flash of magic seemed to pass between them.

A light cough and a shuffling of feet brought them back to earth.

"Your tagine and couscous, madam," said Ahmed, placing two bowls in front of them. Then bringing brightly patterned ceramic plates and spoons, he added "Please enjoy."

The lamb smelt and tasted delicious. For a while they ate in silence. Finishing their meal, they sat back and sipped glasses of mahia.

Relaxed and emboldened by the alcoholic drink, Ron looked up and asked "So, what's a nice girl like you doing in a place like Casablanca?"

In their short time together, Maggie had rather taken to this tall dark Indian who had a likeable personality and a cheeky grin, so instead of cutting him off with a snub, she replied.

"Well, if the truth be told, I'm here because I wanted to get out of Doncaster, where I grew up." She sighed and then continued, "If you must know, I was married there… far too young to a chap who turned out to be a prize idiot. Didn't have a brain cell in his head and wanted me to be the same. One day he even set fire to all my books so as to stop me reading! Anyway, I left and that's all behind me now." Maggie played with her spoon for a few seconds before continuing, "Then the war started and I joined the WAAF really to get away from the past."

Maggie paused to have a sip of mahia, "I became a WAAF map plotter. You know the job? Listening to instructions in your headphones and then pushing numbered wood symbols of aircraft movements around on a large grid map?"

Ron nodded, "Yes, I know that it's an extremely pressured job. I have been in several ops rooms. I worked in telecoms, you know. There is quite a lot of overlap."

Maggie continued, "Anyway, It turned out that I was a very good plotter. Gifted with a photographic memory I was told. That, along with my fluent French, was probably the reason for SOE approaching me with an offer that sounded exciting. And so here I am!"

Ron quickly apologised, "Sorry. I didn't mean to pry. Actually I escaped too, from Simla, in India where I was born. You see, there was a homely girl that my parents were keen that I married. But I wanted to see the world, follow my dreams, and hear music performed by Chevalier, Dorsey…" Ron broke off and smiled, "I'm a bit of a romantic pirate at heart."

"It's strange that we come from such different worlds, but here we are working together in another world altogether," mused Maggie.

They raised their glasses in toast. "Here's to our partnership," said Ron. As he placed his glass back onto the table, his fingers brushed Maggie's hand. For a long moment their fingers remained in contact, Ron's dark skin contrasting vividly with Maggie's pale colouring.

Soon it was time to leave. They paid what seemed a ridiculously small amount for the meal and then, after offering Ahmed their heartfelt thanks, they walked out into the cool night air. The streets were much less crowded now as many of the shops had closed for the day. As they strolled along, Maggie linked her arm with Ron's.

Ron hummed a tune as they went along. Encouraged by Maggie he started singing softly:

"Hear my song, Magdalena
Hear my song beneath the Moon
Come to me in my gondola
Waiting on the old lagoon."

Maggie laughed and playfully poked him in the ribs as she heard him switch the name in the song from 'Violetta' to her pseudonym.

"You devil...." she began but was interrupted by a sudden sound to her left. There was the roar of a powerful motor and moments later an unlit motorcycle appeared out of the darkness of the alleyway on her left. It was heading directly at her and was only a few yards away. She was rooted to the spot in shock and surprise.

A split second before the machine was about to hit her, a strong arm pulled her backwards and the motorcycle whizzed a few inches past her. As it sped past the left wing mirror clipped Maggie's hip but fortunately it was only a glancing blow. She let out a sigh of relief and nodded her thanks to Ron who still had his arm around her.

They both watched the motorcycle as it disappeared down the opposite alleyway, one of its wing mirrors sticking out at an unusual angle after its fleeting collision with Maggie's hip. A headscarf obscured the rider's face and left no clue to his identity.

"Are you OK?" asked Ron with a look of concern. Maggie rubbed her hip gently.

"Nothing broken, but my side may be black and blue for a few days."

"That's a relief! But let's get a move on now." said Ron urgently. "That was no coincidence. Someone seems to want us out of the way!"

Maggie had quickly regained her composure. "Yes, it seems that way, doesn't it," she replied slowly. "I'll put out a few feelers tomorrow."

They reached the Citroen without further incident.

Maggie dropped Ron off at his digs and as he opened the door to get out, she said quietly, "Thank you for a nice evening. I enjoyed it a lot more than Rick's Bar! And thank you for saving me from that motorbike." She gave his hand a quick squeeze.

Ron stepped out of the car and raised a hand in farewell as she drove away.

**A clandestine visitor,
Friday 5th December 1941**

It was nearing midnight and the street was deserted except for the two figures wearing dark djellaba robes and loose headscarves. To one side of the street was a row of rather plain whitewashed houses whilst on the other side ran a solid concrete wall, about ten metres high. The wall formed one of the sides of the compound around the imposing four storied Italian consulate building. An Italian flag hung limply from the flagpole above.

The two figures stopped at a house opposite the consulate's concrete wall and knocked on the door. The door opened and they quickly entered.

"It is good you see you both. Are you sure that you were not followed?" asked Yusuf.

As Maggie pulled off her djellaba, she replied, "All clear, I think. We parked the car several streets away and we doubled back on ourselves a few times to check for any tails."

Under her robe Maggie wore tight black leggings and a fitting long sleeved shirt, also black. From a small string bag she pulled out a balaclava and a pair of soft rubber soled shoes.

"Give me a few minutes to warm up," she said, and commenced upon a series of gymnastic stretches.

"We will await you on the terrace upstairs," replied Yusuf and beckoned Ron to follow him.

The stairs led up onto the flat terrace of the three storied house. They were now well above the level of the compound wall across the street and they could look down on the Italian consulate building as well as some of its surrounding gardens.

After Maggie had spied the important looking map at the Italian consulate some days ago she had persuaded Ron and Yusuf that a clandestine nocturnal visit to the consulate was required in order to inspect the maps more closely. She had then presented them with her plan - she would use her advanced gymnastic skills to gain entry, with an electric cable to be used as a tightrope! At first Ron and Yusuf had both tried to dissuade her from this risky undertaking but Maggie had insisted that it was a workable scheme and had refused to be persuaded otherwise.

"You have chosen this location well, my friend," whispered Ron to Yusuf. "I'm sure it was not easy to find an unoccupied building just where we needed it." As he spoke he made sure that he kept his profile low against the roof's parapet wall.

Yusuf smiled, "Indeed. And do you see the most important feature?"

Inches away from the edge of the roof was the top of a sturdy wooden post. The post arose from the street below and from it, almost touching distance away from them, radiated a number of thick wires - cables which fed electricity to the houses in the immediate vicinity.

Ron took out a pair of binoculars from his haversack and scanned the area around, his eyes finally coming to rest on the Italian consulate. The building was mainly in darkness with just a few lights visible on each floor. There were also some lamps on posts dotted around the surrounding gardens. Near the front entrance Ron saw a match flicker briefly as a guard lit a cigarette in the shadows.

Hearing a sound behind him, Ron lowered his glasses and saw that Maggie had joined them on the terrace. She had put on her balaclava and rubber shoes. All in black, she blended well into the darkness of the night.

She came over to look at the electricity post. From it, one of the cables stretched across the street, over the compound wall and ended on a fixing point on the consulate's third floor. The cable was significantly broader than the other cables, presumably because it served such a large building.

"When exactly does the electricity go off?" asked Maggie in a muffled voice. The balaclava covered her mouth and nose and only her eyes were visible through the balaclava eye holes.

"Do not worry," responded Yusuf. "On the stroke of one o'clock, Abbas will short circuit the feed to the consulate from the junction box at the end of the street. It should take the technicians at least a couple of hours to replace the main fuses."

Ron, who was trained in telecommunications, added reassuringly, "That sounds okay. Actually, you're perfectly safe using a live wire as a tightrope so long as you don't touch a grounding point at the same time. We see birds perched on live wires all around without any problems. But what I'm really concerned about is the strength of the cable."

"Only one way to find out," replied Maggie.

Ron removed a couple of items from his haversack and handed them to Magge who placed them into a small backpack which she slung across her shoulders. Glancing at his watch, Ron saw the luminous hands approach one o'clock.

Suddenly they heard a sound rather like a small firework, and all the lights in the consulate went off.

Maggie stepped up onto the parapet surrounding the roof and looked out at the compound wall about twenty metres away. She had tight-rope walked across that distance many times before, though never over a hard tarmacked road. She took a deep breath, spread her arms wide and stepped out onto the electric cable.

The cable swayed slightly beneath her weight but held. Maggie's rubber soled shoes gripped the wire and she slowly, with arms still outstretched, began walking across the void.

Ron and Yusuf watched as Maggie moved away from the rooftop and moved forward slowly but without hesitation and reached the wall. Ron watched with bated breath as she continued onwards until she had reached the anchor point on the consulate wall.

"Smart planning, girl," said Ron under his breath when he saw through his binoculars that the cable anchor point was right next to a third floor window.

Maggie hooked a line from her belt to the anchor point and was now dangling free of the cable. Reaching into her backpack she extracted the long flexible lock-picking device that Ron had given her. The third floor windows were not designed to stop burglars, and so it was easy for Maggie to insert the device between the window and its frame. She flipped the latches open, hauled herself up and slipped inside.

The room into which she had made her entry was entirely in darkness. Maggie was aware of the guards below and so knew that she must be extremely careful to avoid stumbling or banging into furniture. She replaced the jimmy into her backpack and took out a small torch. The face of the torch was covered with black tape with just a pin hole for the light to emerge.

She quickly scanned the room; it was a dining room. She smiled slightly when she spotted a divan behind which hung a large painting of David and Goliath. Moving out of the room and into the main staircase landing, she stealthily descended a couple of floors to Captain Andretti's office. The door was unlocked.

She quickly moved over to the map table where a map was still open as if it had just been recently studied. Maggie fished a small camera out of her backpack, and holding the torch between her teeth, took a number of photos of all the maps on the table - including the one with German lettering which she had caught her eye earlier. She then rifled through the stack of documents on the table and noticed that a few also were stamped "VERBOTEN" and had a German army insignia. She systematically photographed them all.

Meanwhile, from across the street, Ron could see that the guards were getting quite animated. All the guards appeared to be Moroccan Goumiers, but amid the Arabic voices trying to work out what was to be done about the electricity failure there was one loud Italian voice and Ron heard the word 'telefono' and 'presto' repeated a few times. He assumed the guards were being instructed by an Italian official on site that they should make some phone calls and get the problem rectified quickly.

Maggie packed the camera away in her small backpack, and feeling quite pleased with herself silently made her way back up the main stairs to the third floor. It was still very quiet inside the building and clearly the guards did not suspect that anyone had broken in.

As Maggie crept into the dining room through which she had made her entry - and then suddenly the room lights came on! She blinked a few times, both in surprise and as a physical reaction to the brightness.

She sat down beneath the window and leaned against the wall.

"Stay calm and think," she mentally repeated to herself. With the power back on she was aware that electricity would now be running through the cable. The only other way out now seemed to be through the gardens which she knew would be patrolled by the guards. And then there was a ten metre high wall to be scaled without a rope - it seemed like a tall order.

She peeped out over the bottom of the window and looked at the rooftop across the street where Ron and Yusuf were concealed. Suddenly she recalled Ron's words about birds perched on live wires. Could she somehow get on and off the live electric cable without touching a ground point at the same time?

Maggie wracked her brains and tried to remember her high school physics about conductors and insulators. Weren't electric wires coated with rubber? That must be an insulator. She looked down at her rubber soled shoes. Would they offer enough protection for that fleeting moment when she would have to stand with one foot on the live cable and one foot on the window ledge? At the far end, she was fairly sure she could jump off the cable and onto the parapet.

It was a very dangerous proposition. A plan which may just work… or she could end up fried and very flat on the ground. All that would be missing would be the chips and tomato sauce!

Maggie made up her mind and gathered her wits about her. She made sure everything was secure in her backpack and stepped out onto the window ledge and pushed the window shut on its spring loaded latches behind her. Across the street from the rooftop she saw Ron raising an arm in alarm.

Ignoring his warning she gave Ron a thumbs up sign and smiled grimly. Then focussing her mind she stepped out on the cable in front of her. Nothing unexpected happened, Maggie's rubber shoes seemed to have provided enough insulation for that brief moment when she still had one foot on the ledge! Quickly bringing both feet onto the wire, Maggie moved onwards assuredly, placing one foot delicately in front of the other.

Now with the electricity back on the ambient light was much brighter which made it easier for Maggie to make her way forward. On the downside she was also now much more likely to be spotted by the guards patrolling the consulate grounds beneath her.

Ron had seen what Maggie had done and was amazed by her audacity and bravery, but he also realised that she was at great risk on the high wire. He scanned the compound with his binoculars in one hand whilst he held his Welrod silenced pistol at the ready in his right hand.

Maggie made her way forwards and had almost passed over the high compound wall when Ron spotted that one of the Goumiers in the garden seemed to have sensed Maggie's presence and was now looking up at Maggie as she walked on the wire above. The guard seemed not to be able to believe his eyes, he shook his head in disbelief and was unslinging his long rifle from his shoulder. Ron did not wait for the guard to shout out an alarm, he swiftly brought his Welrod up, aimed carefully and fired. The pistol made a soft 'phut' and the guard's head exploded in a mist of red. He went down without a sound.

Meanwhile Maggie remained completely unaware of what had occurred below her and a few tense moments later she arrived at the electric post. Ron was very careful not to offer her a helping hand off the wire, as this would have made a fatal ground contact. Maggie leapt nimbly from the wire and onto the parapet from where she scrambled onto the rooftop.

Maggie dropped to the ground beside Ron and he wrapped her in his arms where she stayed for some moments breathing deeply and trembling slightly.

"Come, we must get away without delay," said Yusuf urgently. "They will soon discover the fallen guard and the search will be on for the assassin. Hopefully if they do not realise that there has been a break-in they will put the guard's death down to a fatal family feud as nearly all the Goumiers always seem to have one or two."

They put on their djellabas and left the house quietly, moving swiftly away through the shadows of the night.

Another cold and wet morning in London, Monday 8th December 1941

Greaves-Mortimer had called Major Smith to his office. "Have a shufti at this lot." He pointed to a batch of photos that had arrived that morning by pigeon post. They showed the maps that Maggie had photographed at the Italian consulate in Casablanca.

The major picked up the magnifying glass and studied the prints in silence for a few minutes. Then he looked up and spoke.

"Hmmm, this is in northeast Morocco. Mainly desert, and these linear lines don't seem like roads, they are more likely to indicate some extensive piping or conduits. Looking at the scale of the map, I'd say that they must cover several miles. Very strange."

"Yes indeed, And over here are some photographs of documents possibly related to this map."

Smith leafed through the photographed documents. "Written in German. I can see the words 'Wasser' and 'Strom' which I believe mean 'Water' and 'Electricity'. But I'll get the documents translated properly."

"Good show Smith. I'll also get Sen to dig around and find out more. The secrecy warnings stamped on the map make me think that this must be something important."

At that moment the telephone on Greaves-Mortimer's desk rang. He hurried across towards the desk and picked up the phone. It was his secretary on the line, "Just had a call from Whitehall, sir. The minister would like to speak to you in his office as soon as possible."

"Got to dash now," said Greaves-Mortimer to Major Smith, "Take those photos down to the lab and see what you can make of them."

An hour later, after a short car ride, Greaves-Mortimer was ushered into the War Office and shown to a seat in the Minister of Defence's office. The minister motioned for Greaves-Mortimer to sit and continued reading a document. After a couple of minutes, he put the document down and took off his glasses.

"Thanks for coming over, Greaves. There is a development concerning Morocco that I want to speak to you about."

Greaves-Mortimer was slightly taken aback as he had only just been discussing Morocco with his chief of staff earlier that morning.

The minister continued, "I take it you are aware of the Japanese attack on Pearl Harbour yesterday and its ramifications?"

"Indeed Sir," replied Greaves-Mortimer. "A nasty piece of work by the Japs. Pretty sneaky, no warning given, as I understand it. But it has forced the Americans to finally show up and join the war effort. About time too, in my opinion."

The minister nodded in agreement and continued, "The Americans are with us now. Out in the open. And they are getting concerned about the situation in North West Africa. As you know, if the Germans control the area then our shipping lanes into Europe are at risk from both the U-Boats and land guns. After all Morocco is on the same latitude as the US mainland, just a stretch of water between them."

Greaves-Mortimer nodded vigorously whilst feeling his stomach rumble. He hoped that he wouldn't be late for lunch at his club. Veal, if he remembered rightly. He tried to focus on the minister's words.

"The Americans seem to be in support of Churchill's plan for a pre-emptive strike. Perhaps even a naval invasion on the Moroccan coast. But this is all unknown territory. So, they have asked for some assistance in preparing the ground in advance of any action. I assume we have some presence there?"

"We have a small team out in Casablanca. By coincidence, I was reviewing some intel back from them only this morning."

"Right Greaves, here's what we need," said the minister, lifting his head to look Greaves-Mortimer straight in the eye. "Get your people to scout the coast to the North and South of Casablanca. We need to know about any sheltered bays, which types of craft are able to use the harbours, enemy fortifications and so forth. Also, and this is of importance, in case of an invasion can we reliably expect support from Sultan Mohammed who we believe has signalled some affinity to the allied cause. I will need to respond to US high command in a couple of weeks, so let's get weaving."

Having made his instructions clear, the minister ended the meeting with a request that he be kept informed of any significant developments.

Greaves-Mortimer carefully put on his hat and coat as he digested the turn of events and this new responsibility which had now been placed on his shoulders. He hurried out into the busy street below. Unusually for him, he seemed to have lost his appetite.

**A meeting with the Jewish elders,
Tuesday 9th December 1941**

It was mid-morning when Maggie's Citroen pulled up outside the Beth-El synagogue. Ron and Maggie approached the closed door and knocked. It was opened by the same elderly doorman who they had encountered previously. He looked them up and down and then without a word shuffled off to one side and returned with his wooden weapon storage box.

Ron shook his head, "Nothing for the box today," he said sheepishly. The doorman gave him a toothless grin, nodded and asked them to wait.

After a few moments a young man with a familiar face appeared. "Welcome Madame Magdalena and Monsieur Ron. Please follow me, the elders are expecting you," said Benjamin with a smile.

They passed through the empty main hall and into the inner courtyard at the back. The same group of Jewish elders they had met last time were assembled around a round table. From his visit there a week ago, Ron recognised Avraham, Nathan, Ezra and three other elders whose names he could not remember.

Greetings were exchanged and Benjamin brought in a tray with cups of mint tea.

"You must be wondering why we asked you to come and meet us," began Avraham. Then without waiting for an answer he continued, "We have heard from the Royal

Palace that they wish you to meet a man named Adil Al-Bakar and they have asked us to facilitate this meeting."

"And who is this man, Adil Al-Bakar?" asked Ron, taking a sip of his tea.

"Adil Al-Bakar is a senior member of the Moroccan Nationalistic Movement. Have you heard of them?" asked Avraham.

Ron shook his head.

Maggie interjected, "I vaguely remember reading that there was some sort of a rebellion against French rule by a nationalist group three or four years ago? Was that them?"

Avraham nodded. "Yes, indeed it was. Although, to no one's surprise, it was rapidly suppressed by the French army."

"So why does the Sultan want us to meet this man rather than with one of his own advisors?" enquired Ron trying to steer the conversation back to the immediate present.

"Ah well, you see our Sultan walks a political tight-rope. On the one hand his Sultanate is protected by the French but at the same time he dreams of complete independence for Morocco. In fact the Sultan is also the head of the Moroccan Nationalistic Movement," explained Avraham.

"This is all very interesting, but where do we fit into this?" asked Ron.

"Well you see, who knows which way this war will go? If the Axis win then of course the Sultan will have to settle for the status quo." Avraham paused before lowering his voice a notch and continuing, "But then consider if the Allies should win. The Sultan hopes that if the Allies are aware that he has in some way aided their war effort then, in return, they may look favourably upon the Sultan's desire for Morocco to be granted independence after the war."

Ron interrupted, "But, it's all internal politics. I can't see what any of this has to do with us."

"Ah," replied Avraham. "Well you see the Sultan believes that the British may have sent you to deliver a message to him."

"Well I'm afraid I carry no specific political message for the Sultan," said Ron.

Avraham leaned over towards Ron and touched the back of Ron's hand, "The palace believes that the message may be a non-verbal one. They think it may be conveyed just by the colour of your skin. The palace wonders if the British have specially selected you because you are a brown skinned Indian and sent you here as a signal."

"A signal?" asked Ron disbelievingly.

"Yes. As you may know the British have more or less guaranteed India its independence after the war. The palace thinks that similarly, in return for the Sultan's support, the British may be willing to consider influencing a similar independence for Morocco as well."

Ron looked incredulously across at Avraham and then down at the brown skin on the back of his hand. "All of this speculation just because of my brown skin! Amazing!"

"The art of diplomacy can be very subtle, my friend," murmured Avraham. He raised a quizzical eyebrow. "So are you willing to meet Adil Al-Bakar?"

Ron looked across at Maggie who nodded imperceptibly. "I suppose there can be no harm in meeting him. Although, I can assure you, I have no political messages to give him," said Ron.

"No matter," replied Avraham, "You see, it could be that instead he has a political message for you."

"Well alright, so when can I meet him?" asked Ron.

Avraham looked up at Ron and met his gaze before continuing, "Just now if you wish to. I took the liberty of asking Al-Bakar to come over so as to coincide with your visit. He is here in the room next door."

Exchanging views with a Freedom Fighter, Tuesday 9th December 1941

Ron did not have any real expectations of what a freedom fighter should look like. Back in India he had fleetingly read newspaper reports about the activities and statements of Indian freedom fighters like Gandhi and Bose. Ron remembered that the press photographs of Gandhi had shown a frail man dressed in just a loincloth and shawl and he looked like a saintly holy man. Then there was Bose whose smart military uniform made him look like a firebrand. So, Ron did not really know what to expect. As it turned out Adil Al-Bakar looked rather ordinary. He was of medium height, wore the traditional djellaba and chachiya and was slim with a craggy face and a long hooked nose.

Adil greeted Ron warmly. "A friend from India, it is an honour to meet you," he said as he shook Ron's hand vigorously.

"Well, from England actually. But yes, I was born and educated in India," murmured Ron in reply.

"India and Morocco," continued Adil as if he had not registered Ron's words at all, "Both great countries with long and glorious histories. But alas, now occupied by foreign powers. Our nations' sufferings have much in common," Adil shook his head in dismay. "But the direction of the wind is changing now, and I have faith that these wrongs will soon be righted."

Avraham interjected, "Come, let us have more tea." He clapped his hands and Benjamin appeared. "More tea for our guests," instructed Avaraham.

Adil looked around the table and addressed the Jewish elders. "As you are well aware, my friends, neither the Sultan nor our nationalist movement makes any distinction between Muslims and Jews. We are brothers." Then turning to face Ron and Maggie he added by way of explanation, "Muslims and Jews have lived together in these lands for centuries. We are like fingers of the same hand."

Avraham nodded in agreement, "Our Muslim neighbours have always preferred to trade with us as we are not part of their immediate families. They know that they can confide in us and talk to us openly as we have no interest in converting this knowledge into an advantage in familial and other social matters."

Nathan, one of the Jewish elders chimed in, "Yes, and is there not an Arabic saying which says that your neighbour who is close is more important than your kinsman who is far away."

Adil and the Jewish elders all nodded in agreement.

Sensing that Ron seemed to be a bit out of his depth, Maggie, looking at Adil, spoke up. "It is of course an honour to meet you, but neither Ron nor I are really quite sure how we can be of help to you."

Adil smiled, "When the Sultan's vizier spoke to me he told me that the British had sent an Indian to Morocco. India has been struggling for its independence for many years and now Britain is on the brink of negotiating terms for India's independence. So we asked ourselves, "Why do the British send an Indian to Morocco if not for political reasons"?"

Ron interrupted, "Monsieur Adil, I am sorely sorry to dash your expectations, but I am afraid that I have no political connections at all. Whilst I grew up in India which is ruled by the British, I am not in any way involved with the Indian independence movement. I fear that you may be wasting your time."

Adil looked across at Ron sharply; he appeared rather crestfallen. "You were not involved with India's independence movement?" Ron shook his head.

"And you have no instructions to discuss Morocco's independence?"

Ron shook his head again and added, "But from having grown up in India under foreign rule, I have seen first hand that there are some brave people who stand up to be counted while others will meekly submit to their masters' wishes. You, my friend, are definitely one of the former and I wish you well in your quest."

Adil bowed his head in acknowledgement of the complement before continuing, "There is an Arabic saying which says that the winds do not always blow the ship in the desired direction. I think I can say the same at this time." He paused to think for a moment and then appeared to regroup his thoughts, "However you are here and we both have a common enemy who we both wish to be expelled."

"That is true," agreed Ron.

"Although you seem to have no head for politics, I like you, my friend. You seem to be a straightforward man."

"There is an expression in England called 'barking up the wrong tree'. Quite applicable here when it comes to me and political missions," said Ron with a grin.

Adil waved his hand in dismissal. "We have another saying which tells us that the roads do not all lead to the orchard," He seemed keen to have the last word on old sayings. Ron caught Maggie's eye and concealed his amusement by taking a sip of tea.

Undaunted, Adil continued, "However, I presume that your superiors in England must have political ambitions of which you are unaware." He went on without waiting for confirmation, "It would be useful to our cause if you could remind your superiors that the Sultan has much authority in this country. Remind them that the local administration and Gourmiers pledge allegiance to him and so his actions could prove to be very beneficial to the Allies."

"I presume that would be in return for support for Moroccan independence?" replied Ron.

Adil smiled, "I thought you said that you were not a politician, my friend." He looked across at Ron and then around the table, "In the meanwhile be aware that if you need any assistance in your work you can always contact me through my Jewish brothers here. After all, as we agreed, we all share a common enemy."

After saying their farewells, Ron and Maggie left the synagogue and were making their way back to the side street where Maggie had parked the Citroen.

They had walked for a few minutes when Maggie stopped abruptly, her attention caught by something she had spotted in a tiny cul-de-sac alley off to one side of the synagogue.

"Hang on a minute. Do you see what I see?" she asked.

Tucked away in one corner of the alleyway, Maggie had noticed a parked motorbike over which had been thrown a loose sheet of tarpaulin. A corner of the tarpaulin had been lifted off by the wind exposing one of the motorbike's handlebars - a damaged wing mirror sat at an odd angle.

"Aha," said Maggie, rubbing her sore hip, "Now that's interesting!"

At the safe house in the Medina, Wednesday 10th December 1941

Ron, Maggie and Yusuf were gathered round the battered kitchen table in their safe house, deep within the Medina. Outside, in his usual shady spot, Abbas was perched on his small stool keeping watch while he rhythmically tossed his prayer beads through his fingers.

"The motorbike with the damaged wing mirror belongs to young Benjamin. You have met him. He works at the synagogue," declared Yusuf.

"Benjamin?" said Ron and Maggie in unison and disbelief.

"Yes, there is no doubt. The damaged motorbike belongs to Benjamin," confirmed Yusuf.

"But that makes no sense at all," said Ron, shaking his head. "Why would Benjamin wish to harm us? He is a member of the Jewish community, he works at the synagogue and has never shown any animosity towards us."

"I wondered about all of that too at first," agreed Yusuf, "Which is why I then made some more detailed enquiries through my Jewish contacts. It appears that everything may not be exactly as it first seems."

"So, what's the score, then?" asked Ron.

"Well, let me put it this way, it appears that there may be some internal disagreements and jealousies within the synagogue's Jewish elders."

"But Benjamin is only a young man and is not by any stretch of imagination an elder," interjected Maggie.

Yusuf nodded, "Yes, you are very correct. But my information suggests that Benjamin was probably only acting on instructions to injure you and put you out of action."

"Instructions from?" asked Ron slightly impatiently.

"Well you see, Benjamin is Ezra's nephew and is like a son to him."

"Ezra? Ezra?" asked Maggie, "Isn't he the elder with the longest beard of all who always wears that waistcoat with all those silver buttons? Are you suggesting that Ezra instructed Benjamin to injure us?"

Yusuf nodded again. "Yes, that is correct. In fact, in that description of Ezra, you may have put your finger on the nub of the matter."

Ron and Maggie both lifted enquiring eyebrows.

Yusuf continued, "You see, in the synagogue the tradition is that the elder with the longest beard is usually the most senior. And this is also the case here. Ezra is the most senior of the elders and so traditionally and in normal times he should have been automatically elected as Leader of the synagogue."

Yusuf paused for a sip of tea before continuing, "But, as you know, these are anything but normal times. And so, a few months ago the synagogue elders defied tradition and decided to elect the most astute and able elder as their leader."

"Who is Avraham, and he is not the most senior," said Maggie nodding slowly in understanding, "Hmm…, so, I can understand why there might be internal politics within the synagogue… but I cannot still understand why that should lead Ezra to instruct Benjamin to attack us?"

"Jealousy and hatred are powerful emotions," said Yusuf, "My informant tells me that Ezra's resentment against Avraham may have led him to decide to put his own emotions above the welfare of the synagogue and his community."

"So, are you suggesting that Ezra is collaborating with the Vichy authorities?" asked Maggie slightly incredulously. She thought for a moment before continuing, "Actually I can't believe that because if that was the case, then we would all have been arrested and interrogated by the gendarme a long time ago."

"Yes, you are quite right, my informants suggest that Ezra may not be collaborating directly with the Vichy. The conjecture is that he may be indirectly sending out snippets of information and doing things designed to undermine any project in which Avraham is involved."

"And you are suggesting that Ezra sees me as one of Avraham's projects?" asked Ron.

"That is quite possibly the case," Yusuf stopped for another sip of tea, "A few weeks ago Avraham had been directly involved in arranging for a batch of Jewish refugees to be smuggled over here from Europe and then to be issued with fake entry papers. However soon after they arrived all the refugees were soon rounded up by the Vichy and sent off to Labour camps in the desert. The speculation is that the Vichy authorities had been tipped off by someone within the synagogue and given a list of names."

"So why do Avraham and the other elders not investigate and act upon this information?" asked Maggie.

"Because this is all speculation. Gossip. So far there is absolutely no proof at all." said Yusuf.

"Except now we have one motorbike with a broken wing-mirror, and I have a bruised hip," said Maggie rubbing her thigh thoughtfully.

Exploring the coast of Morocco, Thursday 11th December 1941

The Citroen chugged along the dusty road heading southwest from Casablanca. Maggie was driving with Ron beside her. As usual Ron was cheerfully humming a tune. Looking at the two of them, one would imagine that they were a carefree couple going away on a romantic holiday. But the reality of the situation was quite different.

The communique from London had been frighteningly clear. America had joined the war, and the Allies were seriously considering an invasion into northwest Africa. A crucial part of planning such an operation was to identify suitable landing sites along the coast. This was the task for the couple motoring along in the car.

Maggie had suggested that they explore south of Casablanca first and their initial destination was El Jadida located down the coast about 100 kms away. Maggie had done a bit of homework and spoke as she steered the Citroen around the potholes in the road.

"OK quiet now Ron, here's what I read up about El Jadida. The guide book said that it dates back to the time when the Portuguese occupied it in the 16th century. They stuck around for a couple of hundred years and apparently the town was called Mazagoa back then. But more importantly for us they built some fortifications around the harbour which is why I put it high on our list to investigate."

"Interesting! Nice work Maggie. Quite a few things to check out, I'm sure," responded Ron.

About an hour later, the sea appeared on the horizon and in the foreground the buildings of El Jadida drew closer. They drove slowly into the town and stopped near a small hotel.

Perhaps this would be alright for one night? What do you think?" asked Ron, looking at Maggie. She shrugged and nodded.

Ron got their small cases out of the boot and led the way into the hotel.

"A double room please," said Ron to the man behind the reception desk.

"Actually, he means two rooms," corrected Maggie quickly, giving Ron a look.

"Let me see… yes I have two rooms available," responded the receptionist expertly ignoring the difference of opinion.

As they walked to their rooms, Maggie whispered to Ron in mock anger, "What are you playing at Romeo, trying to get me into bed already?"

Undaunted, Ron grinned "Got to keep up appearances as a happy couple. For king and country!"

After quick showers, Maggie and Ron ventured out into the town. It was late afternoon and this gave them a few hours to explore. The incident at the reception desk had not dampened Maggie's good humour and she linked her arm into Ron's as they strolled along.

As they approached the harbour they passed through a narrow stone gateway with high fortified walls on either side. Enquiring from a street vendor they learned that this was Bab el Bahr which translates as 'Sea Gate'. The name seemed quite appropriate as it formed a natural funnel through which anyone approaching from the harbour had to pass.

Beyond the gate, the harbour lay before them. They climbed up some steep steps that led them up to the ramparts of the mediaeval fortifications and surveyed the sparkling blue sea and the harbour walls. A number of small vessels and boats were moored at the jetties.

Maggie discretely took out her camera and took some photos of the key points of interest from a military perspective. As she was doing this Ron spotted a couple of gendarmes approaching below. Swiftly he drew Maggie to face him and embraced her firmly, the camera concealed between their bodies.

Maggie quickly realised what was happening and relaxed in Ron's arms. She rested her head on his shoulder and closed her eyes. The gendarmes passed by with smiles of amusement, presumably somewhat taken aback at the unusual sight of a white lady in the arms of a dark-skinned man.

After a few minutes they glanced around and decided it was safe to move on.

"I think we've seen enough here," said Ron. "Let's get back to the central area."

Hand in hand they walked into the town centre. By now it was beginning to grow dark and so they found a small restaurant. The aroma emerging from the kitchen was promising.

They ate a simple but enjoyable meal of grilled sardines on a bed of couscous and roasted vegetables while mulling over what they had seen at the harbour.

"The Portuguese did a good job of fortifying this port," mused Maggie.

Ron nodded "And that Bab el Bahr gate would form quite a challenge for any invading force to get through. A small company of soldiers could probably hold off large numbers approaching by sea."

They had also discussed how all the boats which they had seen moored in the harbour had been quite small, suggesting that the channel into the harbour was probably not very deep. They were rapidly coming to the conclusion that El Jadida would not be a favourable landing location.

Feeling replete after the tasty meal, they made their way back to their hotel.

"I'm pleased with our recce here," said Ron. "Even though it turned out to be a damp squib."

"Yes, can't expect to be lucky the first time I guess," agreed Maggie. "Let me see, next we have Ovalida, then Cap Beddouza and then Safi. If my memory serves me right."

They made their way back to their rooms, located next to each other.

"Fancy a nightcap? I've got some rather nice scotch whiskey in my bag," asked Ron with a smile.

"You don't give up, do you sailor?" responded Maggie raising her eyebrows and shaking her head in feigned amazement. "Not tonight, thanks. Perhaps next time I will be tempted by the scotch though. Goodnight, Ron."

She swiftly moved closer to Ron, gave him a light kiss on the cheek and disappeared into her room.

Ron rubbed his cheek in bewilderment and stared at Maggie's closed door. Once in his room he poured himself a measure of scotch, kicked off his shoes and lay back on the bed while sipping his drink thoughtfully.

More exploration along the south coast, Friday 12th December 1941

The next day Maggie and Ron continued their recce along the coast. They had left El Jadida behind them and were now headed to their next port of call. Oualidia which was about 80 km away.

It had just turned 11am when Maggie's trusty Citroen pulled into the town centre. She nosed around and parked down a small side street.

"From what I've read up, this is a fairly small town. I'd suggest we have a quick scout around and then decide whether we need to stay overnight."

Ron gave her a quick thumbs-up and they headed to the waterfront. Drawing closer, it was clear that while there were only a few small fishing boats around and there was no harbour of any note. This rather confused Maggie, whose earlier research had suggested otherwise.

Ron walked over to a little stall selling nuts and olives. While buying a bag of mixed nuts he chatted with the vendor.

"Ah yes," said the man responding to Ron's question. "There was a harbour here many years ago. Bigger boats used to dock here. I remember that it was good for business. But then the ocean currents caused the channel to silt up and the harbour died away as did the size of my shop."

Ron nodded his understanding as he munched on an almond.

"But if you are visiting here," the man went on, "You must not miss the chance to see the lagoons. The flamingoes are beautiful."

Ron thanked the vendor and joined Maggie who was standing in the shade some distance away.

"Not much doing here," said Ron, holding out his bag of nuts to Maggie. "Hasn't been a proper harbour here for ages. He says that there are plenty of pretty feathered birds here though. But I don't think we have got time for that."

"OK, let's crack on," agreed Maggie. "Our next stop is El Beddouza. Just 25 km from here. We should be there in time for lunch."

Soon they had reached El Beddouza which was located on a promontory. Its main feature was a large lighthouse, but once again there was no port. The lighthouse caught their interest though, as they thought that it could provide an excellent navigational landmark for ships approaching the area.

Ron and Maggie found a secluded spot on the beach from where they had a good view of the lighthouse and

Maggie discretely took a few photos while Ron sketched a rough map of the location.

In the town they grabbed a quick meal of lamb kebabs wrapped in pita bread. As they ate, Maggie summarised things. "OK, no dice here either, although the lighthouse seems a good landmark. Now, on to our next stop. Safi is only a short drive away."

"Even I've heard of Safi," added Ron. "I saw it on a map just before I left. It's quite a large town as I understand it."

Discovering the delights of Safi, Saturday 13th December 1941

Maggie and Ron had arrived in Safi the previous evening. Weary after their road trip covering Oualidia and El Beddouza they had stayed overnight.

The next morning found the two of them seated in a little cafe having breakfast. The morning sun streamed in through the windows and lit their table which bore fresh bread, fruit preserve and coffee. Maggie was browsing through her tourist guide book while Ron had his nose buried in a local newspaper grabbed from a rack in the cafe. His long legs were stretched out under the table and occasionally brushed against Maggie's ankles.

They seemed very much at ease in each other's company, and a casual observer would have surmised that they were either a married couple or in a close relationship. Perhaps the fact that last night Maggie had accepted Ron's invitation for a nightcap in his room, had some bearing on this comfortable scene.

"Right ho, listen up! Here's a bit of general background about Safi," said Maggie, giving Ron's hand a gentle slap.

"I'm all ears," responded Ron, putting down his paper and taking a sip of his coffee.

"Well, Safi is one of the main centres for woven carpets which are said to be quite sought after all over the world. And here's something really weird, they have goats that climb trees!"

"You're pulling my leg, old girl!"

"Nope.. it says here that there are these Argan trees and the goats have learnt to climb them so as to eat the nuts off the branches. Perhaps that's what makes the goats go nuts," said Maggie with a laugh.

"But here is something more interesting from our point of view," she continued reading aloud from her guide book, "Safi is one of the country's main fishing ports, especially for sardines". She skimmed through the text, "It says that this harks back to the time when the Portuguese came here in 1488, and you know how the Portuguese love sardines. Apparently the Portuguese fell in love with the place because of the sardine fishing capabilities and then built a big fortress to defend the town."

"Hmmm, sounds like we may have some investigating to do here," said Ron thoughtfully.

Quickly finishing their coffees, Ron paid the bill and the couple ventured out into the street.

They didn't need to walk far before they were treated to the strange sight of the tree-climbing goats which Maggie had read about. Up in the tree the goats nimbly jumped from branch to branch, nibbling at the nuts. Maggie was about to take a photo of the goats but then decided not to when Ron reminded her that the camera roll would end up with Mortimer-Greaves in London!

Passing through the Medina, they passed shops displaying beautiful carpets made from wools dyed in vivid shades of blue, orange, purple and red. They stopped at one shop to briefly admire the carpets and the shopkeeper insisted that they come inside. He led them towards the area at the back of the shop where the carpets were being made.

Before they reached the workshop they first passed through a storage area with shelves laden with canisters full of multicoloured dyes. Among the dyes Ron spotted many large canisters of hydrogen peroxide.

"What's the hydrogen peroxide for?" he asked the shopkeeper.

"Traditionally we prepared the natural dyes with different shades of colour," explained the shopkeeper, "But nowadays we use hydrogen peroxide to bleach some of the dye out of the yarn should we desire the colour to be less intense."

"Ah, I suppose that's progress. Modern chemistry meeting tradition handicraft," commented Ron.

In the backroom Maggie and Ron were treated to the sight of several women working at large wooden frames on which they were expertly tying various coloured yarns into tiny knots. From these thousands of intricate little knots would emerge the rug's complicated multi-coloured patterns.

They gazed at this beehive of activity for a few minutes observing the workers' dexterity. Then Maggie nudged Ron, who took the hint and turned to the shopkeeper, bowed slightly and thanked him for taking the time to show them this fascinating traditional handicraft.

"One day we will return and buy a carpet," they promised as they stepped back out into the bright morning sunlight and continued on their way through the town.

The street meandered along and after a while the smell of sea and fish wafted through the air. Turning a bend they spied the shimmering deep blue of the Atlantic Ocean ahead of them. As the harbour came into sight, they could see that it docked a large number of boats, many of quite considerable size.

Ron let out a low appreciative whistle, "It's big, perhaps big enough for what the top brass are looking for. Let's get down there and have a closer look."

Maggie took Ron's hand as they made their way along the steep path leading down to the waterfront. A panoramic view opened up before them and off to their left they saw the imposing battlements of a large fortress. The Portuguese had clearly done a good job on its construction as the towering structure seemed in good repair despite the centuries.

"So many boats!" exclaimed Maggie, "I can't begin to count them, Ron."

"Blimey, you're not joking. Let's get some photos and let the boffins back in Blighty do the sums," responded Ron.

Making their way to a quiet spot in the shelter of an old, abandoned dwelling, Maggie brought out her camera and fired off a series of snaps covering the bay in sections.

Motioning Maggie to stay put, Ron made his way casually to the one of the largest boats in the harbour. He made a visual estimate of the boat's dimensions and then quickly made a rough count of the number of boats of similar size.

Rejoining Maggie, he winked and took her hand.

"Let's make tracks, I think we've got enough. I've got a good idea of the size of those biguns. It should be possible to extrapolate those measurements into the boats' draft."

"Draft? Have you got your mind on a pint already?" asked Maggie with a smile.

"Well, just in case you need to know, the draft I'm talking about is the distance between the waterline and the deepest point of the boat," explained Ron.

"You can sometimes be a bit of a boffin!" said Maggie good naturedly.

"I'm not sure about me being a boffin but a ship's draft could be a key factor in determining if this harbour is suitable for landing craft. With your photos and my guesswork, the real boffins back home may have enough info to make a decision about this place."

And with that they strolled back through the town arm in arm, making a point to circumvent a couple of gendarmes they spotted on the way. It would not be wise to be caught with a camera full of dubious photos.

After lunch, they spent the afternoon walking around the area, pretending to look round the shops whilst mentally noting potential access routes from the harbour into the mainland for troops and vehicles. They were pleased to find a couple of reasonably wide roads which seemed to have sturdy surfaces and Maggie even managed to get a few discrete photos of these possible approach avenues.

Some hours later after a tasty dinner of the ubiquitous sardines served with saffron flavoured rice and roasted peppers, Maggie leaned forward in her chair and smiled at Ron over the rim of her glass.

"Hey brylcreem boy, I can see you're pleased with what we've found here."

Ron grinned, he smoothed back his jet black hair and nodded in agreement. "Good teamwork! I think the bumf we've gathered here will go down well in London. And as for our exploratory jaunt, I think we've gone as far South as is useful for our objective. It's back to Casablanca tomorrow."

"Mmmm … whatever you say, dear. Come on now, it's been a long day with all that walking around. Let's get to bed," said Maggie stifling a yawn.

They arose from the table and they made their way back to their hotel where they climbed the steep stairs up to their rooms. Ron unlocked the door to his room and was taken aback when, without an invitation, Maggie entered and pulled Ron in behind her. She then gently back-heeled the door and they heard the latch lock on the door shut behind them with a firm click.

Many questions but, as yet, no answers, Sunday 14th December 1941

Avraham, Ron, Maggie and Yusuf were seated around the ancient rather battered dining table in the safe house located deep within the Medina.

Ron addressed Avraham, "I will not beat about the bush, Avraham, as you must be curious to know why we have asked you to meet us here urgently and in secrecy rather than in the comfort of the synagogue."

Avraham nodded, "Yes, naturally I am curious. Obviously, what you wish to discuss is something that you wish to say to me alone."

"Yes, that is correct," continued Ron, "What I am going to tell you is for your ears only."

"Please continue," replied Avraham gravely.

"A few days ago, there was an attempt to injure or kill Maggie and me and we have evidence which indicates that the perpetrator has links to the synagogue."

Ron then went on to relate to Avraham the details of the motor bike attack and how they had been lucky to have escaped without any significant injury. He described how the motorbike's wing mirror had been damaged and how they had accidentally spotted the same damaged motorbike parked near the synagogue.

Yusuf picked up the conversation, "Avraham, I am sorry to have to inform you that the motor bike, without any question, belongs to young Benjamin, the attendant at the synagogue."

"Could it be that the motor bike just appears to look similar to Benjamin's?" asked Avraham.

Yusuf shook his head, "No, there is absolutely no doubt. We have also discovered that Benjamin was trying to conceal the damage and we also hear that he was arranging to have the wing mirror repaired."

"So are you suggesting to me that there is treachery within the synagogue?" asked Avraham grimly.

Maggie added softly, "Yusuf informs us that there has recently been some disharmony in the synagogue which could have led to bad feelings and jealousies within the ranks of the elders. Is that true?"

Avraham sighed wearily, "In any organisation there will be some disagreement, but in our community we are so close. We have hundreds of years of history behind us and have very strong family bonds. So, some disharmony perhaps, but treachery - that I cannot believe." He paused in thought, "Perhaps someone stole Benjamin's bike and then returned it?" He added hopefully.

Ron shook his head, "If that was the case then surely Benjamin would have reported it stolen or, if it was borrowed without his knowledge, then he would have told someone that he had found it damaged. Instead he tried to conceal the damage."

Yusuf spoke softly, "I understand that there may have been some resentment in the synagogue after you were elected leader recently. Perhaps some ill feelings?"

Avraham sighed again, "You seem to have your ear to the ground, my friend. But yes, you are right. As you seem to have heard, quite recently in order to deal with these tricky times there was a break with tradition and I was elected leader. I accepted the role only on the condition that when our community was no longer under grave threat I would pass the role back to the senior-most elder who, by tradition, should have been appointed."

Ron added softly, "And the senior elder, who would traditionally have been appointed leader, is Ezra?"

Avraham nodded sadly.

"And Benjamin is Ezra's beloved nephew?"

Avraham nodded again.

Ron continued, "Yusuf also told us that there was recently an incident regarding the arrest of a group of European Jewish refugees who had been provided with fake

Moroccan identity papers by the synagogue. Did that raise any suspicions in your mind?"

Avraham sighed and then continued, "Yes, that has been playing on my mind quite a lot. In the matter you are referring to, all the refugees were rounded up and arrested by the Vichy in one swoop." He paused, "In the past year, that is before I was elected leader, we had provided similar fake papers to many refugees and none of them had been discovered by the Vichy."

"Did that make you suspect that someone in the synagogue may recently have started tipping off the authorities by giving them a list of the refugees?" asked Ron quietly.

"Sadly, yes," answered Avraham bitterly. "Although I still do not want to believe that it could be true."

"It seems as if all these actions may have been designed to undermine your authority and standing within the synagogue," added Maggie.

"No doubt I am worried and concerned about all of this, my friends," said Avraham. "But this is very delicate ground, and I cannot take any action without more firm proof."

"Benjamin's motorbike with the broken wing mirror?" asked Ron.

"I agree that that seems very suspicious, but I am sure many explanations can be offered. I cannot take any action without some harder proof."

"Well," said Ron, "We thought that you might say that, so here is a plan we came up with. See what you think. If you are agreeable it might provide enough proof upon which you may be able to take definite action."

"So, what is your plan?" asked Avraham.

Casting a net in the Beth-El synagogue, Sunday 14th December 1941

The Jewish elders were gathered in the synagogue's inner courtyard for their weekly evening meeting. Benjamin brought in fresh cups of tea.

The elders had already discussed matters related to repairs to one of the synagogue's outer walls and they had just finished addressing the issue of additional subsidised food rations for the city's Jewish community.

Avraham was winding up the proceedings, "Finally, I have one more piece of information to give you. As you are aware for some time now we have been expecting a small group of influential French Jews to be smuggled here by boat from Marseille. We have accepted the task of giving the group refuge for a few days while arrangements are made for them to be smuggled onwards to Lisbon from where they will make their escape to America."

All the elders nodded. "Yes," said one of the elders, "I think the latest news was that their arrival is planned for the next new moon night, which will be in two weeks' time. Correct?"

"Well," continued Avraham, "I have just heard that there is going to be a change in that schedule. The group's current hiding place in France is at such a high risk of being discovered by the Vichy that they have to set off immediately. They have already set sail in a fishing boat earlier today and will arrive at our usual pick up point in the harbour tonight."

Ezra, the elder with the longest beard interjected, "Impossible. There will be no time to make the arrangements. They need to be met, transported and housed."

Ezra, obviously annoyed, first looked towards the other elders for support before addressing Avraham, "You must immediately tell them to call off their travel until we can get these things organised here."

"I am afraid that we have no choice in the matter, Ezra. I was given no option but to agree to this new timetable. Fortunately, this time we do not have to arrange the pick-up, Adil Al-Bakar and his men from the National Freedom party have already volunteered to handle the pick up and they will also house the group for the night. Tomorrow the group can be dispersed to safe houses within the Mellah as was previously planned."

"Adil Al-Bakar, is incompetent and not to be trusted!" snorted Ezra.

"It should be a straightforward pick-up," said Avraham, "And I am sure Adil Al-Bakar is entirely capable of organising it and after all he is our ally."

Ezra snorted again, "What a shambles!" He declared before storming out of the meeting.

Outside the synagogue Ron, Maggie and Yusuf had positioned themselves at the tops of the various streets radiating away from the synagogue's small square. They spotted Ezra emerge.

Ezra seemed deep in thought and did not seem to even register the heavily veiled woman bent over a pram, he did not spot the stooped djellaba clad man smoking in a doorway and nor did he pay any interest in the overweight man seated on a low wall as he fingered the beads of his tasbih.

Ezra seemed in a hurry as he glanced at his watch and moved quickly down the Route de Mazagan. Abbas, nonchalantly arose from his seat on the low wall and followed in Ezra's footsteps while the hooded and gowned Ron adopting the stooped gait of a man twice his age made his way down a parallel road to the right of Route de Mazagan. Maggie meanwhile negotiated her pram down the first parallel road to the left. The chase was on!

As Ezra turned off the fairly busy Route de Mazagan he seemed to have no idea that he was being followed in turn by either the veiled mother with her pram, the stooped djellaba-clad hooded man or the stout man with the tasbih beads.

At one point Ron thought that he might have lost him but then when he quickly retraced his steps he spotted Ezra who had turned down a narrow street to one side.

After about ten minutes, Ezra reached a small park which appeared to be his destination. Although he seemed preoccupied and somewhat agitated he paused and stopped to look around the park. He scanned the few couples and the families enjoying the evening air. However, his gaze did not settle for more than a second on the veiled woman who had followed him into the park while pushing a pram before her. The same woman who was now making her way towards a nearby park bench while jiggling her pram and making soft cooing noises, ostensibly to soothe her baby.

In the centre of the small park stood a tall water fountain covered by a flat stone canopy. Ezra went up to the fountain and held his hand out for a drink of water. He stood up and once again glanced around. Seeming satisfied that he was unobserved he reached into his pocket, drew out a piece of paper and standing on tiptoe he reached up and placed it on top of the fountain's flat canopy where it was hidden out of sight.

While Ezra was doing this the veiled woman had been positioning her pram and bending over it, to all intents and purposes to adjust her baby's position. In fact Maggie was reaching inside for her camera which had been set up so that its lens was aligned with a small round hole cut in the pram's side. As Ezra placed the piece of paper in its hiding place Maggie rapidly took several photographs. "Gotcha!" thought Maggie.

Without looking around Ezra rapidly strode away and left the park.

Maggie cast a look to one side and spotted Ron lounging in a doorway some distance away. He made a slight gesture as if to say "Wait."

She did not have long to wait. Five minutes later the clock in the Medina's tower chimed six, then a European man dressed in a lightweight suit and Panama hat entered the park. and made a beeline for the fountain. He reached up to the canopy and retrieved the piece of paper which Ezra had deposited there. The veiled woman fussed over the contents of her pram and the camera shutter opened and closed several times. "Bingo!" thought Maggie.

Early morning at a Casablanca bay, Monday 15th December 1941

Two identical black Renaults with French army markings were parked off the road and under the trees on a low ridge overlooking a deserted bay.

In the rear seat of one of the cars Major Schmidt leaned back against the comfortable black leather. As there was only a faint ambient light his jet-black SS Officer's uniform blended into the car's dark upholstery leaving only his pale face visible and creating the impression that his disembodied head was eerily floating in the air.

In the front seat of the car, next to the driver, sat the same light-suited and Panama hatted Frenchman who had picked up Ezra's letter from its hiding place in the park earlier that evening.

Schmidt was in a foul mood, and he was making the Frenchman nervous.

"It is now almost three o'clock and you assured me that the fishing boat with the Jewish scum would arrive before one," he said in an irritated tone while looking at his wristwatch.

The Frenchman, who was a junior officer in the French army intelligence group, shifted uncomfortably in his seat and raised his binoculars to scan the sea beyond the entrance to the harbour. "It could be that the tides and currents have delayed their arrival, sir."

In the driver's seat, next to the Frenchman, sat Sergeant Jager. Jager was Schmidt's driver, aide and fixer all rolled into one. When Germany had invaded Russia earlier that year he had been with one of the SS units charged with rounding up and killing Jewish civilians in Ukraine, but his career in extermination had been cut short by a ricocheting bullet. A ricocheted bullet from the skull of one of his victims had found its way into Jager's leg where it had shattered his tibia. After a spell in hospital, he had been transferred to less active duty in North Africa.

Jager was well used to being at the receiving end of Schmidt's acid tongue and for a change he was quite enjoying seeing someone else in the firing line. He was quite relishing sensing the Frenchman's obvious discomfort.

"Your division assured me that an underground network was going to smuggle in several prominent French Jews this evening. On your assurance I decided to be here, and this was only because your unit has so far proved itself to be most ineffectual in carrying out proper arrests," continued Schmidt.

"We are fairly confident that our information is reliable, sir," replied the Frenchman slightly nervously.

"Earlier you told me that you were very confident, now you say you are only fairly confident," retorted Schmidt angrily as he extracted a small silver hip flask from his jacket's inner pocket and took a large swig.

"The Jew loving scum who run these networks both here and in France need to be dealt with immediately and firmly. Which is something which you people seem incapable of doing," continued Schmidt accusingly.

"But sir, so far, we have only had the opportunity to arrest the European Jews some time after their arrival. By the time we can extract the details of their networks from them the information is out of date and the trail has gone cold," replied the Frenchman on the defence.

Schmidt continued as if he had not registered what the Frenchman had just said, "And then after an ineffectual interrogation all you do is to disperse them to labour camps. They should be summarily executed!"

"Sir, as you know we have strict orders, directly from General Nogue himself, not to execute any of the prisoners," replied the Frenchman.

Schmidt snorted, "There are many ways to perform an execution. You should speak to Sergeant Jager here. He has been with the SS units operating on the eastern front and he will tell you how an execution can easily be manufactured. Shot while attempting to escape being an obvious one. Please captain, do not tell me about orders which have only been given to appease some native so-called sultan!"

In the darkness the Frenchman rolled his eyes, but trying to keep calm replied, "It is not just that, sir. The Goumiers, although vicious fighters, would recoil from shooting defenceless civilians. They would not baulk from gouging out a man's eyes or cutting out a tongue if they thought the crime merited it, but they would not execute a man without justification."

"So you are now abiding by instruction from a worthless black sultan and by the so-called morals of his worthless native army," snarled Schmidt in disgust. "Which is why I have decided to be here personally today so as to show you how such an operation should be conducted!" he added grimly.

For perhaps the hundredth time the Frenchman raised his binoculars again and worriedly scanned the horizon. Under a setting half-moon he saw only an empty sea. It was now getting close to four o'clock.

Earlier that night on the hillside over on the other side of the same bay Ron, Yusuf, Avraham and another elder named Nathan had sat crouched in bushes under a tree. Just after one o'clock they left a nearby abandoned shepherd's hut and had made their cautious way to this spot. In the dim moonlight they had a good view of the bay below them.

"We must be very careful and remain very silent as the Goumiers will be looking out for a reception team which they believe will be coming to pick up the refugees," whispered Yusuf. "We can take a quick look to see what's happening and then we should quickly get back to the hut."

Ron nodded in agreement as he passed Avraham his binoculars. "I don't think we will need to spend much time here. Avraham, if you look carefully at that area to the right of the big rock and then also to the left of the main clump of trees you will notice Goumiers concealed in the shadows."

Avraham placed the binoculars to his eyes as Ron continued, "And if you look across at that low ridge across the bay you should be able to spot two army staff cars and a covered truck parked under a patch of trees."

Avraham looked intently through the binoculars for a minute or so. He let out a long sigh and then handed the binoculars to Nathan, "I have seen enough. Take a look for yourself, Nathan and then let us head back."

Nathan reached for the binoculars and raised them to his eyes. After half a minute he lowered them shaking his head. "Had I not seen this with my own eyes I would never have believed that Ezra would have betrayed his own people!" he whispered with sadness in his voice.

A secret German installation east of Oujda, Monday 15th December 1941

The deep throated roar of the Junker JU52's engines grew louder and out of a cloudless sky the three-propellered aircraft made its cautious descent towards the rough makeshift runway in the desert. To call it a runway would be actually an overstatement as it really was just a strip of land where some attempt had been made to clear the larger shrubs and to compact down some of the soil.

The JU52 touched down with a small bounce and its tyres raised a puff of desert dust and then the propellers were stirring up a mini sandstorm. At the end of the strip the plane slowed to a halt, turned and then taxied towards the small group of men who stood by a staff car. Immediately behind them were half a dozen or so prefabricated buildings which made up the camp. In the perimeter corners, just outside the huddle of buildings rose four watchtowers. A few six wheeled armoured cars bearing the palm tree and swastika insignia of the Afrika Korps were parked at intervals around the camp.

In the swirling desert sand Major Schmidt held a handkerchief to his mouth and nose and wished that he had stayed inside the car and out of the dust until the plane had landed.

As the JU52's propellers slowed and then stopped turning the dust began to settle, Schmidt used his handkerchief to brush off some of the sand which had settled on his black SS uniform. He wanted to look his best today and had arranged for his uniform to be freshly laundered for the occasion. It was not an everyday event for him to be visited personally by the immediate deputy to the SS Obergruppenfuhrer himself!

The JU52's back door opened and a short set of steps were lowered. A couple of junior officers and soldiers clambered out of the Junker and stood stiffly at attention by the steps and a couple of minutes later SS Standartenfuhrer Walter Muller emerged from the aircraft. He was a tall, slim man with hunched shoulders, a stoop and a rather loping gait. Under his SS officers cap with its central silver skull and crossbones badge his long nose was hemmed in by prominent cheekbones. On his left upper arm he sported a red and black swastika armband. Despite all his military paraphernalia Muller's appearance had more than a fleeting resemblance to an Afghan hound rather than a high-ranking Nazi officer!

Major Schmidt smartly walked up to Muller and threw him a tight elbowed Nazi salute. Muller responded with a languid limp raise of his right arm, it had been an early start for him and the long flight had left him feeling rather tired.

Schmidt introduced himself while a junior SS Officer and Sergeant Jager, Schmidt's aide, stood stiffly to attention by his side. None of them had ever been in the presence of such a high-ranking SS Officer before and they were all somewhat in awe.

Schmidt ushered his guest into the camp area. The Afrika Korp soldiers, in their distinctive olive-green fatigues, on guard stiffened to attention as they passed.

A few minutes later Schmidt, Muller and the junior officer were seated around a table with coffee cups before them. Sergeant Jager stood to attention by the door.

Muller began speaking, "As you are aware I am here on a fact-finding exercise which has been personally authorised by Obergruppenfruhrer Heydrich himself."

Schmidt nodded, "Yes, I am aware of this, sir."

Muller continued, "To cut to the nub of the matter I am producing a dossier on various poisonous substances which can be used against civilian populations. I have just been to Serbia to observe our scientists work on carbon monoxide and before visited laboratories producing cyanide and mustard gas. But today I am here to see, at first hand, the work you are carrying out."

Schmidt turned towards a portly man with a bristly moustache who was standing discretely to one side, he wore a long white lab coat embellished by a swastika armband, "May I introduce to you Doktor Roth who is our Chief Scientist here," said Schmidt.

Muller nodded curtly, "So Doktor, tell me what you are doing here."

The doctor cleared his throat and in a high-pitched voice set off into what clearly was a pre-prepared account, "Of course, Herr Standartenführer. In 1888 a talented German scientist called Stillmark discovered…"

Muller interrupted, "Doktor, I have not flown a thousand miles to be given a history lesson. I asked you to tell me what you are doing here - now."

The doctor looked flustered and struggled to regain his composure after this criticism, "Forgive me, Herr Standartenfuhrer. Of course… err… well, in this plant we are experimenting with extracting and purifying Ricin poison from Castor plants."

Muller nodded, "Good. That's better. Tell me how long does Ricin take to kill?"

"It depends on the dose and the form of exposure. Death usually occurs a few hours if the poison is inhaled as an aerosol or a day or two if the poison is ingested by mouth," replied the doctor.

Muller sighed, "Nearly all the scientists I have spoken to seem to believe so far have told me that a quick lethal effect is most desirable. So would not two days be overly long?"

Schmidt interrupted, "Herr Standartenführer, as I mentioned in my report, we have an unusual political situation here in Morocco which may actually make this longer lethal duration more desirable."

Muller sighed, "I have stacks of reports to go through, so please enlighten me."

"Yes, of course, Herr Standartenführer. You see, unlike in Europe, here the Moroccan Jewish population is extremely well integrated into the local society. Inexplicably they are valued by the Muslims as fellow citizens and to make matters even more difficult the Moroccan Sultan sees no difference between his Jewish and the Muslim subjects."

"So why not topple the Sultan, impose martial law and round up the Jews," suggested Muller.

Schmidt shook his head, "We are told that there would be a major uprising if we were to do that."

"So, what is your alternative plan, then?"

"The Jews, though well integrated in social life here, still live in discrete communities called mellahs. If we wish to rid ourselves of these Jews we could arrange to selectively contaminate their local water supply with Ricin and then pass off the ensuing deaths as being due to an unfortunate epidemic due to an infection," explained Schmidt.

"Hmm… that could be a very clever strategy," said Muller, scratching his nose in thought, "In fact this could prove to be a template which could be replicated elsewhere in areas where there are similar unusual social conditions." He smiled "As the saying goes, there are many ways to skin a cat!"

Muller abruptly rose to his feet, "Now, show me around the facility."

Doctor Roth led the small group of men into one of the adjoining buildings. Half a dozen scientists and laboratory technicians all wearing long white lab coats emblazoned by swastika armbands stood at attention by the entrance. In unison they threw Nazi salutes as the group filed past and into a room off the central corridor.

In this room a dozen attractive looking leafy plants, each about two or three feet tall, stood in wheelbarrows. The doctor pointed at the plants, "These are castor plants which grow wild in the desert. We have already begun cultivating several acres of desert."

"Actually, we are only interested in harvesting these seeds," continued the doctor, indicating the bright red spiky looking seed pods.

He then led them to the next room which was dominated by a large iron cauldron fitted with gauges and knobs. A control panel with more dials and knobs stood against one of the walls.

"This is the emulsifying chamber," explained the doctor. "Here the pods and seeds are crushed and reduced to a paste. The hard sediment sinks to the bottom and the rest is syphoned off through this pipe which runs into the next room."

The next room contained a shoulder height square stainless-steel machine which was fed by the pipe which ran from the emulsifying chamber through a hole in the wall.

"The emulsion will be dried in this chamber, and from here crystals of the final product will be distilled off and then gathered and packaged into vials here," said the doctor indicating a covered lab bench next to which hung a full body protective suit.

Schmidt now took over "That is the end of the guided tour here, Herr Standartenführer. I am sure that you will have more questions for us, but perhaps you would like to do this over some light refreshments back in the office?"

Muller nodded, "That would be ideal," he said as he made his way out of the room. He was beginning to tire, and this made his shoulders even more stooped and his gait yet more loping.

Back in the prefabricated office, bread, cheese and fruits had been laid out on the table.

"We have an excellent Bordeaux," said Schmidt. Muller needed no encouragement to accept, it had already been a long day for him and he still had a long flight ahead of him.

"Tell me, Schmidt," began Muller chewing on a piece of cheese, "How much Ricin have you produced, and have you tested its efficacy?"

"Well, Herr Standartenführer," replied Schmidt rather hesitantly, "We have actually not produced any Ricin yet."

Muller stopped chewing, "What? After all of this you are now telling me that there has been no production at all?"

Schmidt shifted in his chair uncomfortably, "There have been a few minor problems which have delayed production. But these will soon be ironed out and we can initiate the program within days if required."

"What problems?" growled Muller.

"Well, Herr Standartenführer, we are experiencing a problem with our water supply. Without a reliable and consistent water supply the machines cannot be run due to the risk of overheating."

"I have never heard such a strange excuse," said Muller irritably.

"Unfortunately, there is no local source of water here and so the water has to be piped in from an oasis fifty miles away. The piping has been engineered by our Italian colleagues whose expertise leads much to be desired," said Schmidt, while in his mind conjuring up an image of Captain Andretti in his plumed hat. "Rather than burying the pipes the Italians decided to run them above ground. The local Bedouin tribal people, who live around here, discovered the pipes and now keep punching holes in them and collect the water as an alternative water supply. But we are working on this problem."

Muller shook his head. "Why did you build this plant out here in the first place? Why not in a town with a reliable water supply?"

"That would not have been possible. The plant had to be top secret. Sadly, this is not Europe, Herr Standartenführer, General Nogues who heads the Vichy administration in Morocco would have vetoed this project immediately. The general tries to appease the Sultan who, for some strange reason, believes that the Jews are to be treated as equal citizens," explained Schmidt bitterly.

Muller cocked his head to one side attentively as Scmidt continued, "We had to locate out here in the wilderness so that no one knows we exist, not even the Vichy French authorities. Furthermore, the cities in Morocco are infested by foreign spies. Everywhere you look there are spies from every corner of the world."

"The spy capital of the world!" said Muller with a sudden smile. "Do not worry once the German conquest of North Africa is complete all of what you describe will change."

Muller lifted his glass of Bordeaux to his lips, "In the next few months, the Reichfuhrer has directed that a very important meeting is to be held in Berlin to decide on a coordinated plan of action related to the control of the Jewish population. Toxicology will undoubtedly play an important role."

Muller paused to take a sip of the wine. "Excellent wine, Schmidt."

"Thank you, Herr Standartenführer. We have a good cellar in Casablanca."

Muller continued, "In the next week I want you to begin production of Ricin and to conduct an experiment on a section of the Jewish population. I expect a full report which can be included in my advice to the very highest level of Reich command."

Schmidt nodded, "It will be done."

"No excuses, Schmidt. I only expect results. Do you understand me?" said Muller.

"I assure you that it will be done. Doktor Roth here is confident that his plant and production team will deliver," said Schmidt. He paused and nodded towards Sergeant Jager who was standing by the door, "And Sergeant

Jager here, who has much previous experience dealing with the Jewish population on the eastern front, has volunteered to personally disseminate the poison."

Doktor Roth bit his lip nervously while Sergeant Jager stiffened to attention with pride.

Half an hour later Muller was walking back out of the main gates towards his waiting plane.

"Will you be flying directly back to Berlin, sir?" enquired Schmidt.

"Not directly," replied Muller as he approached the Junker's steps, "I am first travelling to Spain where I will be inspecting a factory which is expert in the production of Sarin gas. General Franco has assembled a team there which has considerable production experience with Sarin."

He turned to face Schmidt, "Do not let me down, Schmidt. Within the ten days I expect you to send me the results of your experiment on at least one Jewish community here."

As Schmidt watched the Junker take off and disappear towards the north he felt a sense of pride at the efficiency of the Nazi enterprise. He felt confident that he could deliver what Muller had asked for.

He turned to his Sergeant Jager, "Come on Jager, let's leave this wilderness and head back for Casablanca," he instructed.

A squirming fish on the sand, Tuesday 16th December 1941

The elders had convened for their daily meeting in the synagogue's inner courtyard.

"Last night Nathan and I spent the night at the landing point for the refugees who were arriving from Marseilles," began Avraham.

"Yes," said one of the elders, nodding, "I remember you told us that the landing had needed to be brought forward from what was originally planned. Did it go well?"

"Yesterday I told you that the arrival had been brought forward," said Avraham gravely, "But that information was not true."

"Not true..?" asked the same elder, taken aback.

"Yes," continued Avraham, "It was not true. You see I only gave you that information as a test because I believe that someone here has been feeding information back to the Vichy French authorities."

The elders looked alarmed and spoke together, "What!", "How?", "Who?"

Avraham lifted his hand up for silence, "Nathan, please tell our friends what we observed last night."

Nathan sighed, "Last night Avraham and I observed the Goumiers and the army lying in wait at the designated arrival point for the refugees." Nathan cast his eyes down, "Apart from all of us here no one else was told that a group of refugees was due to arrive yesterday."

"So, I am sorry to have to say that there is a spy among us," said Avraham.

The elders looked at each other in confusion and once again spoke all together, "A spy among us? Among us elders? It cannot be!"

Avraham held up his hand again in a gesture asking for silence, "Does anyone here know anything about this?" he asked.

There was much shaking of heads and furrowing of eyebrows. "A spy?", "Among us?", "Never!", Impossible!"

Avraham leant forward and faced Ezra whose face was looking ashen. "Do you know anything about this, Ezra?" asked Avraham softly.

Ezra did not meet Avraham's gaze and he shook his head without saying anything.

"Ezra, a few days ago our British friends were attacked by an assailant on a motorbike. Do you know anything about that?"

Ezra looked down at the ground and shook his head again.

"Nathan, can you please show Ezra and the others the photographs?"

Nathan produced a large envelope and from it extracted two black and white photographs which he placed on the table.

Avraham continued, "These photographs were taken yesterday evening by our British friends. They were taken in the Park Monceau a few hours after I fed you the fake news about the refugees' imminent arrival."

Avraham stood up to point at one of the photographs, "In this photograph, which was taken from a place of concealment, you will see a person placing an envelope on the canopy of the fountain in the park," he paused to then point to the other photograph, "And then in this one, taken a few minutes after the first, you will see the same envelope being collected by someone who I can inform you is a French agent."

The elders leaned forward and peered at the photographs. "But that is Ezra!", "Ezra!", "Ezra, is this true?", "What!!" They exclaimed in confusion.

Ezra sat with his shoulders hunched, his face grey.

"Ezra, why did you do this?" asked Avraham in a soft voice.

Ezra sat looking down at his hands and then, after what seemed an age, spoke in a strangled voice, "It is true, I have betrayed you all and brought suffering to innocent people." He looked around the table, "Yes, I have brought shame to myself and to my family. I have betrayed your trust and each time I betrayed you I told myself it would be my last betrayal."

Ezra's shoulders slumped even further, and tears now flowed freely down his face and wet his beard, "I was filled with hate against all of you because I believed that you had conspired to deprive me of my rightful position. I was touched by so much hatred that to teach you all a lesson I betrayed my own people. I knew that what I was doing was wrong, but my pride and jealousy was too strong. And all the time I knew in my own heart that I had become a monster!"

Avraham leaned over and placed his palm over Ezra's hand. "Ezra, you must leave this town and go somewhere remote, somewhere very far away from here. Benjamin, who was your partner in deceit, must leave with you and neither of you must ever return."

The elders nodded in agreement as Avraham continued, "If you agree to do this, then I promise that your deceit will stay a secret among us elders. No one else will learn of this, not even your family," he paused before continuing, "But, should you refuse or should you betray us again, then these photographs will be circulated widely and you and all your family will be brought to infinite and eternal shame."

Avaraham turned to the other elders, "Do you agree with my decision?"

All the grey beards looked at each other and then nodded in unison.

Ezra slowly got to his feet and in a voice which was barely audible said, "After today, I swear that none of you will ever see me again. I pray that you will forgive me although I doubt if I will ever be able to forgive myself." And with that he stood up and shuffled unsteadily out of the courtyard, a broken old man.

Dancing in the devil's den, Tuesday 16th December 1941

Maggie and Ron were having a lazy breakfast together when they heard a knock at the door. Their coded signal, three quick knocks repeated twice.

Ron ushered him in, "Welcome Yusuf, it has been a while since we've seen you, my friend, hope you are well?

"Yes, I am well, Hamdullah. I hope that your visit down the south coast proved fruitful?"

"Pretty good show. We spotted a few things which may be of interest," responded Ron noncommittally. "But come in, come in, will you have some breakfast with us?"

"Just a cup of mint tea for me. Hello Maggie, I see Ron has brought you back safe and sound," said Yusuf with a smile, as he entered the living area.

Maggie poured tea for Yusuf and they settled down around the small dining table.

"I have some news for you," Yusuf took a sip of tea, "A message has arrived from Hamid Hakim. He indicates that it would be beneficial for you to meet him again."

"Ah, our friendly tribal chieftain! Perhaps he has some information from his scouts in the North," said Ron. He turned to Maggie, "You remember I told you about my visit to his camp a few weeks ago."

"Oh yes, I do. And reading between the lines, it sounded like you had quite an eventful little jaunt. Well, if you're going there again, I'm coming with you this time," replied Maggie with a sweet smile.

Ron could see that Maggie wasn't going to take 'no' for an answer, and besides, with the light of new love in his eyes he was quite pleased for her to be at his side wherever he went.

"OK Yusuf, we'll set off to make contact with Hamid as soon as possible, maybe even later today. It could be important. Maggie and I can drive there in the Citroen. I think I remember the way to his camo but I think it would help if you could mark it on the map for us."

Yusuf had astutely worked out that the relationship between Maggie and Ron had changed and had now blossomed into romance. So, he merely smiled and nodded his agreement to the proposed plan.

"As you wish Ron. But take care my friend, it can be treacherous out there in the desert. Now, if you show me your map I will mark the route for you to follow."

As Yusuf made the markings on Ron's map he also mentioned a few key landmarks which would help to guide them along the way. Finally after he had finished his tea he rose from his chair, wished them good luck and left.

Later, with no fixed commitments for the day, Ron and Maggie set out on the road out of Casablanca to visit Hamid's camp. They took the precaution of carrying supplies of food and water, and filling up an extra jerry can of petrol.

The Citroen followed the road east from Casablanca towards Meknes. Maggie was driving with Ron acting as navigator, the map open across his knees. The small car bounced around on the rough road and even with the windows open it was hot inside but on the plus side being inside kept some of the dust away.

After about an hour on the road, Ron put a hand on Maggie's knee. "OK, slow down now. We will need to take a turn off to the left soon. I'm watching out for the distinctive cluster of palm trees that Yusuf mentioned."

Maggie slowed and shifted down a gear and as the car moved along slowly, Ron kept his eyes peeled so as not to miss the landmark.

"Ah, here it is," he said, pointing. "Turn off into that trail down to the left. Gently does it, it's a rough track."

Half an hour later, they came upon the fallen tree trunk which blocked their way along the track. They came to a stop and seemingly out of nowhere two armed men appeared. Ron thought he recognised them from his last visit and Ron had the impression that the camp guards also seemed to recognise him. It seemed that they may have been told to expect him. So this time, it was a fairly amicable encounter and after just a cursory pat down and several appreciative glances at Maggie's breasts, the guards waved them off the road and walking in front of the car they guided them into the camp.

The Citroen slowly approached the main campsite and following the guards directions Maggie parked not far from the largest tent.

"That's where Hakim will be," said Ron with a wry smile. He squeezed Maggie's hand reassuringly, "Now prepare yourself for a trip back in time, Mags."

They climbed out of the car and dusted off as much of the desert sand from their clothes as they could. Their escorts then led them to the big tent.

Hamid was in his usual position, reclining against cushions placed on an intricately patterned rug. A scantily clad buxom woman was by his side and from his last visit to the camp Ron recognised that it was Rachida. Maggie's eyes opened wide and she closed her mouth which had fallen open in surprise.

"Ah, welcome my friend," said Hamid, rising to his feet and brushing Rachida aside, "And you have brought a companion I see." He looked Maggie up and down, nodding appreciatively.

"Good to see you, Hamid," said Ron, trying to adopt a business-like tone. "Allow me to introduce my colleague and friend, Mademoiselle Maggie."

Hakim gave a slight bow and did not seem to notice the hand that Maggie extended, "Perhaps Mademoiselle would like to join Rachida and her companions in the women's tent? They have some beautiful jewellery, fabrics and costumes that would be of interest I'm sure."

Maggie shot a glance at Ron and spoke under her breath, "Does this guy want a poke in the eye, or what?"

Ron quickly jumped in, "Monsieur Hakim, my colleague and I both need to speak with you together. Mademoiselle Maggie is a key part of our operation here in Morocco."

Hakim shrugged and waved them both to sit down on cushions placed on a rug in front of where he was seated, "I am aware that some of the western ladies are different from ours. Here, we find that our women excel at but a few skills, you know, cooking, dancing…"

Ron interrupted Hakim before he could finish, "Indeed, I am sure we each have our own cultures and ways. But Hakim, we are here as we heard that you desired us to visit you because of some new information. As you can see we came straight away and so let us not tarry."

Hakim called out for refreshment to be brought for the guests.

A few minutes later, the ubiquitous tray of fruit and mint tea had arrived. Sipping on a glass of mint tea, Hakim looked across at Ron and Maggie, "You did well to visit so speedily," he said.

Hakim then launched into a monologue about how skilled his scouts were in tracking activity across the desert and how strong his herd of horses and camels had been bred to become. This was then followed by a disparaging description of the other tribal groups in the region in comparison to his own.

Finally, Hakim broached the topic that Ron and Maggie had travelled to hear more about. "There has been more word from my lookouts to the north. Over the last few weeks a further convoy of several large German military trucks crossed the border from Algeria a few weeks ago. My scouts discovered that they have now established a site about 50 kilometres south of Saidia which is on the coast. My scouts report that the Germans have erected a number of prefabricated buildings and barracks there."

"Do you know the number of personnel involved in this activity?" asked Maggie.

Hakim shook his head slightly, as if bewildered that a woman should be discussing matters meant for men, but he responded nonetheless, "Mademoiselle, we believe there were no more than a hundred men in the convoy. But of particular interest is that not all appeared to be soldiers. Some appeared to be wearing civilian clothing."

"Hmm, could be technical guys. Possibly scientists?" Mused Ron. Maggie nodded in agreement.

"This is another matter that may be related. From Saidia, some pipelines have been laid that lead in the direction of the same German settlement."

Maggie and Ron exchanged glances. They were both thinking about the maps, marked "secret", that Maggie had discovered in the Italian consulate. They were aware that the maps had also included linear markings in the same general area. Lines which could possibly relate to piping installations.

"Have your scouts got a feeling about what may be going on in the settlement?" asked Ron.

"They are not paid to think, but just to look," replied Hamid dismissively. "But my view is that the Boche may be building big guns or even a rocket site. They may have brought the cannon in the trucks and from where they are located they could attack a number of places in the battlegrounds to the east."

Maggie looked unconvinced at Hakim's theory. Ron thanked Hakim nonetheless, "This is important information, Hakim, and we thank you for it. But now we must leave as it is a long way back to Casablanca."

However, now that business was concluded, Hakim suddenly became more effusive. "No, no. Unthinkable! You cannot leave without us taking some food and drink together. Let it never be said that the Arabs are poor hosts."

As there did not seem any question of them turning down Hakim's hospitality Ron followed Hakim to the central hub of the campsite whilst Maggie allowed herself to be led away by Rachida so as to freshen up before the meal.

Dusk was falling and the torches illuminating the central space were already beginning to cast flickering shadows on the surrounding desert scrubland. Cauldrons of food bubbled away, throwing spicy aromas into the evening sky and one of the tribal musicians plucked out a plaintive tune on an oud.

Ron took a seat next to Hakim and savoured the sultry ambience. He took a deep sip from the glass of mahia that had appeared at his side.

After listening to the music and sitting together in companionable silence for a while, Hakim rose and clapped his hands. From the left emerged a string of women wearing flowing robes. Ron watched with a smile on his face but then his expression turned to astonishment when he realised that Maggie was among the dancers!

Ron stood up and held out a hand to Maggie. She shimmied over to him and he wrapped her in an embrace, much to the amusement of the onlooking crowd who applauded loudly.

The oud player had now been joined by a few more musicians including one who played an ancient looking percussion instrument. He broke into a faster beat, rather similar to a Latin American rhythm.

"Shall we show them how it's done, old girl," smiled Ron, adopting a classical dancing stance.

"Where you lead, I will follow, Ronnie," responded Maggie, moving smoothly into his arms. What no one there, including Ron, knew was that Maggie was an accomplished ballet and ballroom dancer. She could manage most things on a dance floor without batting an eyelid.

The pair held each other closely, made eye to eye contact and stepped out into the centre of the gathering. Ron launched into the first steps of a tango. Maggie's leading leg flashed bare and high as she wrapped it around Ron's.

The musicians sensed the excitement of the moment and spurred each other on to play more creatively while keeping the rhythm.

Maggie and Ron had not danced together before but the chemistry between them made it appear as if they had practised and danced with each other a thousand times.

The tribal crowd watched mesmerised as the couple moved through a sexy tango, taut with emotion and desire. They rocked through various cross steps and clinches as the music reached a crescendo and then climaxed. Even after the music had stopped Ron and Maggie stayed locked in embrace together for several moments, breathing heavily. The men clapped and the women made a high pitched ululation in appreciation.

Ron led Maggie back to the central rug and they collapsed there, sweating profusely.

"Well done, my friend," exclaimed Hakim looking at Ron. "Your colleague has many fine skills. And it is also now clear to me why my Rachida was of little interest to you!"

Maggie let that last comment pass her by without comment. But it was reassuring to hear nonetheless.

Drinks arrived, food was served and Maggie had to admit that it was all excellent. The exotic company and location seemed to have spiced the dishes with some extra flavour.

Sometime later, after Maggie had changed back into her own clothes Rachida came and sat by her side and pressed a cloth bag into her hands. It contained the robes that Maggie had worn during her dance with Ron. "Keep these, as a memory," said Rachida. Strangely the two women had got on well with each other in their brief encounter. It was as if they had recognised and acknowledged each other's individual strengths.

The evening drew to a close and farewells were exchanged. Finally, with Maggie behind the wheel of the Citroen they slowly made their way out of Hakim's camp. The little car bumped along the desert trail for a while and then turned right on to the road leading west to Casablanca.

A secret German installation - east of Oujda, Tuesday 16th December 1941

Doctor Roth, the chief scientist at the Ricin production plant, stiffly extracted his rotund body from out of the backseat of the squat open topped Afrika Korp Kubelwagen.

The medical orderly held open the Kubelwagen's door.

"I hope your journey was comfortable, Herr Doktor?"

"As good as could be expected, I suppose," said the doctor carefully taking off his protective eye goggles which were encrusted with a heavy dusting of desert sand.

In reality the doctor wished that he could have been issued a comfortable Renault staff car for the long, hot and dusty drive from Casablanca. Instead, he had been informed in no uncertain terms, that the staff cars were reserved only for the use of more senior officers like Major Schmidt.

The doctor dusted off the fine red desert sand from his hat and jacket sleeves.

The orderly continued, "We have prepared a bath for you, Herr Doktor. Unfortunately the shower is still not working as the water pressure is once again too low."

Fifteen minutes later the doctor was half sitting in a metal tub of warm water which was already turning orange from the desert sand as he scrubbed the grime out of his hair and from between his toes. "Water pressure!" said the doctor softly to himself. He shook his head, "Damn water pressure!"

In fact his four hundred mile car journey had been purely in order to address the issue of the water pressure. In Casablanca, he had accompanied Colonel Schmidt for a meeting with the Italian Captain Andretti.

Andretti, as on every previous occasion, had once again proved himself to be utterly incompetent. "Whoever was responsible for placing Andretti in charge of the camp's water supply has a lot to answer for!" thought the doctor to himself darkly.

The doctor recollected that, true to previous form, Andretti had arrived at the meeting half drunk and over the course of the next two hours had managed to get through several glasses of wine all on the pretext of toasting Mussolini and the Fuhrer multiple times.

Andretti had spent most of the time rambling on about the glories of Italian engineering and how the ancient Romans had built aqueducts all over Europe! On more than one occasion Major Schmidt had needed firmly to steer Andretti back to the issue of the low water pressure.

Finally, it had been concluded that, in order to keep to the new tight schedule, there was now insufficient time for the Italian engineers to bury the fifty miles of piping which ran from the oasis to the production plant. Major Schmidt had been scathing in his criticism of Andretti, "If your marvellous Italian engineers had not tried to cut corners when they were initially laying the piping we would not be facing this problem now!" Schmidt had thundered. However, the Major's angry comments had just seemed to wash off Andretti like water off a duck's back.

As the doctor scrubbed the sand out from between his toes he recollected that at the meeting it had been concluded that inspection teams would repair the damaged pipes whenever discovered, but it would be impossible to guard the entire length of piping in order to put an end to the local Bedouin tribesmen from puncturing the pipes and pilfering the water.

A workable solution had been finally decided upon - a solution initially suggested by the doctor but then promptly claimed by Andretti to have been his idea all along! Engineers from the Afrika Korp would immediately procure and install additional and stronger water pumps at the oasis. The increased volume of water pumped into the pipes should improve the overall water pressure despite the leaks.

"It better work," thought the doctor to himself grimly as he stepped out of the orange bath water and dried himself on a rough towel, "We are scheduled to begin production tomorrow!"

A few hours later the doctor, freshly bathed and refreshed after a good meal, was in the office block briefing his six-man production team on the latest plan of action.

"Very powerful water pumps, secretly brought over the border from Algeria by the Afrika Korp, are today being installed at the oasis. No more puny Italian pumps, this time they will be proper and efficient German pumps - Siemens!"

His team, dressed in their long white lab coats, all nodded appreciatively. "Siemens," they murmured approvingly.

"As you know our work here is pivotal and of monumental importance to the Reich. You all saw for yourself only a couple of days ago that we were visited by the Standartfuhrer himself!"

His team nodded again.

"This evening we will begin the process of harvesting the castor pods from the plants," the doctor pointed to two members of the assembled team, "Hoffman and Klein, that is your department."

"Yes, Herr Doktor!"

"Then by tomorrow morning the new pumps will have been installed and the water pressure will be restored.

Becker and Schulz, in anticipation of switching on our machines tomorrow I want you to make sure that the generators are fully charged and that all the production equipment is completely ready for immediate use."

"Yes, Herr Doktor!"

"And Schneider and Braun, I want you to check that your measuring scales, packaging vials and storage units are functioning perfectly."

"Yes, Herr Doktor!"

"Now, before you get to work, are there any final questions?" asked the doctor.

The technician Schneider, who appeared to be the youngest member of the team, tentatively raised his hand.

"Yes, Schneider?"

"Herr Doktor, what should we do if there is an unexpected sudden drop of water pressure during production?"

The doctor raised his eyebrows and his moustache bristled, "Schneider, that is exactly why production has been delayed for so long and which is why I explained the great lengths we have gone to rectify the issue."

The doctor paused before continuing, "As you know we require a steady supply of water to keep the castor emulsion at a steady state of consistency." He gestured towards one of the other technicians, "Which is why Becker here, will be constantly operating the Particle Size Analyser and the Rheometer in order to ensure we reach and control the optimal consistency. In case of any compromise in consistency we will immediately review the situation."

Schneider raised his hand again. The doctor sighed wearily and nodded at him. "What is now, Schneider?"

"Herr Doktor, the machines are cooled by circulating water pipes. Presumably a drop in water pressure, especially in the drying chamber, would cause catastrophic overheating and …"

The doctor raised his hand and irritably cut the young technician off mid-sentence. "Have you not been listening to what I just said, Schneider? The new Siemens water pumps are in the process of being fitted at the water source. This has been achieved at great expense and after huge effort. Once the new pumps are in action there will be no question of a drop in our water supply. Now, any other questions before we start work?"

The team shook their heads in unison.

"Well get to work then!" ordered the doctor.

Later that evening the medical orderly knocked on the doctor's bedroom door, "Herr Doktor, your presence is requested in the telecommunications room. Colonel Schmidt is on the field telephone."

The doctor quickly threw a dressing gown over his pyjamas and rushed over to the telecommunications room. Once there he grabbed the handset from the Afrika Korp signaller who was seated before his radio equipment. The Feldfernspecher line crackled with background static,

"Hello. This is Roth speaking."

Major Schmidt's voice was distinct although it sounded faraway.

"Roth, is that you?... Good… Just to inform you that everything is now in place. The new pumps will be in action from exactly 0200 hours tomorrow morning so you can begin production first thing tomorrow morning."

"All our equipment is ready and we are all set to begin, sir."

"Send me a full field report once production has begun and remember the importance of your task. You must not fail."

"You can rely on me, sir," said the doctor before passing the handset back to the signaller.

"Good night, Herr Doktor," said the signaller as he replaced the handset on its stand over the Feldfernspecher.

Speaking with the mothership, Wednesday 17th December 1941

It was morning and Ron was busily packing his belongings into a kit bag. He hummed a tune as he folded up his cotton shirts and trousers. Clearly, the dangerous mission which he was embarked upon had done nothing to dampen his cheerful mood.

As he packed his bag he sang softly. The tune followed the song 'Peanuts', currently his favourite, but the words were made up on the spot.

'In Casa, this merry maid, wakes up to a serenade,
Ronnie, he's nice and hot,
Ronnie, you'll love him a lot,
If you haven't got Bogart don't be blue,
Ronnie's right here waiting for you!'

He ran out of words and, with a chuckle, turned his attention to completing his task quickly. He looked around the room to see if had forgotten anything and spotted his carpet slippers under the bed. Bending down, he picked them up and shoved them into the bag. Satisfied that nothing was left behind, he shouldered the kit bag and made his way to the street outside.

A few minutes later Maggie's Citroen pulled up by his side.

"Hop in soldier. I think you're going my way," said Maggie with a grin. Ron tossed his bag into the rear seat, slid in beside Maggie and gave her a quick kiss.

"Let's drop off my kit and then go on to Yusuf's place. It's time we had a chat with London."

"Roger," acknowledged Maggie.

The previous evening, Maggie had suggested that Ron might move in with her, and Ron hadn't needed any persuading. He had jumped at the idea. He missed the nights on the coastal road when he had shared Maggie's warm bed.

Having made a stop at Maggie's apartment to drop off Ron's bag, they then made their way into the Medina and finally pulled up on a side street which led into Yusuf's safe house. Across from Yusuf's door sat Abbas, perched on his low stool and tossing the beads of his tasbih. He nodded at them in greeting as they approached. "Yusuf is already here and waiting for you," he said.

Once inside they were soon seated and sipping on the ever-present mint tea.

"Good to see you both safely back from your trip into the desert," said Yusuf.

When Yusuf left the room for a moment, Ron leant over and whispered to Maggie.

"Why can't we get a decent cup of milky cha in this country!"

"When in Rome…" responded Maggie smiling.

Yusuf returned, bearing a small tray of flat bread, olives, dates and hummus.

As they ate, Ron and Maggie gave Yusuf an account of their recent trip to Hakim's camp.

"There certainly seems to be something afoot in the northern desert area," said Ron thoughtfully, "Hakim thinks that the Germans may be building big artillery guns or constructing a rocket site."

"It is true that the Boche are very good engineers, and they would love to have the ability to attack towards the direction of Libya from that location. Perhaps Hakim is correct and they are constructing some sort of launch platform or a long range cannon," said Yusuf tossing a plump olive into his large mouth.

"It's no use speculating," interjected Maggi, "We will have to somehow get to the bottom of the matter soon."

"Agreed," nodded Ron, "But for the moment let's get on with a pressing matter. Yusuf, we need to speak to London. Could you please set up the wireless."

Yusuf took a quick look outside to check with Abbas for any suspicious activity. Satisfied that all was quiet he re-entered the room, closed all the window shutters and kneeled on the stone floor. Gently he prised up the loose flagstone and lifted out the Marconi wireless transceiver.

Maggie helped Yusuf string up the aerial wire across the room and Ron turned on the wireless radio. After a few moments the valves inside came to life, emitting an amber glow.

"We cannot stay on the radio for more than 10 minutes," warned Yusuf. "The Vichy authorities are not that diligent but they do sometimes scan for transmissions."

Ron nodded and picked up the microphone while Maggie tuned the dial into the frequency that was monitored continuously by SOE in London.

"Sabre calling mothership, Sabre calling Mothership."

All they heard was a layer of white noise emerging from the speaker. Ron tried again.

"Sabre calling Mothership, Sabre calling Mothership."

More static, and then a faint response.

"We hear you, Sabre. Mothership listening. What is your reply to Stairs? Sierra, tango, india, romeo, sierra."

Ron consulted his silk handkerchief adorned with his special codes.

"My reply is Pears. Papa, echo, alpha, romeo, sierra," replied Ron.

The radio crackled once again. Roger, Sabre. You are now clear to speak. Over."

"Is it possible to patch in Headmaster? Over." Ron responded using the code name for Greaves-Mortimer, hoping that he might be able to speak directly to Greaves-Mortimer although he doubted if he would be available at short notice.

"Hang on Sabre." After about thirty seconds of silence the loudspeaker crackled to life again, "Roger Sabre, Headmaster is connected. Go ahead."

"Sabre to Headmaster. We have news on our coastal mission."

"Excellent, Sabre. Headmaster here. What have you found?"

"Best southern location appears to be Safi, I repeat Safi. Sugar, Alpha, Foxtrot, India."

"Headmaster here. I read you Sabre. Good work. Will communicate to cousins across the pond."

"Roger. We will be sending photographic reconnaissance and further details by our usual courier channel."

"We will be ready to process immediately on receipt. Any more to report, Sabre?"

"Yes. Something strange is afoot in the northeast. Reports indicate that the enemy is establishing some sort of a secret site in the desert. Purpose currently unknown."

"Get to the bottom of it, Sabre. We can't have anything jeopardising the master plan we spoke about."

"Roger, Headmaster. Will investigate and report at my earliest." responded Ron.

"Thanks…. and… good work team. Now, over and out."

Yusuf hurriedly crossed over and switched off the wireless set.

"Well done on keeping the communication down to just a few minutes," said Yusuf as he dismantled the aerial and carefully stowed away the transceiver in its hiding place under the flagstone.

The three of them were silent for a few minutes, mulling over the dialogue with London.

Ron looked at the other two, "Well, this confirms that our number one priority now is to recce the mysterious German site up north."

"That may not be so easy, Ron," responded Yusuf. "The location you mentioned is at least 400 kilometres away."

"And I doubt if my little car is up to that sort of journey," added Maggie with a little shake of her head.

"Yes, that's true. Any ideas on how we do this?"

After a few moments of thought Maggie spoke, "Ronnie, do you remember that chap we met in the synagogue? The one who is hell bent on getting independence for Morocco… the chap who thought that you were an Indian freedom fighter?"

"Yes of course… Adil, I think that was his name."

"Adil Al-Bakar is the man you mean," confirmed Yusuf, "I know him well."

Maggie continued, "Well, he seemed quite keen to be of assistance and he or his organisation must have some facilities. I would imagine that they must have transportation and probably armaments as well. I'd suggest we try to get him involved on this mission in the north. After all, as he said many times, we all have a common enemy."

"Good thinking, old girl," nodded Ron approvingly, "Adil will have valuable local knowledge of the territory as well. Yusuf, would it be possible to get in contact with Adil and without revealing too much, ask if he would be willing to join us on our exploration. You could mention that we need a vehicle and must leave soon, within the next couple of days at the latest."

And with that, Maggie and Ron took their leave of Yusuf and walked over to the Citroen parked on a side street nearby. Ron jumped into the passenger seat and Maggie drove them through the cobbled streets towards her apartment across town.

"You won't need to drop me off this time," said Ron with a smile.

Maggie feigned surprise and gave Ron a dig in the ribs "Well, I hope you do not prove to be a messy man, Flight Lieutenant Ronnie. My mess would not be able to cope with yours! No, that just would not do at all!"

They both burst out laughing and then lapsed into a companionable silence.

The secret German installation east of Oujda, Wednesday 17th December 1941

Doctor Roth awoke feeling groggy as he had hardly slept at all that night. He knew that it was entirely his own fault but he had not been able to resist the urge to set his alarm clock for two in the morning. Once awoken he had reached for his glasses, padded over to the bathroom and then turned on the tap over the sink. To his dismay he had been greeted only with a disappointing rusty dribble of water.

He had then remembered that although the new Siemens pumps were going to be switched on at 0200 hours, it would take a while for the head of water pressure to travel the fifty miles through pipes across the desert. He had left the tap open and sat on the toilet seat staring at the tap in anticipation.

Then, about fifteen minutes later he had been treated to a series of loud belching and sighing noises from the tap. A few minutes later after a deep gurgling sound he was rewarded by the tap spluttering to life. To the doctor's delight, within a few more minutes the intermittent spurts of water had converted into a flow of water which was strong and steady.

Satisfied that the water pressure was good the doctor had returned to bed but he found that sleep evaded him as he mentally went through every detail of the Ricin production and it was not until four o'clock that he had finally managed to fall asleep. He then dreamt that he was in an echo chamber and that Major Schmidt's words were being played to him over and over again, "Remember Roth, you must not fail!"

When his alarm clock went off at six he woke feeling rather heavy headed.

At eight o'clock precisely he crossed over to the production barrack where his team was already assembled.

"Everything is in place, Herr Doktor," announced one of the senior technicians.

"Good. And, as you might have observed when you bathed this morning, we now have good water pressure." He turned to face Schneider, the young technician who had raised concerns about the water pressure the evening before, "This is despite young Schneider's concerns about Siemen's engineering capabilities."

Schneider turned bright red with embarrassment.

"In the future you must learn to have more faith in German technology, Schneider. Now, everyone, to work," instructed the doctor.

Within a few minutes the production rooms were hives of activity.

One of the technicians began heaping spadefuls of the bright red Castor pods out of a wheelbarrow and into the iron emulsifying chamber. Meanwhile another technician was methodically adjusting the chambers controls, studying its gauges, then making notes on his clipboard.

In the room next door the stainless steel drying chamber had been turned on, and the technicians could hear the gurgling sound of water circulating through the tubes which controlled the heating element's temperature. Here too, the technicians were busy adjusting knobs and studying dials.

Once the emulsifying chamber was sufficiently filled with the castor pods its iron lid was lowered and bolted into place.

The doctor gave the order for the machine's main switch to be put on and the machine came to life emitting a loud grinding sound as the castor pods were smashed, mixed with water and emulsified into a thin paste. It would take a few hours before the emulsion, after rigorous testing, was deemed appropriate to be syphoned off into the drying chamber.

"What is that awful smell? I know it well, but I can't place it," asked the young technician Schneider of his more senior technician colleague.

"You probably remember it from your childhood, Schneider. That's what your grandmother used to feed you. It's unrefined castor oil!" replied his colleague with a chuckle. "It's a byproduct of the manufacturing process. But don't worry we won't force you to drink it!"

The doctor, who was carefully overseeing the process, moved between the rooms and was pleased with the way the production was progressing. By mid-day the technicians were reporting that the emulsion consistency was almost at optimal level.

When he was satisfied that the emulsion was ready, the doctor gave the order for the syphon machine to be activated and the castor emulsion began to slowly flow into the drying chamber.

As the emulsion warmed and solidified a soft flow of steam rose out of the chamber, traversed an intricate series of glass piping which then fed into the hooded laboratory bench.

Schneider sat perched on a stool at the bench and the doctor peered over Schneider's shoulder as the first crystal of Ricin materialised. Schneider carefully used a pair of tweezers to lift the small white crystal and delicately placed it onto a tiny set of laboratory weighing scales which sat enclosed in a small glass cabinet. He noted down the weight and then carefully lifted the crystal off the scales and transferred it into a small stoppered glass vial.

"What was the weight of that crystal, Schneider?" asked the doctor.

"Zero point zero eight milligrams, Herr Doktor," Schneider replied.

"Good. Now you can begin weighing the crystals in batches of ten," instructed the doctor.

By two o'clock the production was proceeding well. Schneider had now collected about twenty of the white Ricin crystals and so the doctor decided that he could afford to take a short break for lunch.

The doctor was in his office wiping the last crumbs of bread and sausage off his moustache when an orderly burst in without knocking.

"Herr Doktor, come quickly! There has been an emergency…," announced the agitated orderly.

The doctor leapt to his feet and raced across to the production building from where he could hear the sound of an insistent alarm.

One of the technicians saw him enter, "Herr Doktor! It's the water pressure! At first it started fluctuating wildly and now it's falling rapidly. Look!" he said gesticulating at one of the gauges.

Another technician ran in, "Herr Doktor, the temperature in the heating chamber is getting too high! Should we switch off?"

Before the doctor had a chance to issue any instructions he looked around to see that Scneider, the young technician, had staggered into the room. His face was ashen and rapidly turning blue as he clutched at his throat with both hands, "It burns… my throat burns…", he said in a strangled voice, before collapsing onto the floor in a heap.

"A book is like a garden carried in the pocket", Thursday 18th December 1941

The motorbike roared along the road from Casablanca to Rabat, its ancient engine making rather more noise than was warranted by the rather leisurely pace at which it was travelling. Yusuf's face was partially obscured by a long scarf wrapped around his lower face in an effort to keep the swirling dust out of his mouth and nostrils. Behind him sat Ron rather incongruously wearing goggles while dressed in a smart shirt, pink bow tie and linen jacket. With one hand he clung on to the pillion strap whilst with the other he clutched a white panama hat.

After having covered about 70 kilometres, they turned into a long avenue lined with well-maintained palm trees. At the end of the avenue, they reached a towering set of wrought iron gates and it soon became clear why Ron had made the effort to wear his best outfit for this visit.

The Dar-al-Makhzen palace of Sultan Mohammed was visible behind the gates. Once Yusuf had brought the bike to a stop, Ron alighted and took off his goggles. He put on his hat, straightened his bow tie and dusted himself off. A guard from the sentry box beside the gates approached him, no doubt a little bemused by the sight of this smartly dressed man arriving on the back of a motorcycle.

"As-Salaam-Alaikum," said the guard in the traditional Islamic greeting, 'Peace be with you'. This was slightly reassuring as the man had a long rifle held at the ready across his chest. "What is your business here?" asked the guard.

"Wa-Alaikum-Salaam," responded Ron. "I am here at the invitation of His Highness Sultan Mohammed. Please inform his vizier, his excellency Karim Halimi that Monsieur Ron Sen has arrived."

The guard retreated into a guard box where there appeared to be a telephone which linked the guard house and the palace, and after a brief conversation to confirm the details, the guard opened the gates and waved them into the palace grounds. Ron directed Yusuf to park the motorcycle to one side and asked him to wait in the compound. Ron then marched briskly down a pathway lined with exotic plants and up the palaces imposing marble steps.

At the main entrance, a man-servant greeted him with a deep bow and led Ron through a series of ante rooms, finally arriving at an ornately decorated living room.

"Please be seated. His Excellency the Vizier will be with you very shortly."

The servant silently left the room and Ron gazed around him, taking in the crystal chandeliers and the intricate golden filigree work on the walls. The windows were framed with velvet curtains and through them he looked out at the exquisite maintained palace gardens. Ron was idly contemplating whether he would actually fancy living in a place like this, when the door opened and Karim Halimi walked in, he was dressed in a richly embroidered flowing robe and a turban.

He advanced toward Ron with arms spread wide. "It is good to see you, my friend. A thousand thanks for coming to visit us. You must have some refreshment. I hear that you arrived on a two wheeled machine. It must have been an arduous journey," he said with a smile.

"Your Excellency. Yes, it was the quickest way to make my way here," responded Ron, taking no offence at the little dig at his mode of transport.

The vizier clapped his hands and soon trays bearing mint tea, cool sharbat cordial, food and fruit arrived.

Once Ron had nibbled on a few dates and they both were seated with cups of tea, Ron leaned forward and looked at Karim inquisitively.

"You know, your Excellency, I am very keen to learn what has prompted you to invite me to visit the palace."

"Ah indeed. You see Monsieur Ron, things are moving rapidly. Since we met last time at the Sultan's banquet, we have heard of various advancing situations that could threaten the peace of the Sultan's regime."

Ron made a few sympathetic noises, but did not volunteer a response. He nodded his head in encouragement.

The Vizier continued. "Let me see...it is as if we are in a tagine with many ingredients. It begins with a few humble ingredients such as indigenous potatoes, carrots, onions. And then we have more invasive flavours such as garlic, dried apricots, tangy tomatoes and a splash of lemon juice."

Ron nodded wisely while at the same time his brain tried to make sense of what the Vizier meant. He guessed that perhaps the indigenous ingredients referred to the local people of Morocco who lived together in harmony. He presumed he was referring to the Arabs, the Berbers and the Jews while the invasive flavours were the external powers such as the Germans, Vichy French, Spanish and on the horizon, the Allies.

The Vizier continued, "In order for the tagine to retain its traditional consistency and authenticity, we must not allow the spices to overpower the basic ingredients."

Just when Ron thought he was getting to grips with these metaphors, the Vizier threw another idiom into the mix.

"We have a saying, 'The one whose hand is in the fire can also be the one whose hand is in the water'"

Ron let that one go, covering his confusion by grabbing a few grapes from the tray. He thought it was time that he brought the conversation down a notch to a level that he could comprehend.

"If I may speak more plainly, your Excellency. You are aware that the Germans currently use Morocco for non-combative activities. I hear that their battle-weary troops are sent here for a few weeks to recover from the taxing battles and conflicts in Libya and Egypt. That is perhaps understandable. But perhaps I speak out of turn, but what is of more concern to my superiors is that our contacts now speak of strange activity in the North of Morocco near Oujda which suggests that the Germans may be gearing up to take a more threatening stance in your country."

Karim raised his eyebrows in surprise. Clearly this was new information for him, and Ron wondered if he had revealed a bit too much. After a moment's silence the Vizier spoke.

"You know, it is said that whoever plays with a cat will find its claws. I trust that you will keep us advised on the sharpness of this feline's claws. Perhaps we can help in finding a way to blunt them."

Ron glanced away briefly and raised his eyebrows helplessly. "Why didn't Major Grimm's lot not warn me about Arabic doublespeak?" he thought to himself.

Speaking aloud he merely responded, "Of course your Excellency, you can rely on that. On another matter, it will not come as a surprise to you to hear that significant action by the Allies in support of Morocco may not be too far away. In the face of the local Vichy French opposition, it is imperative that my superiors can rely on the Sultan's assistance in our endeavours especially in those regions which may be entrance points."

The Vizier nodded, "His Highness Sultan Mohammed, blessings be upon him, understands that the Allies have indicated that they wish to advance his peaceful rule in Morocco." The Vizier paused for a sip of tea, "But of course our assistance should be reflected by the Allies support for the Sultan's desire for Morocco's independence. An independence under the stewardship of the Sultan's legitimate and continuing regime."

Seeing a little opportunity to throw in an idiom of his own Ron said, "I understand your excellency. We have a little saying that goes: "You scratch my back and I'll scratch yours."

"Rather crude but the sentiment is correct I believe," replied the vizier rising from his seat, "I am also aware that you have met Al-Bakar and I presume that you must have already conveyed back what he had to say to your superiors."

"Yes, your Excellency. My superiors have been informed of his sentiments."

That is good, Monsieur Ron. No doubt you will immediately inform me if you hear of any specific response from your superiors regarding this matter, especially now that America has joined this war."

Ron nodded, "Of course, your Excellency."

The Vizier stood up, "Now, please excuse me, I must attend to some matters of state. This has been a fruitful and frank discussion which I am sure you will also convey to your superiors in London. Thank you again for making the time."

With farewells exchanged, it wasn't long before Yusuf and Ron were on their motorcycle heading back on the road to Casablanca. Ron was keen to get home before dusk, especially because he knew Maggie was cooking shepherd's pie for their dinner. A simple and wholesome British dish which seemed far less complicated than a Moroccan tagine!

The secret German installation east of Oujda, Thursday 18th December 1941

The doctor was addressing his technicians. The previous day had seen the young technician, Schneider die following an accident in the Ricin production plant and so the atmosphere was subdued.

"As you know, yesterday during the production process there was a sudden unexpected drop in water pressure which led to an overheating in the drying chamber. This led to Ricin escaping in an aerosol form," He scanned his teams faces intently, "As you are aware our colleague, Schneider, who was harvesting the Ricin crystals at the time, inhaled the aerosolized Ricin and this led to his unfortunate death due to catastrophic lung damage."

The doctor paused to take off his wire glasses and carefully wiped the lenses before continuing, "Like all of us here, Schneider was dedicated to the Nazi cause. He was an excellent colleague and died for the advancement of the Fatherland. I have recommended to Major Schmidt that he should be posthumously awarded the Iron Cross."

The doctor replaced his glasses, "But now we have a job to do. We must put yesterday's incident behind us. The temporary failure of the water supply yesterday was due to a malfunction of one of the new pumps, but Major

Schmidt has given me an assurance that there is no chance that such a malfunction will recur again."

A couple of the assembled technicians shuffled uneasily.

"Furthermore as an additional precaution gas masks must be worn at all times in the drying chamber room," the doctor added.

The shuffling stopped.

The doctor continued, "I can also inform you that at this stage we have been ordered to produce only a small amount of Ricin for a preliminary clinical trial. Production of the required quantity of Ricin should only take us two full days to complete."

The doctor glanced around his technicians and raised his chin, "And remember that your work here is of vital importance to the Fatherland and you should rightfully consider yourselves as heroes of the Reich. Together our work here will make the Fuhrer proud!"

With that the doctor extended his right arm in a Nazi salute and the assembled technicians saluted him back.

"Heil Hitler!"

Strange happenings in the Mellah, Friday 19th December 1941

Ron and Maggie entered Casablanca's Mellah through its ancient arched gate. In days gone by the wooden gates would have been closed and locked every night at dusk but in recent times they were rarely, if ever, shut. The mellah, inhabited exclusively by Casablanca's Jewish community, was surrounded by thick stone walls and within it a labyrinth of narrow cobbled lanes snaked out at every angle.

On either side of the lanes stood houses one or two stories high, many of them with elaborate overhanging wooden balconies which sometimes almost touched the balcony across the street. Street gates, which were hardly ever shut, led into common courtyards which provided entry to the houses. These homes had belonged to families for generations and the dwellings which led off from a shared courtyard very often housed several generations of the same family.

Interspersed between the houses, shops spilt out onto the street. Displayed under oil lamps were an assortment of items - fabrics, hats, toys and kites which jostled and competed for space alongside heaps of dates and sacks of spices. Everything was piled high.

"Avraham's message said that he lives on Rue De Capitaine," said Maggie as they navigated their way through the mella's busy streets. Families were out in force, strolling along while harassed mothers tried to pull excited children out of the path of carts pulled either by hand or donkey. "I believe it's just off this main lane."

Ron noticed that a broad candelabra stood displayed in a window of every house. Six lit candles or oil lamps glowed from each candelabra, one from the highest branch and the others at a lower level.

"That specially shaped candelabra is called a menorah in Hebrew," said Maggie pointing to the lamps. "You can see that the menorah holds nine candles. The highest candle is called the shamash and differentiates the holy lights from any other light. During Hanukkah one new candle is lit every night, so tonight, from the six lit candles you can tell that it is the fifth day of the festival."

"Hmm… Interesting. You are like an encyclopaedia of knowledge, Mags! How do you know all of this?"

"Oh, I don't know. I once worked in a library and so had the chance to read a lot of books." replied Maggie with a laugh.

"In India we also have a festival of lights," said Ron, "It's called Diwali and oil lamps are also lit by the doors and windows - but in our festival people can light as many lamps as they want to, the more the merrier!"

"Yes, the same goes for Christmas lights too. I guess it's a common religious theme - light in the midst of darkness," replied Maggie before pausing and pointing to a street sign, "Here we are, Rue de Captaine. Now look out for number 7."

Ron and Maggie were in the mellah at Avraham's invitation. The leader of Casablanca's Jewish elders. Avraham had not seen them since Ezra's treachery had been uncovered and, given that it was the festival of Hanukkah, he had invited them to his home for refreshments.

The entrance to number 7, Rue de Captaine led into a small courtyard. An elderly woman in a long gathered skirt and with a woollen shawl draped over her shoulders was raising water from a small well to one side of the courtyard. "Excuse me, Madam. We are looking for the home of Avraham," asked Maggie.

The woman paused midway through filling her bucket and nodded, "Welcome. Avraham is my brother-in-law. This is our family's ancestral home which we all share." She pointed to one of the many doors leading off from the central courtyard, "And that is where Avraham and his wife live."

They thanked the lady and knocked at the door which was opened by a teenage boy. "Please come in. Yes, my grandfather said that we should be expecting you.

Unfortunately though, my grandfather is not well today and he is confined to his bed."

"Oh, we are so very sorry to hear that. We can always return another day," said Maggie, "I hope that it is nothing serious?" she added with concern.

The boy shrugged his shoulders noncommittally, "My grandfather is expecting you though, and specifically asked that you be taken up to his room when you arrive."

A grey-haired woman dressed in a pleated skirt, shawl and headscarf came bustling into the room. "You must be Avraham's friends whom he told me about… please, come in and please sit down. We were expecting you. I am Avraham's wife."

She gestured to the chairs in the sparsely furnished living room and then turned to the teenage boy, "Avi, where are your manners? Quickly, bring out some refreshments for our friends."

Soon Ron and Maggie were biting down on a crispy fried doughnut sprinkled with sugar. "This is sfenj, it is a traditional snack for Hanukkah," explained Avraham's wife. "Can I pour you some mahia to go with it. Our mahia is specially brewed from figs, it's made just for Hanukkah."

"Thank you," said Ron, "Yes, I would love to try the mahia."

"I'm afraid that mahia is a bit too strong for me," said Maggie with a smile, "Just a glass of water will suit me fine."

Once they had their sfenjs, Ron's washed down by a glass of mahia and Maggie's by water they were taken upstairs to visit Avraham who was resting in his bed.

When they entered the bedroom they were taken aback to see just how unwell Avraham looked. He appeared tired and weak, the skin below his eyes was puffy and his complexion looked waxen. As they entered Avraham tried to haul himself up to a sitting position but the effort seemed too much for him and so he lay back on his pillows.

"Thank you for coming, my friends and I apologise for being in bed," said Avraham in a weak voice. "But I have not been well since yesterday."

"What is wrong?" asked Maggie with concern.

"It all began with some stomach cramps and sickness yesterday and today if anything I feel much worse," said Avraham. "Look, at how my feet have swollen up so much," he said pointing at his exposed bare feet which looked puffed up like little balloons."

"Do you have a fever?" enquired Maggie.

Avraham shook his head, "No there is no fever."

"I hope the doctor has been to see you?" asked Ron.

"Avraham nodded. "Yes, the doctor came to see me today. I suspect that he is not quite sure what is wrong, but he did say something about my kidneys and my liver not working properly. He has given me some medicines which I am sure will help."

The effort of even this short conversation seemed to have tired Avraham. Sensing Avraham's exhaustion Ron and Maggie rose, wished Avraham well and promised to return to see him once he felt better.

As Avraham's wife was showing them out, she said in a worried voice, "I do hope he recovers soon, He has hardly ever been ill in his life and I have never seen him quite so unwell. The doctor thinks that he must have caught some sort of an infection as Avraham's elder brother who lives next door has also developed quite similar symptoms since yesterday. I believe it was his wife who sent you to our door as she was drawing water from our well."

Ron and Maggie bid their farewells and left. They had been rather taken aback to see just how unwell Avraham had looked.

"Did you notice the colour of the whites of Avraham's eyes?" asked Maggie.

"No, I didn't notice," replied Ron.

"They were quite yellow, jaundiced," said Maggie, "That's usually a sign of liver failure, I believe."

"I am amazed by how much you know, Maggie, about nearly everything," said Ron appreciatively.

"Oh, as I told you before I was just lucky to be able to read a lot of books in the library," replied Maggie.

As they were passing out of the small courtyard through the gate and into the lane outside, Maggie's eye was caught by a dog which lay curled up under a lamp to one side. The dog was trembling and whining softly.

"Hello doggie," said Maggie, approaching the dog. "What's wrong, doggie?"

She squatted by the dog and then gestured to Ron to come over. "Ronnie. Come over here. Do you see what I see?" she asked.

Ron peered over Maggie's shoulder.

"Look at the whites of the dog's eyes," said Maggie, "They are distinctively yellow. This dog's also got jaundice! Just like Avraham!"

Debilitation and deliberations, Saturday 20th December 1941

Maggie, Ron and Yusuf sat around the small dining table in Maggie's apartment.

Yusuf's face was grave. "I am afraid that I am the bearer of bad news. There appears to have been an outbreak of disease in the Mellah and our friend Avraham is very ill," he announced grimly.

Ron and Maggie nodded. "Yes, we are aware of this. In fact, only last night we were in the Mellah visiting Avraham and he looked very unwell when we saw him," said Ron.

"Even worse news, I'm afraid. Last night there were two deaths in the Mellah and others have now fallen ill. Among the dead, sadly, is Avraham's elder brother and I hear that Avraham's wife and two of his children have now also fallen ill today."

Ron and Maggie looked at each other, "Well, after our visit to see Avraham yesterday evening Maggie woke up last night feeling unwell with stomach pains and nausea. She threw up a few times but has felt better since then," said Ron.

"How do you feel now, Maggie?" Yusuf asked, looking worried.

"A bit drained but otherwise fine," answered Maggie. She thought for a while, "Members of Avraham's whole household are affected. Hmm.."

"I presume there has been some sort of infectious epidemic like typhoid or perhaps food poisoning from something the whole family ate?" mused Ron.

"And presumably I also caught a small whiff of it?" added Maggie.

Yusuf continued, "It's rather strange. From what I've heard the illness seems to have been restricted to only three families who live within the mellah. It seems to begin with vomiting and diarrhoea and then the weaker and older members of the family go on to become more severely affected than others," said Yusuf.

"I doubt if it could be food poisoning if it is affecting families who live in homes well away from each other," commented Ron.

"Unless the contamination is from a common source," suggested Maggie, "Like from a common meal which was cooked in one house and then shared among all the affected families."

"From what I've heard the families affected were not related and in fact each lived in completely different parts of the Mellah," said Yusf.

Ron cocked his head in thought for a moment before asking, "Could it be that raw food has been contaminated from the source they bought it from? Like meat from a diseased animal at the butchers."

"That is a possibility," agreed Yusuf. He thought for a second, "Maggie, I presume you ate something at Avraham's house when you visited?" he asked.

Maggie thought for a few seconds. "All I ate there was a sfenj, which is just a fried doughnut sprinkled with sugar. That couldn't have been contaminated from the butchers. And Ron and I both ate it and he was fine."

Ron suddenly sat upright. "I just remembered something," he said thoughtfully, rubbing his nose.

Maggie and Yusuf looked at him expectantly.

"It just occurred to me that I only drank mahia at Avraham's house while Maggie drank the water. And when we were there I noticed that there was a well in the courtyard, presumably used by Avraham's entire extended family. Could that be it? Could the water in the shared family well have been infected?"

"I suppose that's possible," agreed Maggie.

Ron continued thoughtfully, "You know when I first came to London I lived in rather cheap digs and to save money I used to walk to my technical college which meant that I had to pass through Soho, which is in the centre of London."

I hope that this is relevant, Ronnie?" enquired Maggie.

Ron continued, "I think that It may be, Maggie. I remember that on a street corner at Great Windmill Street in Soho there was an old water pump which had a plaque on it. The plaque said that this single water pump had been responsible for a big epidemic of waterborne disease in London. I think it was cholera. A physician, the name John Snow, sticks in my mind, had worked out that every person who had fallen ill had consumed water from that same water pump. It turned out that the water pump had been contaminated by sewage water."

Yusuf looked a bit bewildered by all of this but Maggie seemed to be following.

"I think what Ron is suggesting is that a few family wells in the Mellah may contain infected water and that anyone who drinks from these specific wells falls ill," explained Maggie.

"Exactly!" said Ron triumphantly. "And Maggie drank the water at Avraham's whereas I only drank mahia! This may be why she was sick last night, and I wasn't."

"And remember that poorly dog who we saw in Avraham's courtyard last night, he may also have drunk water from

Avraham's well," said Maggie thoughtfully. "Your water contamination theory might just be right, Ron."

Yusuf narrowed his eyes thoughtfully, "The illness has affected a few families. This must mean that all the wells used by the affected families must have the same contamination."

"Perhaps there is a leaking sewage pipe which runs through the same water source feeding the affected wells?" suggested Maggie.

"Although we don't know if our theory is correct we should urgently contact the Jewish elders and explain what we think to them," said Ron. "It would make sense for the affected wells to be at least temporarily sealed off until the water in those wells has been properly tested."

Yusuf nodded and stood up. "Yes, and if that is going to be done then there is no time to waste. I shall go to the synagogue immediately and explain all of this to the Jewish elders and suggest to them that the affected wells be sealed and investigated for contamination."

An exchange of SS memos, Saturday 20th December 1941

To: SS Sturmbannfuhrer Schmidt, SS Kommandant, Morocco.

From: Doktor SS Hauptsumfuhrer Roth. Project Director. Morocco Poison Production Programme 71.

Subject: Ricin Poison Production Programme.

1. Following some early technical issues related to a stable water supply Poison Production Programme 71 was successful in growing and harvesting Castor plants which are native to the Moroccan desert.
2. Poison Production Programme 71 was also successful in extracting and manufacturing 21mg of purified Ricin crystals derived from the Castor plants.
3. As a preliminary experiment 7mg of the purified Ricin crystals were added to each of three family wells situated in the Mellah at Casablanca.
4. It was observed that some members of the families who drank from these wells suffered from acute kidney and liver failure, and a few died. Most others only suffered from transient gastrointestinal symptoms. Morbidity and mortality appeared to

depend on the recipient's previous state of health and possibly the dose of Ricin ingested.

It is now recommended that further immediate experiments on the Jewish community of Casablanca's Mellah be authorised in order to address:

1. The correct dose of Ricin needed to create the desired lethal effect on all recipients.
2. The dilutional effects on Ricin related to the size of the well and the volume of water held within it.

Heil Hitler!

To: Doktor SS Hauptsumfuhrer Roth. Project Director. Morocco Poison Production Programme 71.

From: SS Sturmbannfuhrer Schmidt. SS Kommandant, Morocco.

Subject: Ricin Poison Production Programme.

Following your successful demonstration that Ricin can be extracted from Castor plants you are now directed to continue with full scale production of purified Ricin.

Within reference to the dose of Ricin to be used in subsequent treatments of Jewish wells in Casablanca you are instructed, on the basis of the available data, to calculate the best estimate of the lethal dose. This calculated dose should then be doubled and then used to poison the wells. This should ensure that all Jews who use the well, regardless of age or state of health, will be appropriately dosed.

Based on the success of your preliminary experiments it is now hoped that it may be possible for the Ricin poisoning programme to be expanded and applied throughout North Africa.

Heil Hitler!

To: SS Standartenfuhrer Muller, SS Headquarters, Berlin.

From: SS Sturmbannfuhrer Schmidt. SS Kommandant, Morocco.

Subject: Poison Production Programme 71. Morocco.

I am pleased to report that the preliminary trials of production and application of Ricin poison have gone well.

Extraction and purification of Ricin poison from the Castor plant has been successful and early application of the poison to the local Jewish water supply has produced encouraging results. The only outstanding issue is of the appropriate dosage, but this is only a technical issue which will soon be resolved.

Heil Hitler!

To: SS Sturmbannfuhrer Schmidt. SS Kommandant, Morocco.

From: SS Standartenfuhrer Muller, Berlin.

Subject: Poison Production Programme 71. Morocco.

Congratulations on your successful implementation of this important programme which you should now continue to expand as planned.

I await your full detailed and technical report which will be included in my final comprehensive report to Obergruppenfuhrer Heydrich. As you know, my report will form an important part of discussions at a meeting in Berlin, which will be attended by the very highest level of Schultz Staffel and Nazi officials.

Heil Hitler!

**A mystery in the Mellah,
Monday 22nd December 1941**

As Ron and Maggie entered the Mellah they noticed that the candelabras displayed in the windows of every house glowed even more brightly than on their last visit. Today all nine candles in the menorahs were lit indicating that it was the eighth and final day of Hanukkah.

Earlier that day Ron and Maggie had received word from Avraham to say that he was making a rapid recovery from his illness and that he was eager to see them. He had asked if they could visit him that evening.

They reached Avraham's family home on Rue de Capitaine and on entering the courtyard they immediately noticed that the family well was now covered over by a tarpaulin which was tied securely down with ropes.

"It looks like they took your theory seriously, Ron, Dr John Snow would be proud of you!" said Maggie pointing at the covered well.

The front door was opened by Avraham's grandson who told them that his grandfather was expecting them and asked them to follow him straight up to Avraham's bedroom.

Avraham lay in bed, propped up by pillows to a half-seated position and it was obvious from his general appearance that he was now much recovered. He raised himself up and attempted to get out of bed.

"Please do not rise, Avraham. Just lie back and rest. With us there is no formality," said Maggie gently gripping Avraham by the shoulder and helping him to lie back on the pillows.

"It is good to see you, my friends," said Avraham, reaching out to shake Ron and Maggie's hand. They were pleased to feel that his grip felt strong and to see that his eyes were now clear and bright with only the faintest trace of jaundice.

"Thank you for coming, my friends," said Avraham, "Forgive me for not rising but I am still weakened from my sickness, although improving steadily by the day."

"That is good to hear," said Ron.

Once Ron and Maggie were seated, Avraham continued. "Although I am much improved, you might have heard that my elder brother who was also affected by the same illness passed away the day after you came to visit."

Ron and Maggie nodded and offered their condolences.

"My brother was very old and frail and therefore very susceptible. At the same time the doctor was also concerned about my condition which he said was a combination of kidney and liver failure. But fortunately this only lasted for a couple of days, although it was a very unpleasant experience. Thankfully, none of the other members of my household were affected as badly as I was and by God's grace they have all now recovered."

"We heard that, besides yours, two other households in the Mellah were also affected by the same illness," said Ron.

"Yes, families in completely different parts of the Mellah. One of the families also suffered the death of an elderly relative who had been unwell for a long while, while others in both families were only somewhat affected, but all with the same symptoms."

"We noticed that your well is now covered over. Was the water found to be contaminated?" enquired Ron.

Avraham shrugged. "We do not know yet. The doctor came and took some water samples which he said that he would send to be tested. He said that he knew of a disease which was transmitted through rats' droppings. He told us that this might cause symptoms of stomach disorders followed by sudden kidney and liver failure. So we decided that the cautious and sensible thing would be to close all the wells used by the affected families until the water in them had been properly tested."

"That seems perfectly logical," agreed Ron.

"Oh, one more thing," said Avraham, "My wife found this lying in the courtyard by our well," Avraham reached into a drawer in his bedside cabinet and drew out a small empty vial. "What do you make of it?"

"It looks like something out of a laboratory," said Maggie examining the vial. "Perhaps your doctor dropped it while he was taking samples of water from the well?"

"That's also what I thought, but my wife says that she is sure that she found it the day before the doctor drew the samples - but she may be mistaken. She's been through a lot recently, what with my brother's death and my illness," said Avraham, "When the doctor next comes to visit I will ask him if he recognises it."

Then after exchanging more pleasantries and wishing Avraham a speedy recovery, Ron and Maggie took their leave.

Outside the Mellah's streets now seemed busier now. Children rushed about talking excitedly, telling their friends of the gifts they had received over Hanukkah and neighbouring housewives, sitting in their elevated covered wooden balconies, gossiped across the cobbled street.

As Ron and Maggie sauntered down the bustling street arm in arm, they did not cast a second glance in the direction of a man who stood in the shadows. The man had the hood of his djellaba pulled low over his head while observing the entrance to the courtyard of a house across the lane from Avraham's.

Then, when the street momentarily quietened, the hooded man slipped into the house's deserted courtyard. A careful observer would have noticed that the man's skin was pale, that he had a slight limp and wore military boots.

Once in the courtyard Sergeant Jager paused to look around. When he was sure that he was alone and unobserved he then quickly crossed over to the open well.

He reached his hand into the pocket of his djellaba. He felt three glass vials and gingerly extracted one of them. Then holding the vial well away from his face he carefully pulled out the stopper, leant over the open well and then with his arm still fully extended carefully tipped the vial's contents into the water.

Sergeant Jager stoppered the empty vial and pocketed it. He drew back into the deep shadows before stepping back out into the busy street and then headed off towards another section of the Mellah.

A further exchange of SS Memos, Monday 22nd December 1941

To: SS Standartenfuhrer Muller, Berlin.

From: SS Sturmbannfuhrer Schmidt. SS Kommandant, Morocco.

Subject: Poison Production Programme 71. Morocco.

I am pleased to report that following further production of purified Ricin we were able to apply the increased dose of Ricin (doubled estimated lethal dose) to a further two wells used exclusively by two local Jewish extended families.

The experiment was completely successful as it led to death in all members of the families regardless of age and state of health.

My full report, including technical details, dosage etc. is attached.

Heil Hitler!

To: SS Sturmbannfuhrer Schmidt. SS Kommandant, Morocco.

From: SS Standartenfuhrer Muller, Berlin.

Subject: Poison Production Programme 71. Morocco.

I am in receipt of your detailed report on the Ricin Poison Programme and I congratulate you on your success.

Your full report will be included in my final comprehensive recommendations to Obergruppenfuhrer Heydrich.

A meeting at the highest level of Schultz Staffel and Nazi officials is scheduled to be held in Wannsee, Berlin next month. The meeting will be chaired by Obergruppenfuhrer Heydrich and at this time all toxicology options will be considered.

Heil Hitler!

A sortie into the NorthEastern desert, Tuesday 23rd December 1941

The road stretched out endlessly before them as the jeep motored along, sending out a plume of dust in its wake. Ron and Maggie sat in the rear seats of the old vehicle. Both were dressed in black, with long scarves wrapped around their heads and lower faces to keep out the flying insects and grime. They had felt every bump along the rough desert road as the poorly sprung vehicle headed in an easterly direction towards the town of Oujda close to the border with Algeria.

"We must have done a couple of hundred kilometres at least," said Maggie shifting on the hard bench seat. "And my bottom can feel each one of them!"

"Stiff upper lip, old girl. We still have some way to go," responded Ron, grimly hanging on to a strap dangling from the roof bar as the jeep bounced along. "Let's hope this trip is worth the effort!" he added.

In the front seat Abbas battled with the driving wheel while Adil sat beside him. Adil held a rifle between his knees while his eyes continually scanned the rugged terrain around them.

A few days ago, Adil had responded to Ron's call for assistance in investigating the Nazi activity that Hamid had alerted them to and through his fledgling nationalist organisation, Adil had rustled up a serviceable jeep. He was more than willing to accompany Ron and Maggie on their reconnoitre. Afterall, he was as keen as anyone to see the Germans ousted from Morocco.

Abbas had volunteered to drive as the distance from Casablanca to Oujda was the best part of four hundred kilometres. Ron had thought that this would be sensible as it would leave the others free to handle whatever surprises their mission may throw up.

In the back of the jeep, Ron was dozing slightly when a change in the sound of the engine jerked him into alertness. The motor revs dropped, and Abbas brought the vehicle to a halt by the side of the road. The reason for the stop was apparent from the cloud of steam which rose from under the bonnet.

Adil looked round apologetically, "I'm afraid there is a small leak in the radiator. The water needs topping up from time to time."

Abbas opened the hood and once the engine had cooled down a bit, he refilled the radiator with water from a metal canister strapped to the back of the jeep and before too long they were on their way again.

A couple of hours later as dusk approached they had reached the outskirts of Oujda. The blood red sun gradually dipped out of sight on the distant horizon as Ron tapped Abbas on the shoulder.

"Abbas, can you stop now please. From here we need to follow the map coordinates that Hamid Hakim gave us."

As soon as the sun had set darkness rapidly spread across the bleak landscape and stars began to appear in the dark sky. Ron jumped off the jeep, extracted a sextant and a compass from his haversack and he took a bearing from a prominent bright star which he identified as Sirius.

"OK chaps. As far as I can tell, we must now leave the road and continue our journey on a bearing of 10 degrees."

"That's almost due north from here," said Maggie stretching and rubbing her backside.

Abbas turned left off the road and followed the direction indicated by Ron's outstretched arm. The going was rougher now and the jeep made slow and bumpy progress across the barren terrain.

After they had traversed a few kilometres, Ron checked his luminous compass dial.

"We are getting close, I think," he said. "Cut the headlights, Abbas. We must now be even more careful. It would be fatal to alert the Germans of our presence."

The jeep lights went out and they moved forward at a snail's pace. As they rounded a small hillock, up ahead in the distance they saw some flickering lights. Abbas silently brought the jeep to a stand still.

"That must be it," announced Ron. "Hamid's coordinates were spot on!"

Ron, Maggie and Adil now climbed out of the vehicle and prepared to move forward on foot. They exchanged their head scarves for black balaclavas and each had a small backpack. Adil was about to sling his rifle over his shoulder when Ron put out a restraining hand.

"That will be of no use, Adil. We can't afford to get into a firefight and carrying the rifle will only slow you down. Silence and stealth are what we need."

Adil nodded and dropped the rifle back onto the front seat. Then with a brief wave to Abbas, who would stay with the jeep, Ron and the other two melted into the darkness.

Adil, being more familiar with desert terrain, led the way. Their eyes were now growing accustomed to the darkness but they still made their way forward cautiously taking care to avoid large rocks and shrubs.

The lights grew brighter as they drew closer and Ron tapped Adil on the shoulder and signalled that they should circle round to the left. Adil moved forward but after a few steps tripped on something and half fell to the ground. He steadied himself up and gave the others a 'thumbs up' to signal that he was okay.

Looking closely at the ground around them, Maggie spied the obstacle that had caused Adil to stumble. A few centimetres above the ground, supported at intervals on concrete blocks was a dark metal pipeline. It was about twenty-five centimetres in diameter and seemed to run from north to south and directly towards the lights ahead.

Ron placed a hand on the pipe. "Hmm… feels cool to the touch," he whispered. He then dropped to his knees and put his ear against the metal. He heard a soft gurgling sound.

"I can hear that some liquid is flowing through it. Sounds more like water than oil to me. Let's follow the pipe, it seems to be leading straight towards that cluster of lights."

Now taking the lead, Ron led the others forward. Maggie followed closely with Adil bringing up the rear. As he walked, Adil fingered the hilt of a curved knife strapped to his belt.

When they were about three hundred metres from the lights they stopped and Ron took out a pair of night vision goggles with which he slowly scanned the area of the lights. The goggles were a very recent invention. He was lucky that Major Grimm had included a pair in his bag of tricks.

Ron whispered to the others, "It appears that there are about half a dozen large prefabricated buildings and a couple of barracks. There is no perimeter fencing and no visible sign of guards either. Perhaps the Germans feel they are secure in this isolated part of the country."

"But the area is quite well lit," said Maggie pointing to the tall towers set at the four corners of the camp. On each tower was mounted a spotlight that illuminated the buildings and ground between them. Ron passed the goggles to her and she could see that some of the buildings had lights showing through the windows and that one had a couple of tall aerials rising from the roof.

Ron nodded in agreement but did not reply. His attention was drawn to one of the buildings larger than the others, it had a prominent chimney mounted on the roof from which, in the beam of the spotlights, a tiny wisp of smoke was visible rising into the dark sky.

Maggie now took out her camera and took some photos of the buildings and towers.

"Let's take a closer dekko at the buildings," said Ron pointing. "Adil, stay here and keep watch while Maggie and I have a look. If you spot anything can you give us a warning signal?"

"I can do a convincing fox growl," responded Adil, white teeth gleaming under his black balaclava.

With Maggie leading, they carefully made their way forward, taking care to keep in the long shadows that the buildings cast across the countryside. Silently they approached the large building with the chimney that had caught Ron's interest. The prefab building was set on large concrete blocks that raised it above the surface of the ground.

As they drew close they realised that the windows were high above their heads and that a ladder would be required for them to look inside. Maggie leaned over and whispered into Ron's ear, "Brace yourself against the wall and I'll climb up on your shoulders."

Ron raised his eyebrows but nodded in agreement. Maggie placed a foot into Ron's cupped hands and nimbly jumped up onto his broad shoulders, balancing herself easily.

Maggie gingerly raised herself to full height and peered through the window. Her eyes were first drawn to a large steel control panel mounted on the far wall. It had a number of switches, knobs, lights and dials. In one corner of the room was a rectangular bin containing some bright red material that looked like plant seeds. She noticed that placed centrally was a large circular iron vessel with a number of pipes feeding into it from below and above.

There was no one visible and the lights on the control panel were not illuminated. Maggie presumed that the laboratory was not presently in use and so seizing the opportunity she carefully unhooked her camera from her belt and quickly took a few photos of the strange manufacturing equipment within.

Silently she climbed down from Ron's shoulders and gave him a thumbs up sign. Ron nodded but then pointed up towards the tower on their right. Maggie could now see that the beam of the spotlight was moving in a slow arc.

"There are guards on the towers," whispered Ron. Maggie was about to respond when they heard a low animal's growl coming from the direction where they had left Adil.

"Adil's signal," mouthed Ron, dropping to a prone position on the ground and Maggie did likewise. They waited motionless, their senses on full alert.

After less than a minute, they heard the faint sound of boots and saw a man emerging from around the next building. He stopped about twenty metres away from them and they heard a match being struck. In the light of the flaring match they saw the forage cap and shoulder flashes of a German soldier.

The German had his back to them, and Ron made a quick decision. He motioned Maggie to wait, extracted an object from his backpack and crouching low, crept towards the soldier.

When Ron was within a couple of metres, the man seemed to sense or perhaps hear someone behind him. He dropped his cigarette and reached for his holster belt, but before he could turn, utter a word or draw his gun Ron had risen to his full height and had swung the lead cosh catching the German full on the side of his head.

Without a sound, the man dropped like a stone. Ron broke the man's fall, beckoned Maggie over and whispered instructions. They swiftly bound the soldier's hands and feet with pieces of strong cord and gagged him with a large handkerchief. Ron could see that the soldier's collar and shoulder insignia were that of a SS sergeant.

They waited for the searchlight to pan far away and then Ron lifted the man's shoulders while Maggie grabbed his feet and between them they half carried and half dragged the soldier's limp body to where Adil was awaiting them.

When Adil saw them approaching, he went forward and took over from Maggie.

"What are you doing, are you mad?" whispered Adil to Ron angrily. "They will discover the soldier missing and realise something is afoot."

Ron nodded "Yes, I know that, old chap. But we need to know what is going on in this place, and pretty damn quick. I thought that this man may be the best chance we have of finding out. Now, let's get back to the jeep and make tracks."

It was quite an effort to move the unconscious German over the pipeline and back to where Abbas and the jeep were waiting. Without wasting a moment, they dumped the inert body in the back of the jeep and clambered aboard.

"Come on, come on Abbas, let's get back to Casablanca," said Adil, clearly quite agitated and keen that they get away before someone raised the alarm at the German camp.

He turned to Ron, "And there you can decide what you plan to do with this prisoner who you so rashly decided to take!"

"Actually, hang on a minute. I have an idea," said Ron thoughtfully. "Hamid Hakim's camp is on our route back. Abbas, we should stop there. I would be surprised if our Arab friend doesn't have a trick or two up his sleeve when it comes to interrogating the enemy."

Maggie raised her eyebrows but said nothing. She turned her head and stared ahead at the rough track which was now dimly illuminated by the jeeps side lights.

A nocturnal visit to Hamid's camp, Wednesday 24th December 1941

It was three in the morning when the jeep pulled up at the sentry point at the border of Hamid Hakim's encampment. This time it needed all of Ron and Adil's persuasive skills to convince the guards of the urgency of their visit at this unearthly hour.

Hamid had not been pleased to be awoken from his slumber. Grumbling loudly, he had roughly pushed away the naked girl sleeping next to him, donned his djellaba and entered the central marquee.

"Monsieur Ron, what is so important that it cannot wait until the sun has risen? I am not used to entertaining guests at this hour," he said in an irritated tone.

Ron gave a short bow, "My extreme apologies for disturbing you like this, Hamid. But the matter is extremely urgent and of the greatest importance I assure you."

He nodded to Adil and Abbas who were standing at the entrance of the tent. "Bring him in."

A few moments later, the two men dragged in the captured German soldier who had now recovered consciousness. He was still bound hand and foot and could not move from where he had been dumped on the floor in front of Hamid and the others.

Hamid's face slowly lit up with an evil grin. He stroked his beard and nodded.

"Ah, Ron, I see you come bearing gifts. You are welcome indeed. Let us take off the gag and see what this pig has to say."

Adil stepped forward, brought out his knife and slashed the gag free. The German spat out some mud and shook his head to clear it.

"I need some water," he croaked, speaking in French. "Please..."

Hamid nodded, and one of his henchmen brought over a glass of water and held it to the soldier's lips. He drank greedily and seemed to recover some of his composure.

Ron walked over to the German. "Who are you?" he asked in French.

"Sergeant Jager. Erkennungsmarken 7539234." Was the reply.

"What were you doing out in the desert?" asked Ron, looking the German straight in the eye.

"Sergeant Jager. Erkennungsmarken 7539234."

"Ok let's try again. What is the function of the camp at which we found you?"

"Sergeant Jager. Erkennungsmarken 7539234. Under the Geneva convention I am required to give you only my name, rank and number."

Ron shrugged and looking at Maggie said in French, "Right Maggie, let's have a little stroll outside, I'll show you the moon and stars while we let Hamid continue with the questions. Now I wonder if he's ever heard of a Geneva convention?"

As Sergeant Jager realised what was happening his face grew taut in alarm. But he said nothing.

Ron and Maggie walked out of the tent and beckoned Adil and Abbas to follow them. As Ron led Maggie to the edge of the camp, she said, "Ron, I'm not so sure we're doing the right thing, leaving that soldier there in the hands of these barbarians."

"You may be right, old girl, but it's a tough game. If we had been discovered back there on our recce, we would have been shot on the spot. There's no time to lose. It is imperative that we learn what's going on at that site and inform London. I just want Hamid to soften the guy up a little until we get some proper answers."

For a few minutes they stood and looked up at the serene sky where the stars were twinkling brightly when suddenly the silence was broken by a terrified cry. A few moments later this was followed by another shriek and then a couple more.

Maggie's fingers dug into Ron's forearm and her forehead wrinkled with concern. She was about to speak when they heard a shout with some garbled words in French. "Non, non,…..arrêt, arrêt!".

"Perhaps he has found his tongue after all. Let's go back," said Ron grimly.

As Ron and Maggie entered the tent again they smelled the odour of burning flesh. The German soldier lay trembling on the ground with his eyes closed. His boots had been removed and a thin wisp of black smoke rose from his scorched bare soles. Hamid was seated a few feet in front of the man, a burning torch in the ground by his side and next to him an assortment of evil looking knives laid out on a dirty cloth.

"Ah there you are Ron," said Hamid cheerfully. "It seems our German canary may be ready to sing us a song."

"Sergeant, I am not going to repeat my questions. It is best, for your own health, that you answer them without delay," said Ron sharply. "What is the function of the installation where we found you?"

The German opened his eyes fractionally and spoke in a hoarse whisper.

"It is a scientific laboratory. The technicians are finding medical cures."

"Medical cures? For what ailments?" barked Ron disbelievingly.

"For many diseases, uh uh, malaria, dengue fever."

"Why have the scientists come all the way to Morocco to research such cures?"

"I don't know, I'm just a soldier, I only do as I am ordered," stammered the Sergeant.

Ron turned to Hamid, "It appears that this canary just has fairy tales for us. I'll go for another walk while you keep him warm."

As Ron walked toward the entrance, Hamid sighed and pulled the burning torch out of the ground. Seeing this the German screamed, "Wait, wait. Okay, I'll tell you what I know."

Ron turned back and dropped to one knee in front of the prone man. "No tricks now. It's your last chance."

"I do not know the details, but I heard that the laboratory is for the manufacture of a poisonous substance. A powder I think."

"But why come all this way to Morocco to make poison?"

"They are collecting Castor plants which grow in the desert. From these pods the poison is extracted and purified. That's all I know. Honest to God."

Ron was taken aback by this revelation but kept his face expressionless.

"What is the laboratory's capacity to produce the poison at present?"

"Very little, I think. I believe there are problems with the water supply. Water is essential for the process to function."

"Where is the water coming from?" asked Ron thinking about the pipeline they had discovered near the plant.

"It is piped down from a town on the Northern coast, I don't know which one."

"Has the poison been tested at all?"

"No, no. Not at all, I swear it."

Whilst not convinced of this last answer, Ron figured that they had got enough useful information from the man. He signalled to Maggie and the others that it was time to leave.

"Hamid, we must be on our way now. We have much work to do now that the purpose of the laboratory is known. Thank you for your assistance. But I fear I will have to leave the sergeant in your hands as we have no means to hold him in Casablanca."

"Do not worry Ron," said Hamid with a humourless chuckle. Raising his hand in farewell he added. "We will take care of this one for you and he will tell us everything he knows.. Perhaps we will take him sunbathing in the desert."

As Maggie and Ron left the tent, they heard the German calling out in a shaky voice, "Hey, do not leave me here with these animals. Have pity. Take me with you!"

The four of them climbed into the jeep and with Abbas at the wheel, they slowly pulled away into the approaching dawn. As they departed Sergeant Jager's desperate cries behind them grew fainter and fainter.

. .

. .

Joining up the dots,
Wednesday 24th December 1941

Maggie and Ron knocked on the door of Yusuf's house. Hearing the coded knock Yusuf quickly opened the door and let them in.

"It is unusual to see you at this early hour, it is barely seven o'clock," said Yusuf with a slightly surprised expression. "But come in and make yourselves comfortable. Unless I am mistaken, you both look quite weary."

"Thanks Yusuf," said Ron, lowering himself onto a divan. Your observation is spot on. We have been awake all night and have covered many hundreds of kilometres in a bumpy jeep."

With a long sigh, Maggie sat down next to Ron and leaned her shoulder against his. She added, "We are lucky to be back in one piece and we've come straight here from our journey. There is evil business involved, and we cannot waste time."

Yusuf raised his eyebrows questioningly, then nodded. "Let me first bring you some tea and then we can discuss matters." With that he disappeared into the kitchen.

Once they were each holding a welcome cup of steaming tea Ron briefed Yusuf on their adventures at the German plant near Oujda and of their subsequent visit to Hamid Hakim's camp in the dead of night.

"We have photographs of the plant. They must go to London immediately for examination and interpretation. The boffins will be able to make more sense of them than we can," said Maggie.

"Of course Maggie, we can do that right after we have concluded our meeting. The pigeons are ready."

Ron continued, "Now we have a pretty good idea of what the plant is producing, thanks to our little chat with the captured Sergeant. I feel pretty sure Hamid persuaded him to speak the truth."

"Well, the photos should help to confirm the purpose of the plant, " said Maggie while she stifled a yawn.

"Yes indeed," agreed Ron. He paused and added, "But you know there is something niggling at the back of my mind. When I asked our prisoner whether the poison had been tested, his denial did not ring true."

The three of them sat in silence for a few moments and then looked at each other with open mouths as the same thought hit them all at the same time.

"The unexplained ailments in the Mellah!"

"The death of Avraham's brother!"

"The glass vial which Avraham's wife found next to their well!"

"And while you were away there were further deaths in the Mellah, again restricted to individual families."

"The Germans have been poisoning the water in the wells!"

Now fully alert to what they had deduced, they discussed their next actions.

Ron took control of the situation, "Yusuf, I need to speak to London right now. We must go to the safe house and set up the wireless. And Maggie, can you get Abbas to drive you to Avraham's house. You must speak to him in person as it's too risky to send a message. Inform him that all wells in the Jewish Mellah neighbourhood must be immediately sealed and guarded. The water has almost certainly been poisoned and so the elders must arrange for drinking water to be brought in from sources outside the Mellah."

Yusuf and Maggie nodded and sprang into action. First Yusuf clambered up to his pigeon coop where he chose the sleekest looking carrier pigeon. He strapped Maggie's film roll to its leg and then released it into the sky with its valuable cargo.

Maggie gave Ron a quick kiss and made her way out into the street. She walked briskly to where Abbas was waiting in the jeep and jumped in next to him. She gave him instructions of where to go and they set off towards the mellah.

Then Ron jumped on the back of Yusuf's motorbike and they rode off to the safe house in the medina where they quickly set up the wireless, and Ron made contact with London. He requested for Headmaster to be patched in. Greaves-Mortimer's voice came over the radio.

"Headmaster here, do you read me Sabre?"

"Sabre here. We have an update on those activities up north. We believe that the Huns are manufacturing a deadly poison in a specially constructed laboratory located in the middle of the desert near Oujda."

"Hmmm. go on Sabre." responded Greaves-Mortimer.

"The lab may not be fully up to speed yet, but we believe that some poison has already been produced and is being covertly tested on the Jewish civilian community in Casablanca. There have been some fatalities."

"Quite a bolt from the blue, not what we were expecting at all," said Greaves-Mortimer in a worried tone. "Do you know the nature of this poison?"

"No, but we have been told that it is a powder extracted from Castor plants which are said to grow in abundance around that area. We have just dispatched photographic film of the lab, via the usual carrier channel."

"Sabre, are you aware of plans to use the poison beyond the suspected test in Casablanca?"

"Negative, Headmaster. One more thing though, there are water pipelines running to the lab site from a town on the north coast. Presumably, given the effort in construction, this infrastructure is vital to the production process."

"Understood. Will digest your intel, discuss it with our team here and respond soonest. Good work, Sabre. Over and out and I wish you and your team a Merry Christmas."

Ron switched off the Marconi wireless set and placed the microphone on the table. Yusuf quickly dismantled the aerial and stowed the equipment away in its hiding place under the loose flagstone.

With their immediate task completed, Yusuf gave Ron a lift back to Maggie's apartment.

Alighting from the bike Ron stretched and said thoughtfully "Thanks Yusuf. I'm pretty sure we'll hear back from London soon and I suspect our work here may not be finished. Not by a long chalk."

Yusuf nodded to Ron, put the motorcycle into gear and gunned it down the street.

The SS Office - German Embassy Casablanca, Wednesday 24th December 1941

Major Schmidt re-read the memo which he had received earlier that day.

To: SS Sturmbannfuhrer Schmidt. SS Kommandant, Morocco.

From: SS Standartenfuhrer Muller, Berlin.

Subject: Poison Production Programme 71. Morocco.

Following discussion related to your detailed technical report relating to Ricin production and its dissemination among the civilian population it has now been decided to consider the expansion of this ongoing project.

The high command is aware that in North Africa and in many areas of France the Jewish population is well integrated into the general population, this may make extraction of the Jewish populations from their homes and into concentration camps difficult. High command is therefore considering using Ricin selectively upon local Jewish populations across the whole of North Africa and then extending this action into France. The fatalities from the poisoning will be presented as localised epidemics of disease restricted to Jewish neighbourhoods.

As there is an abundant supply of Castor plants in your area it has been decided to consider expanding the Moroccan Ricin production plant. This will involve increases in both infrastructure development and manpower.

In order to discuss the feasibility and schedule of this project I will be making a visit to the production plant on 31 December 1941. My final arrival time will be signalled in advance.

Heil Hitler!

Schmidt put down the memo and scratched his nose. He had mixed feelings about this. On the one hand he was proud that his efforts had been acknowledged and considered so important. But on the other hand he felt that he was being roped into a role of full time factory manager. He did not fancy that, especially when the factory was to be located deep in an isolated part of the desert!

There was a knock at his office door and a soldier informed Schmidt that they had now managed to get Doctor Roth at the production plant on the radio. Schmidt nodded and walked down the corridor to the telecommunication room.

Schmidt picked up the handset, "Roth, is that you?"

The doctor's voice was clear despite the background static, "Yes, Herr Sturmbannführer, this is Roth speaking."

"Roth, I just have had a message from Standartenfuhrer Muller to say that he will be paying us another visit in the next few days. I will inform you of the exact details nearer the time but in the meanwhile you will need to make sure that the runway is cleared of all debris and that the plant looks shipshape."

"Standartenfuhrer Muller! Again? He has only recently visited! Do you know why he is returning, Herr Sturmbannfuhrer?" asked the doctor, taken aback.

"It appears that our project has performed so well that high command is considering expanding the project and making us the central hub for major production."

"That is excellent news, Herr Sturbannfuhrer!" exclaimed the doctor, obviously excited.

"Are there any issues with production which I should know about, Roth?"

"No, Herr Sturbannfuhrer. No issues with production… but can I enquire if you have seen or heard anything from Sergeant Jager?"

"Jager? Why should I have heard anything from Jager? He should be there with you at the plant collecting a further consignment of Ricin."

"Yes," stammered the doctor, "He was here, but now he seems to have disappeared."

"Disappeared? Disappeared where?" said Schmidt incredulously, "You are in the middle of the desert, there is nowhere to go. How can he have disappeared?"

"But there is no sign of him, Herr Sturbannfuhrer. He had dinner in the mess last night but after that he has not been seen at all and his bed has not been slept in."

"Is his vehicle still there?"

"Yes, Herr Sturbannfuhrer."

"Have you searched the camp and the area around?"

"Yes, Herr Sturbannfuhrer. There is no sign of him anywhere."

"Was there any unusual activity around the camp last night?"

"No, Herr Sturbannfuhrer. Nothing unusual," said the doctor nervously, "The Afrika Korps guards here think that he may have gone for a walk in the desert and got lost."

"A walk? In the wilderness? Nonsense!"

"According to the guards it is not unusual for the vast desert to evoke melancholia in a soldier resulting in unusual behaviour. They say it is quite common for being away from home at Christmas to cause such melancholia."

Schmidt snorted, "Jager, melancholic! Now I have heard everything! What a load of rubbish!"

"The Afrika Korp guards also said that they thought it was possible that Jager may have been bitten by a venomous snake… There are many vipers and cobras out here and it is easy to step on one in the dark. Or on a poisonous scorpion… You know we found a snake in one of our production chambers the other day. The Afrika Korp guards say that they have heard of soldiers becoming disoriented and confused after a snake bite and then inadvertently walking out into the desert."

"Tell the Afrika Korp guards that they should just concentrate on locating Jager quickly. Send out more search parties and, Roth, keep me updated. I do not want anything to interfere with Standartenfuhrer Muller's visit."

"I will do my best, Herr Sturbannfuhrer."

"You better find Jager and also don't forget to have the runway cleared."

"Yes, Herr Sturbannfuhrer. Hiel Hitler!"

The line went dead, and Schmidt put down the receiver. Schmidt had an intense and pathological fear of snakes and the mention of cobras and vipers had shot up his anxiety levels. Now the thought of high command designating him to be the poison plant's factory manager filled him with a new dread - he imagined being stuck out in the middle of the desert surrounded by masses of slithering venomous snakes and by creeping scorpions! The thought of this made Schmidt shudder involuntarily.

A high level meeting in Whitehall, Friday 26th December 1941

It was nine o'clock on Boxing Day morning when Greaves-Mortimer arrived at his desk in Whitehall. He hadn't slept well and had woken up with a nagging headache, perhaps due to those few extra glasses of sherry on Christmas day.

The conversation that he had with Casablanca a few days earlier had been playing on his mind. He pressed the button of the intercom on his desk.

"Morning Lydia, some coffee please. And a couple of Aspirin, if you can get your hands on some."

There was a big day ahead and Greaves-Mortimer needed a clear head. He had called an urgent high-level meeting later that morning to discuss the recent intel from Flt Lieutenant Ron Sen.

After a few minutes, there was a soft knock on the door and Lydia came in with a cup of coffee and a small plate.

"Here you are, sir," she said cheerfully. "I had some Aspirin in my drawer, and I brought you a couple of mince pies. I hope you had a nice Christmas, sir."

"Thanks… err Lydia. Very nice, thank you. That will do nicely," responded Greaves-Mortimer distractedly while reaching into a buff folder on his desk from which he extracted some large photos.

He sipped his coffee and swallowed the aspirin. Then picking up a magnifying glass, he studied the photos. They showed the inside of what looked like a laboratory or processing plant and some surrounding buildings. For a long moment, he stared at the photo of the large containers of Castor pods, before finally replacing them into the folder and placing the folder into his briefcase.

At ten to eleven, Greaves-Mortimer picked up his briefcase and left his office. He took the stairs to the top floor and entered a well-appointed meeting room.

A couple of the meeting attendees had arrived already. One was his own Chief-of-staff Major Smith and the other he recognised as Group Captain Fotheringham. They shook hands.

"Hope you are well gentlemen, I'm sorry to have had to drag you out on Boxing Day. Do help yourselves to some refreshment." said Greaves-Mortimer waving to the sideboard that had been laid in advance of the meeting.

On the dot of eleven, three other officers entered the room. Once they were all seated around the meeting table with cups of tea and biscuits, Greaves-Mortimer suggested that they introduce themselves.

"Group Captain James Fotheringham, 226 Bomber Command, RAF Northolt. Hello chaps."

"Commodore William Ambrose. Fleet Air Arm. Based out of Portsmouth. Got a train up this morning. Bit of a trek, I can tell you."

"Morning. Major Smith here. Chief-of-staff for Mr Greaves-Mortimer."

"Mike Brown. From the Toxicology and Poisons Division at Porton Downs."

"Pleased to meet you, gentlemen. I'm John Worthington. SOE Assistant Director, London."

"And I believe that you all know who I am," concluded Greaves-Mortimer. "Thank you all for making the time at such short notice. But the matter is of the utmost urgency and I must act quickly. It goes without saying that our discussions here must remain strictly between yourselves."

Over the following half an hour, Greaves-Mortimer outlined the mission that he had initiated in Morocco, and the information that had been received from Ron following the coastal and inland reconnoitres. Major Smith chipped in with his assessment of the photographic evidence received to date.

Greaves-Mortimer continued, "Our operatives on the ground have done a sterling job of exploring the coastline for potential landing sites. This has been passed on to the relevant parties, most significantly our American allies."

"Do we know if an invasion has been confirmed?" asked Commodore Ambrose.

"I am not privy to that information," replied Greaves-Mortimer, "but we must assume that it may happen, and soon!"

He looked around the table, "So, now let's focus on the next matter concerning a poison production facility. This seems to be an urgent and major threat."

He took out the buff folder from his briefcase and passed around the photos Maggie had taken of the German processing plant.

"Have a look at these. They arrived last night by carrier pigeon. Brown, who is from Porton Downs, has already had a look at these this morning along with the other intel. Could you tell us what to make of these, Brown?"

Brown leant forward on his elbows, "I understand the operatives in Morocco have learnt that the poison is being extracted from Castor plants, which grows wild in the Moroccan desert. The operatives have also indicated that the poison has been used to contaminate the local water supply."

Brown leant back in his chair and steepled his finger-tips together, "Castor plants are the source of a poison called

Ricin, contained within the plants' pods. In case you are not aware, Ricin is one of the most poisonous substances known to man."

The assembled group took a few minutes to digest this piece of information and to look at the supporting photographs.

Brown then continued, "Ricin can be produced in either an aerosol form which, when inhaled, causes immediate lung damage and death. Alternatively, it can be manufactured in a crystalline powder form which, if drunk or eaten, causes gastrointestinal symptoms. If the dose is high enough, then the gastric symptoms are followed by liver and kidney failure which can be fatal. From what we know I suspect we are dealing with the crystalline form of Ricin here and the equipment in the photographs of the factory would be typical for this sort of production."

"If the Germans are producing enough of this stuff and have proved its efficacy, then the ramifications are enormous," said Worthington thoughtfully. "They could begin using the poison in all sorts of other locations, France for starters."

"Another possibility is that German spies bring in concentrated amounts of poison to use here in Blighty," added Major Smith.

Brown raised his hand to speak, "May I also add that there is no known antidote against Ricin."

Greaves-Mortimer nodded, "Very worrying indeed. Fortunately, it appears that the water supply, which is crucial to the production process, has been flaky. It has to be piped in from a city on Morocco's northern coast. This may have somewhat limited the quantity of poison that can currently be produced. But I suspect that this may be a temporary glitch."

"In any event, there seems no time to lose," said Group Captain Fotheringham briskly. "I say we rustle up a few Lancasters and bomb the hell out of the place. Your chaps on the ground have provided good location coordinates for us to work from."

Commodore Ambrose spoke, "Another option is to pull up a Fletcher-class destroyer from Gibraltar. Sounds as if the plant could be in range from the north coast. Our heavy artillery on board can strike targets at 25 miles or perhaps further."

The meeting went on for a while, discussing the pros and cons of the various ideas that each person put forward. Then Greaves-Mortimer raised a hand.

"Gentlemen, gentlemen, thank you. However, notwithstanding all your suggestions, there is one overriding factor that we cannot ignore. The elephant in the room, if you will."

"Ah… of course, the possible invasion," murmured Commodore Ambrose with a slight smile.

"Exactly!" exclaimed Greaves-Mortimer, "We cannot jeopardise such a major allied operation by pre-emptive use of overt military force. An attack on the plant by RAF bombers or Naval artillery from the Mediterranean, would put the Germans on full alert. It would transform Morocco from being on the fringes of the war into a full-fledged battle zone. I have no doubt that the Huns would respond by increasing their presence in Morocco, and bolstering up their defences which could scupper the success of an invasion. This would go down like a bomb with the Yanks."

The room fell silent for a few moments, while they mentally grappled with this dilemma.

"So, is it full circle, back to the SOE then?" asked Major Smith, looking questioningly around the room.

The senior SOE officer, John Worthington nodded in agreement, "Yes, it looks that way doesn't it. The destruction of the poison production facility must be a clandestine operation. Our chaps on the ground must come up with a plan of action that would leave the German high command thinking there was an unfortunate accident."

"Yes, I agree," added Greaves-Mortimer. "In any event, we must keep the Allied involvement concealed."

There was a general nodding of heads in consensus.

Realising that the meeting had come to a conclusion, Greaves-Mortimer rose to his feet and inclined his head.

"Thank you, gentlemen, thank you for your time. I needed your views and experience on this tricky and deeply sensitive situation. You have all provided these admirably. Now excuse me, I must make haste and get things moving. I wish you all a safe journey back."

The men dispersed to go their separate ways, but a couple of minutes later there was a soft hesitant knock on Greaves-Mortimer's door. It was Mike Brown, the scientist from Porton Downs.

"A brief word, sir?" he asked.

"Of course."

"You know you mentioned that it would be for the SOE agents on the ground to deal with destroying the Ricin poison plant."

"Yes?"

"Well," said Brown, "I think your agents may be interested in some of the chemical aspects of Ricin production which may prove to be useful."

"I'm all ears, Brown. Go on."

Not your traditional Moroccan handicraft, Sunday 28th December 1941

Ron and Maggie woke early, and after a quick shower, had breakfast on the little patio outside. They had a busy day ahead.

Their conversation with Greaves-Mortimer the previous night had left no doubt of the enormity of the task before them. His words had been frighteningly stark.

"The poison plant poses a grave threat and must be completely obliterated. And due to circumstances which I am not at liberty to divulge, this must be achieved without leaving any trace of allied involvement. Awfully sorry Flight Lieutenant, but this means that London cannot overtly assist on this."

Over breakfast Ron and Maggie mulled over this directive, and bounced a few ideas off each other.

"To start off with, we can't manage this without some local help," said Maggie, buttering a piece of toast.

"Agreed," responded Ron. "Let's see … we have Yusuf and Abbas of course. But I'm pretty sure we'll need more brawn as well as brains to do this."

"Your wild man in the desert could provide the brawn all right," Maggie gave a small grimace remembering their last encounter with Hamid Hakim.

Ron nodded, "Yes, no time to be squeamish. Hamid's men will need to be drafted in. And for the more skilled tasks, I think we must have a word with Adil Al-Barker, our freedom fighter chappie."

Ron stirred his cup of tea thoughtfully, "But before we contact anyone, we need a clear plan. Mags, I have an idea or two in the back of my mind, but it's not yet making much sense yet. I could probably come up with something better if we could visualise the plant somehow. Perhaps I could draw something on paper?"

Maggie thought for a moment and then smiled, "Ah, I can do better than that. Leave it to me. Come on, we need to do a little shopping, then I can show you what I mean."

They cleared up the breakfast dishes and were soon on their way in the old Citroen. Maggie pulled up outside a stationery shop and dashed inside whilst Ron waited in the car. After ten minutes or so she emerged carrying a large bag. They continued on their way, then parked a couple of streets away from the safe house in the Medina.

Taking the usual precautions to ensure they were not being followed, they reached the front door which Maggie quickly opened with her key.

Once inside the house, Maggie told Ron that she needed a couple of hours to prepare and suggested that he walk over to Yusuf's house and bring him over. Ron raised his eyebrows, but decided to trust Maggie on this, though he was none the wiser about what she was up to. He kissed her and headed outside.

Once alone, Maggie went over to the dining table and pulled out the contents of her shopping bag. There were several large sheets of cardboard and stiff card-paper. A box of paints, a bottle of glue, a ball of string, a bunch of thin wooden sticks and a pair of scissors completed her purchases.

Maggie laid out the items on the dining table and started to work.

As she cut and folded the stiff paper she recalled her previous role as a plotter in the WAAF. Before joining the SOE, she had worked around a huge map table receiving information of aircraft coordinates through her headphones. Then, using a long wooden pole moved small blocks on the map, to show enemy and friendly aircraft positions on the map. This visual representation had helped the senior RAF officers, looking down at the map from a gallery above, to make quick decisions about which squadrons to scramble to intercept the enemy, send out air-raid warnings and so on.

Her experience as a plotter had given Maggie an idea about how to create a visual design from which to develop a plan. She was building a replica of the poison plant site based on what she had seen on their recce mission. Maggie had a phenomenal photographic memory which helped her accurately to recreate the plant's layout.

Over the next hour Maggie constructed little models of the buildings, towers, the pipeline and other topographic details that flashed up in her mind.

Each miniature piece slowly took shape using the craft materials that she had purchased. She painted the pieces in suitable colours and glued them into place on a large thick sheet of light brown cardboard whose colour did a good job of representing the desert sand.

Finally, Maggie finished her task, stood from the table and inspected the mock-up from a little distance away. It looked surprisingly life-like, and she allowed herself a satisfied smile.

At that moment there was a coded knock. Maggie opened the door to Ron and Yusuf.

While Yusuf went off to brew some tea, Maggie grabbed Ron's arm and pulled him over to the dining table. There she showed him the model she had created.

Ron examined it for a couple of minutes then with a wide grin, turned to Maggie and gave her a hug.

"Well done old girl, it's just the ticket! I can already see why some of my half-baked ideas just wouldn't fly. But there are still a couple of ideas in my mind that could possibly work. Let me think for a moment."

He pulled up a chair and sat down in front of the reproduction of the poison plant. Rubbing his chin, he studied the model intently from various angles. Muttering softly to himself he tapped it at various points and traced imaginary paths with a finger as he mentally married up his initial ideas to the physical realities highlighted by the model. Then with a deep sigh, he leaned back and looked up at Maggie and outlined the plan taking shape in his head.

When Ron had finished, Maggie's face looked worried. Ron could tell that she was rather concerned by what he had just told her.

Yusuf returned from the kitchen with the tea. Though he had also been listening to Ron's words he showed no reaction on his inscrutable face.

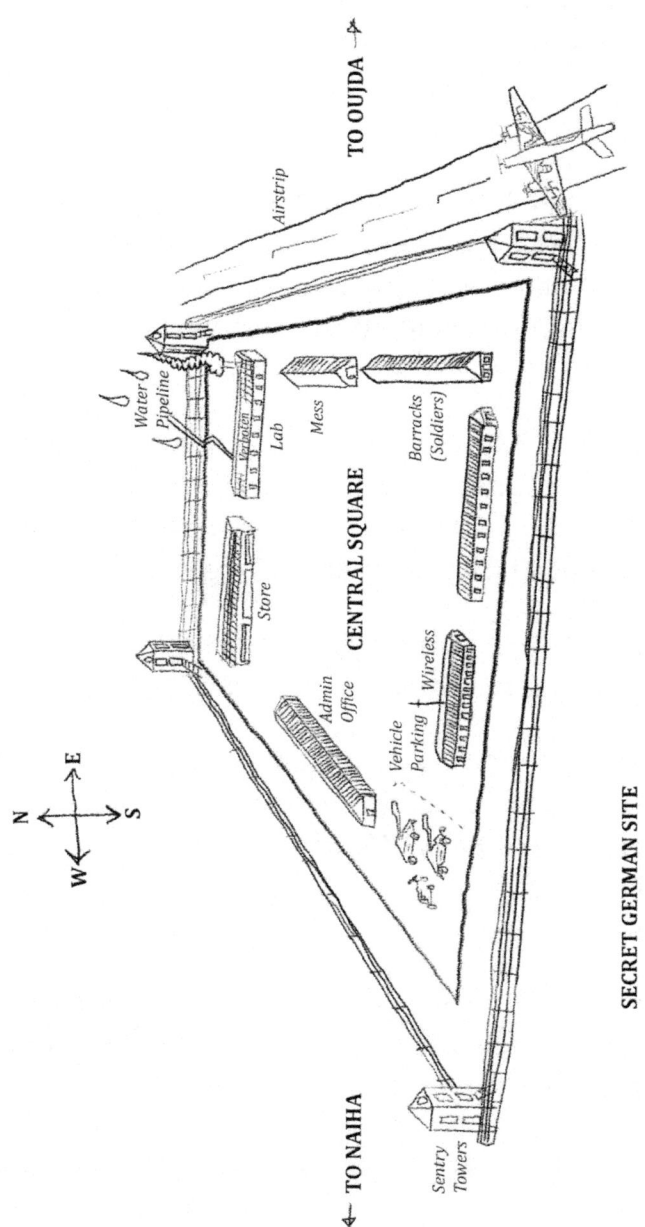

**Brothers in arms,
Monday 29th December 1941**

Ron and Maggie had arranged to meet Adil Al-Baker at Yusuf's safe house set deep in the medina. Over a cup of ubiquitous mint tea Ron and Maggie outlined to Adil the latest information and directives which they had received from London.

"As you already know the Germans are extracting the poison from the Castor plant. The experts in London tell us that the poison is called Ricin and that it is one of the most lethal known poisons," said Maggie.

Adil nodded, "I see, and the Germans have already begun poisoning the Jewish wells in Casablanca."

"Exactly and London believes that this is just the start, and that communities all over North Africa and in France are also at risk of attack. Which is why we must destroy the plant as soon as we can. But can we count on your help?" asked Ron.

Adil nodded vigorously, "Of course! The Germans are murdering my fellow Morrocans. It is my national duty to assist you as best I can. This is my battle!"

"Excellent. With Yusuf's help we are building a plan of action. Of course, it's going to be a trickier and a bigger operation than the one when we were out there last time," explained Ron.

"Of course," agreed Adil.

"Come, let me show you something, added Ron. He rose from the sofa and motioned towards the dining table which was covered over with a delicate white cloth. They all gathered around the table and Maggie carefully pulled away the cloth to reveal the mock-up she had made of the poison manufacturing plant.

Adil leaned forward and peered at it with interest, recalling their trip there a few days earlier.

"What a good idea!" exclaimed Adil. "This should prove very useful in understanding exactly what we need to do. Just looking at this brings a vivid recollection of our night-time visit to that awful place."

Maggie smiled and made a little hand gesture, acknowledging the compliment to her handiwork.

"We are planning another surprise night-time operation. Once again on a dark and moonless night," said Yusuf.

"Our current thinking is that we will mount a multi-pronged attack. Small teams striking here, here and here," said Ron tapping and tracing a finger across various points on the mock-up.

"But this time we will need more than just your vehicle, Adil. Our plan will also need a few of your men and some hardware," added Ron.

Adil nodded, "I will do my best."

"Do any of your men have any technical experience? Nothing extraordinary needed. A plumber or a carpenter?"

"Yes, we do indeed have volunteers from both of those trades," replied Adil.

Ron produced a piece of paper with a short list of items and handed it to Adil. "We can go through how these items will be used in a minute, but first do you think you can get these for us?"

Adil scanned the list, "Hmm… plastic explosives with timers. Very tricky, but I have an American contact who may be able to help. The Americans have helped with such a request in the past although they are obviously very careful that explosives are never traced back to them. You know that thus far they pretend to be neutral in this war."

"That's good," said Ron. "Actually, the plastic explosives are probably the most difficult item on that list."

Adil looked at the list again, "Metal cutters, a metal drill and a large funnel. That should be easy to get." He returned to consulting the list, "Hydrogen peroxide…Hydrogen peroxide? What's that?"

"It's a chemical. It's like a bleach. It's also the stuff they use to dilute natural dyes and I seem to remember that I saw many canisters of it in a carpet factory which Maggie and I recently visited. Do you think you will be able to get us several gallons?"

Adil smiled broadly, "If it's something which is used in the production of carpets then I should be able to get you as many gallons as you desire!" he declared.

"That's excellent," said Ron, sipping his tea. "Now let's go through the other items, then I will tell you about your part in the plan."

Ron moved over to the mock-up of the poison site and as he spoke he pointed to various locations across the model. Adil listened, observing intently, while nodding and occasionally asking a question.

Gathering of the clans,
Wednesday 31st December 1941

It was ten o'clock when Ron, Maggie and Yusuf arrived at the agreed rendezvous point outside the village of Naima, about 10 kms west of the German secret installation. Yusuf brought the jeep that Adil had loaned them to a standstill and after the long drive from Casablanca, they were all pleased to be able to jump out and stretch their legs. The countryside around them was deserted. They were the first to arrive.

Maggie and Ron wore black trousers and jerseys while Yusuf had on a dark coloured djellaba. In the back of the jeep were three backpacks containing the equipment they would need for their mission.

It wasn't more than five minutes before a small dust-covered truck pulled up alongside their jeep with Abbas in the driver's seat. Adil opened the passenger door and stepped out raising his hand in greeting.

"Good timing, Adil," said Ron, giving a thumbs up sign. "Are your men here, the ones we need?"

"Hello Ron, Maggie, Yusuf. Indeed, they are here," replied Adil, as he beckoned to the two men clambering out of the back of the truck. He introduced one of them as a mechanical technician and the other as a chemical engineer."

Handshakes and bows were exchanged. Then Ron stepped back and addressed the little group around him.

"Ok chaps, let me recap our plan. Our first strike team is codenamed Sabre. Sabre will consist of Maggie, Yusuf, Adil and me. The second team is Freedom, formed of Abbas who will drive, and two of Adil's men, the technicians. And as for our third team, unless I'm mistaken, I think I can hear them approaching."

In the stillness of the night, a faint thrumming sound could be heard. It grew in volume and was soon identifiable as the beat of horses' hooves on the compacted sand.

A group of four riders came into view and reigned in their horses. As the horses snorted and stamped on the ground, the lead rider raised a hand in greeting.

"Monsieur Ron, we are here and ready to fight," said Hamid with an evil grin. "These are my best fighters," he said, indicating the other horsemen.

Ron gave a brief bow, "Welcome Hamid. We are all here now." He noticed that the riders had brought with them four extra horses. Swapping horses periodically must have made their two-hundred kilometre journey from near Meknes possible. He introduced Hamid to the other teams.

A few days previously, Ron and Yusuf had made the journey to Hamid's camp and had explained to him their plan to neutralise the German poison production site. Hamid had been more than eager to participate in any action against the Nazis.

Ron nodded. "Hamid's team will have the call sign 'Star'. Now here are the walkie talkie units, one for each team. This is so that we can communicate."

Ron handed out a walkie talkie to Hamid and one to Abbas, "Let me show you how these work. Remember only to use our code names when we communicate."

Once the team leaders had grasped how to use the walkie talkies, Ron encouraged everyone to synchronise their watches. He then, once again, ran through the salient details of their plan of attack being careful to emphasise the key times when specific actions were required.

Hamid and his men listened to Ron's instructions with slight impatience. They seemed to view the mission more like a rough night out with the boys and were keen to jump into the fray.

In contrast, Team Freedom which consisted of Abbas and the two technicians, seemed more subdued and the men looked a bit worried. Clearly the complexities of their tasks and the possible dangers weighed more heavily on their shoulders.

Ron's team, which had some experience of this sort of action, seemed calmer and better able to focus on their final preparation.

It was 22.30 hours when the three teams split up and headed out into the dark desert night. The 'Freedom' truck rumbled towards the north-east while the 'Star' horsemen galloped off south-east, between them forming a sort of pincer movement. Meanwhile the 'Sabre' jeep drove due east, on a direct bearing to their target.

After a few minutes, Ron pressed the talk button on his handset to test the comms.

"Sabre calling, Sabre calling, come in Freedom. Come in Star. Do you hear me?"

Almost immediately there was an answering crackle, "Freedom here. We read you loud and clear, Sabre."

"OK, Freedom. Maintain radio silence until required. Sabre to Star, do you read me? Come in Star"

After half a minute, the radio crackled into life.

"Yes, yes Star here. I had to rein in my horse before I could start this telephone," said Hamid with a throaty chuckle.

"OK, teams. Good luck. Over and out," responded Ron before clipping the walkie talkie back onto his belt.

Yusuf kept the jeep moving ahead at a slow but steady pace, carefully avoiding the rocks and bushes that sprang out of the desert gloom in the dim light of the vehicle's sidelights.

New Years Eve at the secret German installation, Wednesday 31st December 1941

A few hours earlier, Major Schmidt and the Doctor had stood by the side of the makeshift runway just outside the poison production camp. Schmidt looked at his watch impatiently, "Fifteen minutes late already. If they leave it too late there will not be enough light for them to make the landing and they will have to divert to Casablanca."

"Hopefully the plane will arrive any minute now, Herr Sturmanfuhrer," answered the doctor scanning the sky to the north.

As if in response they heard the first faint drone of an aircraft engine and then the JU52 appeared as a speck in the sky.

"Did your staff prepare bedrooms for Standartenfuhrer Muller and his staff?"

"Yes, Herr Sturmbannführer. And one for yourself too."

"And I hope they checked the rooms thoroughly for snakes and other venomous creatures."

"Yes, Herr Sturmbannführer. As I told you earlier, the snakes like warm areas and so the beds will also be checked later in the evening."

The doctor had worked out that Schmidt had a fear of snakes, and so he was enjoying playing up to Schmidt's phobia. Ever since Jager's disappearance in the desert, Schmidt had been imagining that he could see a snake under every bush out here in the desert.

The JU52 was now lining itself for the runway and it made a slightly bumpy landing in the failing light. A few minutes later Standartenfuhrer Muller emerged from the plane to be greeted by Schmidt and the doctor who threw him Nazi salutes.

"It's been a long day," said Muller as he walked with his peculiar loping gait towards the camp with the others.

The table in the administrative office had been covered with a white tablecloth and set for dinner. When he had set off from Casablanca, in anticipation of this dinner, Schmidt had brought with him several bottles of champagne and fine French wines.

"A glass of champagne before dinner, Herr Standartenfuhrer?"

"Thank you, Schmidt. And I think a toast, both for the New Year and towards your success here, is in order."

An orderly popped open the champagne's cork and poured the bubbling wine into shallow glasses.

Muller raised his glass to Schmidt and the doctor, "Congratulations on your success in manufacturing Ricin and testing its potency."

"Thank you, Herr Standartenfuhrer. Happy New Year. Heil Hitler!"

Muller had a sip of champagne and sat down before continuing, "On the basis of your preliminary efforts we now plan to expand this operation by ten-fold. Tomorrow I will explain to you exactly how this site is going to be developed both in terms of infrastructure and personnel."

Muller paused for another sip of champagne, "You will be pleased to hear that the Reichfuhrer himself, has decreed that this facility is going to the central hub, from which Ricin will be sent for use throughout North Africa and Southern France."

The doctor nodded vigorously. Schmidt also nodded but looked more circumspect. If he was going to be put in charge of this facility he would have the snakes to contend with here in the middle of the desert.

"But more of that tomorrow," continued Muller, taking a generous sip of champagne. "What is on the menu for our New Year dinner tonight?"

Team 'Freedom' - 2 km north of the German installation,
Wednesday 31st December 1941

Abbas carefully steered the truck which was now some distance north of the German camp. The truck bumped over the rough terrain and its dimmed headlights illuminated the ground that lay before them.

The three men scanned the ground in front and around them as it was illuminated by the dipped headlamps' pools of light and suddenly they spotted what they had been searching for.

"Stop, stop. There it is!" One of the technicians instructed with urgency in his voice.

In fact Abbas would have had to have halted anyway as a thick black pipeline stretched right across the terrain, blocking off their path. The pipe was raised about half a metre off the ground and ran as far as they could see in both directions. In the distance to the right, they could see the lights on the camp's towers.

Abbas killed the truck's engine and turned off the headlights. They descended and approached the pipeline and a careful examination by torchlight followed.

"Iron, probably. I would say one centimetre thick and forty centimetres in diameter," said one of the technicians, tapping the pipe softly with a small spanner.

"More or less what we expected. Ron's description was quite accurate. I can also see that the pipeline is slightly inclined in a north to south direction. No doubt that is to aid the flow of water towards the camp," added the other technician.

"Okay, let's get to work."

The three men hefted down two heavy loads from the back of the truck. The first was a small petrol-fed generator and the other was an electric cutting tool with a circular blade.

They dragged both items over to the pipeline and the cutting device was plugged into the generator while Abbas shrouded the generator under a thick blanket. A starter cord was pulled and the generator chugged into life.

The blanket did a good job of deadening the generator's noise although it still sounded alarmingly loud in the silence of the desert.

Losing no time, one of the technicians hefted the circular cutter, turned it on and applied the blade to the metal pipeline. Sparks flew as metal struck metal, but the cutter blade made rapid progress easily slicing through the iron pipe. As the pipe ruptured, water began to spurt out, though not very forcefully.

As the pipe was cut through further, water from the pipe began to flow more freely into the desert soil. The technicians gave each other a thumbs up sign and they cut the generator motor.

The two men then ducked back into the rear of the truck and brought out a few more items. The first was a circular metal sheet with clamps around the edge.

With the pipe now completely bisected they could push apart the two cut ends and place the circular piece of metal over the end of the pipe through which water was flowing. They tightened the holding clamps and the device capped off the flow to a small trickle.

The technicians stopped to wipe their brows.

"Now for the important part."

One of the technicians picked up another circular metal plate edged with clamps as before. But this plate was slightly different to the first one as it had a fist sized spout welded into its centre.

He carefully clamped this plate to the end of the pipeline that snaked away in the desert towards the enemy camp.

The technicians then uncoiled a hosepipe from the back of the truck - one end of the hosepipe was already attached to a stopcock which led off from a large tank of liquid in the back of the truck. They then carefully fixed the free end of the hosepipe to the spout which now protruded from the metal plate attached to the pipeline heading towards the German camp.

After they had rechecked that the pipe connections were secure one of the technicians climbed back into the truck and opened a lid in the top of the tank of liquid. Using a hygrometer and torch he tested the specific gravity of the fluid inside. Satisfied that the readings were as expected, he nodded to himself before jumping off the back of the truck and gave Abbas a thumbs up sign.

"Everything is in order," he declared. He checked his watch; it was 23.15 hours.

Abbas went over to the front seat of the truck, picked up the walkie talkie, and pressed the speak button, "Freedom calling Sabre. All is ready. We are good to proceed on your command."

The handset crackled and Ron's reassuring voice came through, "Sabre to Freedom. Understood. Stand by for my order. Over and out."

Having given the Freedom team the instruction to stand by Ron recalled the conversation he had over the radio with Mike Brown, the scientist from Porton Down during which Brown had said, "I am pretty certain that the external water supply feed to the factory will have a twofold usage. Firstly, as a cooling agent piped around the distillation chambers, but more significantly for us, it will be used in the emulsification process itself as the Castor pods will almost certainly be emulsified using a solution containing Acetone diluted by water." At this point Brown had paused before continuing, "Now, Sen, here is the important part, so listen very carefully. Acetone is normally an innocuous substance, but if combined with certain other chemicals in the correct concentration it will react extremely violently. One of these compounds is Hydrogen Peroxide."

Back by the truck Abbas put down the walkie talkie, and called out to the technicians. "Let us pack away your tools now. Once our task is done here, we must be ready to flee at once."

As they loaded their equipment back into the truck, Abbas glanced at the yellow hazard label on the side of the tank of liquid. Clearly visible were the letters H_2O_2 - the chemical formula for Hydrogen Peroxide!

Team 'Star' - south of the German installation, Wednesday 31st December 1941

Hamid and his three henchmen galloped in a south easterly direction, followed by the four riderless horses tethered behind them.

After moving at a steady pace for half an hour, Hamid turned his horse due east and it was not long before the tower lights of the German camp appeared in the distance on their left flank.

When the group were roughly a kilometre due south of the camp, Hamid held up a hand and brought the horsemen to a halt.

"We leave the horses here and proceed on foot," he said softly to his team. Pointing to one of his men he added sternly, "You will stay here with the horses. Stay alert and watch for our return. If I catch you asleep, I will make sure that you sleep forever!"

The man nodded vigorously and busied himself with securing the horses.

Hamid then spoke to the other two men, "Check your weapons but remember we can only use the rifles as a last resort, if we have been discovered. We must approach the camp in complete silence, make any noise and I will personally slit your throats. Our target is on the south side of the camp."

Hamid slung a rifle over one shoulder and a cloth bag over the other. He pointed a finger forward and the three men melted into the darkness, stealthily moving toward the lights in the distance.

When they had come within a hundred metres of the camp Hamid held up a hand and dropped to one knee. He took a pair of binoculars from his bag and scanned the area ahead. The spotlights on the towers illuminated the buildings well and so Hamid quite easily spotted what he had been looking for - the glint of a long metal pole rising from the roof of one of the smaller buildings.

He beckoned his henchmen to draw near and spoke in a whisper, "That hut over there is our target. We may encounter two or perhaps three men inside. No more, I think. We must act swiftly before anyone raises the alarm."

The two henchmen nodded and drew their daggers from the sheaths tied to their belts.

The trio moved forward in a crouch. As they neared the hut, it was obvious that the metal pole rising above it was a wireless aerial. Hamid nodded at his men, confirming they were at the correct location.

Suddenly a searchlight from the tower on their left swung around and panned across the desert. It illuminated the wireless hut for a brief moment and the three men quickly pressed themselves against the wall of the next hut, to avoid being caught in its beam.

The searchlight then moved to a static position over the central area of the camp. Hamid nodded to his men and they crept round to the side of the wireless hut, where they could see a couple of steps leading up to a door.

Hamid reached the door and tried the handle on the door. It was locked. He knocked on the door sharply.

"What is it?" asked a voice from inside in German.

"Message from the officer...." replied Hamid in a gruff voice, also in German.

He heard a chair being pushed back and the sound of a key being turned in the lock. Before the door was opened, Hamid slammed the door into the person behind it, knocking him flat and in a flash the three Arabs were inside the hut.

The man that Hamid had pushed over was lying on the ground clutching a bleeding nose. Another man wearing headphones sat at a desk behind a couple of large wireless radio sets. He had turned in his seat towards the door, a startled expression on his face.

Hamid and his men said nothing but wasted no time executing their task with brutal efficiency. They clearly had much practice. Their daggers sliced across the throats of the two wireless operators, silencing them permanently.

While his men moved the two dead soldiers to one corner of the hut, Hamid examined the wireless equipment. Remembering Ron's strict instructions, he first located the main switch and turned both sets off. He then pulled off the wire mesh covers and gently, and as quietly as possible, he used his rifle butt to smash all the glass vacuum tubes inside.

Hamid nodded to his men and pointed to the door. At that moment the searchlight moved over the hut, briefly illuminating part of the interior through a window. The men dropped to the floor and waited in silence realising that they would certainly have been spotted if the door had been open when the beam of light had passed over the wireless hut!

A couple of minutes passed, then Hamid gave the signal and swiftly led his men out of the hut and into the desert. They moved away rapidly and were soon at a safe distance from the camp.

"Good work," said Hamid with a gleaming smile showing crooked teeth. "It was time we gave those Nazis a taste of their own medicine."

He then pulled out the walkie talkie from the cloth bag over his shoulder.

"Hello, hello, Star team here. Are you hearing me, Sabre?"

He heard the sound of static, but then a familiar voice came through, "Sabre here. I read you, go ahead Star."

"All is done as you wished, Sabre. But I fear it may not be long before it is discovered."

"Okay, Star. I understand. Now get to your agreed position. Over and out." AS Ron put down his walkie talkie he checked his watch. Its luminous dial read 23.30.

Hamid switched off the walkie talkie and replaced it in his bag. He signalled to his men and the three of them continued to move briskly away from the camp in the direction of their companion and their horses.

Dinner at the secret German installation, Wednesday 31st December 1941

Schmidt thought that the evening dinner with Standartenfuhrer Muller was progressing well. Despite the wild location of the plant, the cook had managed to produce an excellent carrot soup, followed by well-proportioned and nicely grilled steaks served with accompanying vegetables.

"You do well for yourselves out here in the middle of the desert, Schmidt," said the Muller, taking a sip of the St Emilion red. "And I must say that your wine cellar is splendid."

Muller was looking relaxed. He had loosened his tie and unbuttoned the top button of his shirt. As he leaned back in his chair the stylised entwined oak leaves on his jacket lapels caught the light from the single candle on the table.

Schmidt replied, "Yes, you are right about being in the middle of the desert, Herr Standartenfuhrer. There is nothing and nobody around us for miles. As you are aware no one, not even the Vichy French, know that we even exist!"

Muller picked up his knife and fork and returned to his steak, "I will speak to you more about this tomorrow with details, but as you already know the Reichfuhrer has given instructions for this plant to be immediately developed." He turned toward the doctor and pointed at him with his steak knife, "You, Herr Doktor, will have an important role here along with other scientists who will join you."

"Thank you, Herr Standartenfuhrer," replied the doctor.

"And you, Schmidt have shown considerable organisational skills and so you will be in overall control of the plant."

"Thank you, Herr Standartenfuhrer. It will be an honour to serve the Reich in such an important role," said Schmidt while internal cursing. He had been hoping beyond hope that Muller would announce plans to bring a technically qualified person in to run the plant and that he would be able to return to Casablanca.

The doctor, who had drunk a bit too much red wine than he should have, felt emboldened enough to be mischievous and play on Schmidt's phobia of snakes. "Herr Standartenfuhrer you may not be aware that this location is also infested by venomous snakes. Perhaps, in addition to Ricin, we can experiment with the extraction of toxic snake venom?"

Schmidt cast the doctor a dagger glance. He mentally decided that very soon he would have to put the doctor in his place in no uncertain terms. But for the moment, he restricted himself. "Herr Doktor, you should concentrate on your current work and allow high command to make the strategic decisions," he said sharply.

"Venomous snakes? Which types?" asked Muller, his curiosity raised.

"Oh, there are various varieties. Cobras, vipers, adders. All with highly poisonous bites," replied the doctor adding to Schmidt's rising discomfort.

As Schmidt seethed internally and contemplated how he would deal with the cheeky doctor, his eyes glanced up at the clock on the far wall. It read 11.30pm.

Team 'Sabre' on the move, Wednesday 31st December 1941

The spotlights on the towers lit up the camp brightly and from a distance it all looked quite jolly. One almost expected to hear the strains of some funfare music in the air and perhaps the sound of laughter.

The four prone figures lying in the shadows some distance away had no such illusions and were fully aware of the evil purpose of the place.

Ron raised his head and using the night goggles, slowly scanned the landscape, tracking across 180 degrees. At one point he stopped and let out a deep breath. Finally, he put down the goggles and spoke softly to the others beside him, "Spotted something that I didn't count on. An aircraft. Must be a landing strip on the far side. No matter, we can deal with that later if need be. Let's crack on with our plan as scheduled."

Ron checked his watch. "Right, it is 2340 hours, we aim to be at the rendezvous point by 00.10 hours at the very latest," he whispered, Freedom and Star have done their bit and now it's time for us to do ours. As planned, we go one at a time, less chance of being spotted than if we move together. Keep your eyes peeled for guards."

Ron tapped Yusuf on the shoulder, "Your targets are furthest away from the searchlights, but still make sure you keep in the shadows. Good luck."

Yusuf moved forward stealthily and circled the camp to the left, as he had been instructed. He reached the eastern perimeter and edged towards the building in front of him. As he moved, he kept a wary eye on the two searchlights on the towers on either side.

Once Yusuf reached his destination, he crawled under the pre-fabricated building which was raised on concrete blocks. He heard voices above his head and surmised that this must be some sort of recreation area or dining room. Then, unzipping his backpack, he pulled out a block of plastic explosive which he moulded around a floor girder.

As he reached into his backpack again, he recalled Ron's instructions, "Use the 40-minute fuses first. Then as you work your way around, use the 35 and 30-minute fuses."

Holding a tiny pencil torch between his teeth, Yusuf armed the explosive with a 40-minute fuse. He then crawled to the next building on his right. More plastic explosive and a 35-minute fuse this time.

Meanwhile the others had now reached the southern end of the camp. Ron had peeled off and snaked his way towards the buildings there and was mimicking Yusuf's actions, on the southern side of the camp.

As Ron was fixing the explosives Adil and Maggie spotted the glint of light on metal, it was heading their way from around the buildings. It was not something that they had expected - a patrolling guard!

They sank deeper into the desert sand. Adil gestured to Maggie to stay down and then, after he waited for the guard to pass by them, drew a dagger from his belt and crept up behind the man. The guard was taken completely by surprise when a large, calloused hand covered his mouth. Adil's dagger flashed twice and the man collapsed to the ground without a sound.

Maggie crawled her way to Adil who was wiping his bloody dagger on the soldier's tunic. "We have no time now, Adil. In a few minutes the guard's absence will be noticed. Let's get on with dealing with vehicles which are parked next to that building on the right," she said in an urgent whisper.

Adil nodded in agreement. Though seemingly outwardly unruffled, Maggie hoped that when Ron returned, he would realise that something had made them decide to set off and deal with the vehicles while he had been away. If necessary, he would make his way back to the rendezvous point alone.

As they entered the camp's perimeter, they could see there was a parked staff car, an open topped vehicle and an armoured car with a mounted machine gun. From her backpack Maggie removed a bag containing thick greasy rags. She handed Adil a handful and moving from vehicle to vehicle, they stuffed handfuls of the rags deep down each of the exhaust pipes.

She sighed with relief when they had finished their task, but as she hefted her backpack over her shoulders, they heard a shout of alarm and the sound of running boots. The dead guard must have been discovered!

A searchlight swung about violently, light snaking about the camp and before they had time to seek the shadows it had illuminated them, blinding them with light. A voice from the tower shouted an alarm and a soldier with a submachine gun at the ready ran towards them.

"If you move or attempt to escape, I will shoot you!" shouted the German.

They put up their hands and waited. The soldier pushed them forward towards the central square, his gun aimed at them the whole time.

Alerted by the commotion, a few more soldiers emerged out of the building at the far side of the square and a corporal moved forward, drawing out his pistol and taking command.

"Ah, what have we here, perhaps saboteurs? Who are you?" he asked roughly.

Maggie stood her ground and said nothing.

The sergeant continued, "A beautiful fraulein with a Berber out here in the middle of the desert. Who are you? Where are your companions?"

Maggie remained silent. Adil squared his shoulders and answered in a loud voice.

"There is no one else with us, sir. I am a local guide and am accompanying this Swiss lady to Oujda."

"Then why have you entered our camp?" asked the corporal harshly.

"Our car broke down some distance away. There was no alternative but to start walking. Seeing bright lights up ahead we came here seeking help. We had no idea that this was an army base. I swear it."

The corporal seemed unconvinced and walked around Adil and Maggie, examining them closely. "An unlikely story. You are both dressed all in black like assassins!" He then barked out an order to one of his men, "Open their backpacks and let me see the contents."

Two soldiers stepped forward and grabbed Maggie and Adil's backpacks. They pulled open the zips and tipped them out onto the ground in front of the corporal.

Meanwhile, twenty metres away in the desert gloom Ron had observed what was unfolding in the camp and could hear the exchange between Adil and the German. His brain raced. He picked up his walkie talkie and pressed the speak button.

"Freedom team, Sabre calling, Release the chemical, I repeat release immediately," he whispered with urgency in his voice.

Back in the camp the German corporal poked his boot at the contents of Maggie and Adil's backpacks which were now lying on the ground before him.

"Knives, rope, survival rations," he shouted. "Why are you carrying these things? You are both spies. Let me ask you again, where are your accomplices?"

There was no reply and so with an impatient snort he raised his pistol and pointed it at Maggie's head.

"I give ten seconds to talk, or I shoot!" He shifted the grip on his Luger, "I am counting."

Ron heard these words and reacted immediately. He flung his backpack, pistol and walkie talkie as far as he could into the desert scrubland and then raised himself up and walked towards the camp with his hands raised in the air.

"Don't shoot," he called out as he walked out from the shadows and into the brightly lit central square.

"Ah, it appears that I was correct, you do have companions after all," said the corporal grimly. He lowered the Luger that had been pointed at Maggie's head and barked an order to his guards.

"Take these three spies to the officers' dining area. I have no doubt that Sturmbannführer Schmidt will wish to interrogate them immediately.

As they were led in the direction of a large building on the far side of the camp Ron spoke softly to Maggie and Adil in Arabic, "Be ready to act when the opportunity arises. Follow my lead."

The 'Freedom' team reacts, Wednesday 31st December 1941

Abbas's walkie talkie had crackled to life before the expected time.

Ron's whispered voice had an urgent tone to it, "Freedom team, Sabre calling, Release the chemical, I repeat release immediately."

Abbas reacted immediately, "Freedom team, here. We will release the chemical immediately, Sabre."

In the darkness of the desert around them Abbas gave the technicians hurried instructions and they quickly ran to the truck and turned open the stopcock on the chemical tank. Immediately the hosepipe filled with fluid and with a gurgling sound the fluid snaked its way into the metal water pipe.

The hydrogen peroxide entered the now empty metal water pipe and flowed down the slight incline in the pipe. As more and more hydrogen peroxide was pumped into the pipe the fluid's speed of travel increased from what would initially have been walking pace into a run and then much faster. The hydrogen peroxide sped along the pipe heading in the direction of the poison plant.

In under five minutes the chemical time-bomb had reached the last sections of the water pipe and was now entering the secondary pipe leading to the factory building. Once in the building the chemical entered yet another feeder pipe leading to the acetone reservoir located under the emulsification chamber.

Team 'Sabre' held at the secret German installation, Wednesday 31st December 1941

Schmidt had pulled out all the stops to ensure that Standartenfuhrer Muller had a pleasant visit to the camp. They had finished their steaks and were now consuming a cheese board accompanied by vintage French cognac.

A few minutes earlier they had heard some commotion outside and the doctor had reassured Muller and Schmidt that it was nothing important.

"Herr Standartenführer, please do not alarm yourself. The men are probably celebrating New Year's Eve and also, some of the men here are also rather shell shocked from their recent battles in Libya and this makes them more edgy. Plus, they are probably quite excited because of your high-profile visit. Now, please do try the cognac, it's the best available in all of France."

Muller took a deep sip and nodded at Scmidt, "Excellent cognac, Schmidt."

There was a knock at the dining room door and without waiting for a reply the door opened and a corporal appeared looking flustered. He clicked his heels and gave a Nazi salute.

"Herr Sturmbannführer, excuse me for interrupting your meal but there is an urgent matter that needs your immediate attention." He turned and beckoned through the open door.

Ron, Maggie and Adil were pushed into the room by the armed soldiers guarding them.

The sergeant continued, "We found these three lurking around the camp. They were carrying knives and ropes in their bags. I suspect that they are spies or assassins and have come to attack our installation."

Schmidt, Muller and the doctor swivelled round in their chairs with startled expressions on their faces.

"Why have you brought them in here, you idiot?" roared Schmidt. "You should have held them and set out a protective ring around the camp!"

"What is this all about? Assassins? How do they know I am here," asked Muller in a worried tone. "Schmidt, what is going on? What is this about?"

Schmitt rose to his feet, "Leave it to me, Herr Standarterfuhrer, I will soon find out."

Schmidt, half-drunk from all the champagne, wine and brandy that he had consumed, got to his feet. He saw this as an opportunity to demonstrate to his superior officer his competency in handling an unexpected situation.

He marched up to where Ron and the other two were standing, "Who are you and who sent you here?"

Ron smiled and replied. "We are employed by Sultan Mohammed. We mean you no harm, I can assure you. After all, if we did, why would we have brought a woman with us?"

"Do not play games with me," shouted Schmidt. "Speak the truth or I shall shoot you, one by one."

To reinforce his words, he drew his pistol out of his holster and pointed it at each of the three prisoners in turn.

Ron smiled again, "It is the truth I assure you." Whilst trying to stay calm on the outside was anything but. The thought of the suicide pill hanging around his neck suddenly flashed through his mind.

Schmidt had heard enough. He strode up to Adil staggering slightly and without another word raised his gun to Adil's head and shot him through the side of the head.

Maggie shrieked as Adil fell to the ground with a thud, a pool of blood slowly forming around his head. Ron wrapped his arms around Maggie. Looking at Schmidt he spoke softly in German, "You bastard!"

Schmidt smiled evilly, "So you speak German now." He walked up to Ron and Maggie and now raised his Luger to point at Maggie's head but before he could say another word a soldier burst through the door, panting. He spoke in a frantic voice, "The wireless operators!" He panted. "I just went to relieve them in the wireless hut and found them dead and the wireless sets have been destroyed!"

Standartenfuhrer Muller rose from his chair, his voice trembling as he screamed at Schmidt, "What is happening, you imbecile. Take control!"

Schmidt shook his head in disbelief, took a deep breath and swung to face Ron and Maggie. He spoke menacingly, "Tell me everything or the woman will be the next to die…"

The laws of chemistry prevail, Wednesday 31st December 1941

At first as the hydrogen peroxide entered the acetone reservoir it gently mixed in with the acetone, but then as more and more of it entered the reservoir the character of the mixing process began to change. Rather than just mixing gently the fluids now began to churn and bubbles erupted with a hissing sound.

As the chemical reaction between acetone and hydrogen peroxide increased apace, trimers of triacetone triperoxide built up and the pressure in the reservoir began to increase. The iron clad reservoir and then the entire metal chamber above it began to vibrate and shake but the vibrations, if anything, only seemed to accelerate the entire process and the clamps and bolts on the iron chamber began to lift and dance under the pressure. Then as the energy in the reservoir built up even further there was a flash of light within the mixture!

**New Year's fireworks,
Wednesday 31st December 1941**

As Schmidt raised his Luger to Maggie's head, she heard a rumbling sound which within a second increased in intensity and she felt the floor below her feet begin to vibrate. It was as if a locomotive train was heading on a course directly towards her. She saw an intense flash of light from outside the window followed a millisecond later by a violent explosion. As if in slow motion the blast blew out all the room's windows and then all the glassware, crockery, cutlery and food lifted off the table and flew across the room followed by the furniture which flew up and then crashed about in all directions.

"Hit the deck, Maggie!" yelled Ron, pulling Maggie to the floor.

As she went down Maggie noticed Muller rising from the table and staggering about trying to extract a steak knife which had flown off the table and embedded itself into the side of his neck. Schmidt had received a face full of flying glass. Then all the lights went out.

The blast had not taken Ron completely by surprise. From the time he had ordered the Freedom team to release the chemicals into the pipeline, he had been mentally expecting an explosion to occur. Despite his anticipation even he was surprised at its intensity and violence.

While confusion reigned in the darkness, Ron grabbed Maggie by the hand and pulled her towards the door. Outside it had gone pitch black but thanks to Maggie's mock-up model of the site, they both had a good mental picture of the camp's layout and before the bewildered Germans could recover and even register what was happening Ron and Maggie were racing diagonally across the central square, past the wireless hut and out into the desert. As they ran, a white flame shot up from the laboratory building's chimney and fire was rapidly taking hold across its roof. Most of the laboratory building's walls had been blown out by the force of the blast.

Ron quickly brought a compass out of his pocket and looked at the luminous dial. "South is that way. Let's scarper!"

The aftermath of the New Year's fireworks, Wednesday 31st December 1941

Schmidt raised himself gingerly off the floor, his ears ringing from the sound of the explosion. Pieces of glass and debris fell off his tunic as he stood up unsteadily and he could feel shards of glass in his face. Someone had switched on a torch and was waving it around in a haphazard manner.

"Herr Standartenführer, where are you?" asked Schmidt. Receiving no reply, he shouted to the soldier bearing the torch.

"Hey, you with the light! Shine it over here."

The beam of light steadied and moved across the floor towards Schmidt. Then the light stopped and illuminated a body lying in front of him. Schmidt could see from the tunic insignia that it was Muller and he realised why Muller had not responded to his call.

Muller's face was a bloody mess. The torch light glinted off a dagger-like shard of glass which protruded grotesquely from one eye socket, deeply embedded into his skull. A steak knife stuck out at an angle from one side of his neck. There was no sign of any movement.

Schmidt shook his head in disbelief, quickly checked himself for injuries but found nothing beyond cuts and bruises although he could feel blood trickling freely down the side of his face. Crunching through glass, he strode over to the man bearing the torch and raised his voice in an effort to take command.

"Everybody who can walk, get outside, now! We must quickly capture the spies to prevent any other attack. The wounded can be attended to later. Go!"

A soldier and the corporal stumbled out of the mess building and into the central square which was now partially illuminated by the flames rising from the manufacturing laboratory.

The blast had brought the rest of the camp out of their barracks and some soldiers were hastily buttoning up their tunics.

"Did you see the intruders escaping?" Schmidt barked at the soldiers.

One man stepped forward, "Yes sir, I was at the barrack window when two figures dressed in black ran across the square." He pointed towards the south, "They went in that direction, past the wireless hut."

"We will follow and catch them. They are on foot. To the cars now! Move you idiots!" shouted Schmidt, striding to the vehicle parking area.

Ignoring the blood which dripped down his forehead from a deep head wound the corporal sprang into action. He marshalled a few of the soldiers together and led them to the vehicles while ordering the rest to form a defensive cordon in the camp.

The corporal and Schmidt leapt into the staff car, whilst the soldiers climbed into the other two vehicles.

Meanwhile, about half a kilometre south of the camp, Ron and Maggie were jogging over the dark scrubland. Behind them they could hear shouts and knew that the Germans would be coming after them.

Then Maggie's shoe found a rock partially concealed in the sand and she stumbled and fell flat onto the ground. Ron quickly lifted her to her feet.

"Are you OK?" he asked worriedly.

"I think I may have twisted my ankle," said Maggie.

"We have to keep going, Maggie," said Ron, putting an arm under Maggie's shoulders. "Lean on me," he said as they moved forward at a walking pace.

Back at the German camp the drivers of the three vehicles revved their engines. The corporal driving the staff car pulled into the central square, manoeuvring the car to point in the direction of the prisoners' escape. Schmidt yelled at the other vehicles to follow him.

The staff car shot forward and then after a few yards, lurched to a halt. Schmidt fumed and slapped the corporal across the back of his head.

"Come on, you idiot. Get this car moving. Now! I command you!"

What Schmidt did not realise was that the armoured cars behind him had also both stalled. Maggie and Adil's sabotage had done the trick in nobbling all the Germans' vehicles!

Meanwhile to the south, as Ron helped Maggie hobble along they had heard the cars start up, and then that the engines had stopped. Ron gave Maggie a squeeze.

"Well done, my darling!" he whispered.

After a few more minutes, coming through the darkness to their right, they heard the sound of a horse's soft whinnying. They headed in that direction and soon located Yusuf, Hamid and his men who had been waiting for them along with the extra horses.

"Good to see you both. But where is Adil? Is he on his way?" asked Yusuf, with concern.

"Sorry. I'm afraid Adil is dead. He was killed by that swine Schmidt. I'll tell you how it happened later but now we must make haste. Let us get going," replied Ron, his voice sharp with urgency and tension.

Ron lifted Maggie onto a free horse and then swung himself into the saddle of another. He nodded at Hamid.

Hamid raised his arm and was about to make a forward sign, when they heard a huge explosion come from the direction of the German camp. A few seconds later this was followed by another and then another.

As the timers triggered the plastic explosives the buildings in the camp blew up one after another throwing debris and flames high up into the air. The searchlight towers came crashing down, the aircraft on the runway was on fire and within a few minutes the whole camp was ablaze - one great burning globular mass of fire.

Ron, Maggie and the others stared at the scene. They had not expected this scale of destruction and neither could they comprehend that they had been responsible for it!

Without a word Hamid pointed in the direction south-west and dug his heels into his horse's flanks. With the others following, he galloped away into the desert night.

A parting of ways,
Thursday 1st January 1942

As the horses sped through the night, their hooves left a cloud of invisible dust behind them. Ron glanced over his shoulder and in the distance could see the glow caused by the inferno of the burning German site. He looked to his left and gave Maggie a grim smile. She responded with a nod, as if to reassure Ron that she was doing okay, and her injured foot wasn't too bad.

The group navigated their way to where they had parked the jeep and they reigned in their horses. Abbas and the engineers had already arrived, and their truck was standing alongside the jeep.

The riders dismounted with Ron helping Maggie to the ground. He put an arm around her and lifted her into the back of the jeep where she collapsed gratefully onto a padded seat and stretched out her legs.

"Ron took a quick look at her ankle with his torch. "A bit swollen but nothing seems broken, old girl. I'll be back in a few minutes. I need to have a word with Hamid and the others before they leave."

"Thank them all for me, darling. They all put their lives on the line and worked brilliantly," replied Maggie.

Hamid's men had gathered their horses together and were feeding them apples and water from large goatskin flasks.

Ron approached Hamid, put his hand on Hamid's shoulder and looked him in the eye, "Well done my friend. We could not have done this without your assistance. You and your men played a vital part in making our plan a success. I will forever be in your debt."

Hamid grinned and raised his hands expansively, "You are welcome. And look at you, you are more like us than any Englishman I have ever met. This expedition has been invigorating. My men and I are happiest when we are out and about doing men's work."

Ron laughed, "Well it has been good knowing you, my friend Hamid. I don't know if our paths will cross again. But England and I give you our deepest thanks."

Hamid stepped forward and embraced Ron in a bear hug.

"God be with you, Ron," said Hamid. "Who knows what fate may hold. Perhaps some years ahead you may be back to visit us and will sing us more songs. And maybe even enjoy lying with the lovely Rachida."

Laughing loudly at his own joke, he stepped away and beckoned to his men. They mounted their horses, waved farewell to Ron and the others and galloped away in the direction of Hamid's camp, towards Meknes.

When he could not see them anymore Ron lowered his arm and slowly walked over to the truck where Abbas and the two engineers were waiting.

"A good night's work, you both executed the technical part perfectly. It is just so sad that Adil is not with us to savour this victory."

One of the engineers spoke, "Indeed, Adil would have been proud to have known that we struck such a telling blow against these invaders of our country."

The other man added, "We will ensure that Adil's memory is never forgotten. The freedom movement will continue in his name."

"He is a true hero," Ron responded. "My country will certainly recognise his sacrifice and will honour him in his death. But please remember that until our battle is won the details of our mission must always remain confidential. It would be detrimental to Morocco and your freedom struggle if the Germans were to find out the truth of how their plant was destroyed."

The two men solemnly nodded their heads and gave their word. Ron shook their hands and bid them farewell.

Abbas and the engineers climbed aboard the truck and Ron watched as its tail-lights disappeared into the distance.

Ron walked over to the jeep where Yusuf and Maggie were waiting, swung himself into the passenger seat and looked over at Yusuf, "It has been a long and eventful night. Let us hope that we have a peaceful journey back to Casablanca."

Yusuf turned on the engine, put the jeep into gear and pulled away into the desert.

.

A gathering back in the safe house, Friday 2nd January 1942

It was afternoon when Ron and Maggie met up again with Yusuf at the safe house in Casablanca. They had arrived back from their mission in the early hours of the morning and had grabbed a few hours of well-deserved sleep.

Ron and Maggie's emotions were a mixture of elation and tension. Elated at having successfully carried out their mission but tense at the thought of any reprisals which may follow. They had no way of knowing if any of the Germans had escaped from the explosions at the poison plant.

Yusuf was, as usual, inscrutable and calm. He brewed tea for them all, and then busied himself in setting up the wireless and aerial, ready for Ron to make contact with London.

Soon the wireless was switched on. The speaker crackled into life as London came on over the airwaves. Ron picked up the microphone and asked for Greaves-Mortimer who was connected immediately. It seemed that he must have been waiting for their call.

"Headmaster here. Go ahead Sabre. Go ahead." said Greaves-Mortimer. His voice sounded unusually strained.

"Sabre to Headmaster. The Ivy has been pruned. I repeat, the Ivy has been pruned," responded Ron.

"Good man! Has the pruning been fully effective, Sabre?"

"Affirmative, Headmaster. The Ivy can no longer flower or flourish. But it's unclear if any of the insects within it survived."

"Understood. Well done to you Sabre and your fellow gardeners."

"Roger, Headmaster. Any further instructions?"

"It is now imperative that you and your associate now return to the motherland immediately. I can arrange a rendezvous with Nautilus tomorrow at 23.00. The usual location. Would you be able to make that?"

"Roger, Headmaster."

"Good luck then, Sabre. Godspeed and over and out."

Ron replaced the handset and switched off the wireless. He looked up at Maggie and Yusuf.

"Well you heard that, the directive from London was clear. Maggie and I must leave Morocco tomorrow night."

Yusuf nodded his understanding. Maggie was used to the itinerant life of an SOE operative, but after having spent over a year in Casablanca, this still came as a surprise.

Ron added thoughtfully, "We knew that the destruction of the poison plant had to appear accidental with no trace of Allied action. I guess it's no surprise that London wants us out of sight tout suite."

"I'll get packing at once, Ronnie," Maggie said.

"Just one bag of personal stuff Mags. Yusuf will have to take care of your apartment, car and so on," replied Ron.

Ron turned to Yusuf, "Also we must inform Avraham about the destruction of the German plant since the poisoned water supply directly concerns his community. Take a message to Avraham, informing that the source of the poison that was contaminating their well water has been located and eliminated. I do not have to remind you to tell him that this is strictly confidential and for his ears only." Yusuf nodded his understanding as he silently packed away the wireless set. He knew that he was going to miss Maggie and Ron.

Farewell to friends at the synagogue, Saturday 3rd January 1942

Ron and Maggie's time in Casablanca was now rapidly drawing to an end. The previous day Yusuf had informed Avraham about the destruction of the poison plant. Avraham had been ecstatic and had replied with a message insisting that Ron and Maggie meet with him and the elders for a special farewell at the synagogue before they depart.

At first Ron had been reluctant to accept the invitation, he would have preferred to have lain completely low until their departure. However, when Yusuf told him of this Avraham had been insistent that Ron and Maggie must make one last quick visit to the synagogue. He had solemnly promised that the elders would only be told that their water supply had been restored and had pledged that details of the poisoning and of the elimination of the manufacturing plant would go no further than himself. Given all these assurances Ron and Maggie finally agreed to visit the synagogue one last time.

It was midday when Maggie and Ron arrived at the synagogue in the old Citroen. When they entered the synagogue's walled courtyard the assembled Jewish elders were all present. The elders all rose to greet them and then each individually came over to shake their hands.

Once they were all seated Avraham rose to his feet and addressed them, "Ron and Maggie, our friends," he said. "On behalf of our community here we bid you farewell and Godspeed."

The elders all nodded vigorously in agreement.

Avraham continued, "For three centuries we have lived peacefully in this land. But, from time to time, because of our faith, we have faced hatred, prejudice and violence. Now these are especially hard times. Our community is facing a new kind of terror, one which is planned and organised and we thank you for standing by us and feeling our pain."

The Elders all nodded in unison again.

"Ron and Maggie, we hope that one day, when all the madness of this war is over, you will both return to Casablanca. On that day it will be our privilege to welcome you back. Shalom."

Later as Avraham escorted Ron and Maggie out of the synagogue he shook their hands again and said quietly, "My friends, once again I thank you from the bottom of my heart. You have, quite literally, saved all of our lives!"

Sultan's Private Offices. Dar-al-Makhzen Palace, Sunday 4th January 1942

Sultan Mohammed raised his head from the pile of papers on his desk, as his Vizier, Karim Halimi, was ushered into the Sultan's office.

"Ah, Karim. Thank you for coming." He gestured to a side table, "Some tea and dates?"

Once the tea had been poured and they were comfortably seated the Sultan broached the subject which was on his mind.

"What is this news of an explosion in the middle of the desert? Have you heard from Adil Al-Bakar?"

The Vizier raised his eyebrows and sighed, "Sadly, your Majesty, the news is that Al-Bakar was killed. By the Nazi's. The reports from his men confirm what was originally suspected."

"Which is that the Nazi's were illegally and secretly producing poison and polluting the wells in Casablanca's Mellah," said the Sultan.

"Exactly so. But as we know the plot was discovered by a British agent, you know the same Indian one who attended your banquet disguised as a Jewish leader," said the Vizier.

The Sultan nodded, "Yes, and we had heard from our sources that he, along with a British woman and Al-Bakar were planning to mount an attack on the Nazi factory."

"That is correct, your highness. And the news is that they were successful in destroying the factory."

"The Nazi's secretly came into my country, built a factory illegally from where they manufactured a poison to be used on our citizens! How could they have even dared to think of doing this!" said the Sultan with disgust.

The Vizier added, "The Nazi's also did this under the very noses of the Vichy French, your majesty. My sources tell me that even the Vichy General Nogues had no inkling of what the Nazi's were up to."

The Sultan shook his head in disbelief, "I was aware that the Nazi's had no scruples, but their contemptuous attitude and their behaviour has no place in our land."

"I agree, your Majesty," said the Vizier.

The Sultan looked into the distance for a few seconds, then nodded his head firmly as if to signal that he had just reached a decision. "Karim, through your contacts you may now inform the Americans that they will have my complete support should they stage an invasion. Inform them that when the time comes, I shall instruct my administration to assist their landings, I will also order our Gourmiers to stand down."

The Vizier bowed his head in assent, "It will be done, your Majesty."

"It would also be useful, when the time is right, to allow the information of the Nazi poison plot to be filtered through informal channels to the Vichy authorities. This may change Nogues mindset as regards the Nazis. No one takes kindly to duplicity."

"Yes, your Majesty."

"And ensure that the family of Al-Bakar is rewarded and that his memory is honoured."

"Of course, your Majesty."

"And also send the two British agents my gratitude on behalf of my country."

"Yes, your Majesty."

Memo from SS HQ, Berlin, Sunday 4th January 1942

To: Acting SS Kommandant, Morocco.

From: Office of the Reichfuhrer, Berlin.

Subject: Poison Production Programme 71. Morocco.

As you are aware there was recently a major incident at the Ricin production plant (Programme 71) in NorthEastern Morocco which led to the complete destruction of the plant. As far as is known there were no survivors yet identified. Unfortunately, Standartenfuhrer Muller, who was on an inspection of the plant at the time of the incident, is believed to be among the fatalities.

Due to the remoteness of the plant, it has been difficult for our forces stationed in Algeria to perform a detailed assessment of what caused this incident. Although sabotage cannot be entirely excluded, our preliminary investigations lead us to believe that the incident was probably due to a major chemical explosion related to the facility's water-cooling systems which were known to be erratic.

The high command has concluded that Ricin production in such a remote area, is too hazardous an operation. The alternative option of developing such a facility within a Moroccan city is not politically viable. Therefore, the

Reichfuhrer has decreed that the entire Ricin production project should be withdrawn henceforth.

You will shortly be receiving details of the replacement for Sturmbannführer Schmidt who we understand was also killed by the explosion at the plant.

Heil Hitler!

A final journey to Fedala Beach, Tuesday 6th January 1942

It was ten o'clock in the evening when the Citroen left Casablanca, travelling north on the coastal road. Abbas was driving, with Maggie sitting next to him while Ron was scrunched up on the back seat, fighting for space with two bags.

Ron glanced over his shoulder, and through the rear window observed a motorcycle tailing them. Although he knew that it would be Yusuf, who had insisted on coming along, he still felt a momentary pang of anxiety at being tailed given all the recent events.

It wasn't long before they reached a clump of trees, by the side of the road close to Fedala beach. The little convoy pulled off the road and stopped in a sheltered spot under the casuarina trees. The luminous dial on Ron's watch read half past ten.

Ron pulled the bags out of the Citroen and slung his duffel bag over his shoulder. Maggie gingerly alighted, not wanting to put too much weight on her recovering ankle, and did the same with her bag.

Maggie turned to Yusuf and Abbas. "The time has come to leave you both," said Maggie. "You have been brave companions and my brothers during my days in

Casablanca. I thank you from the bottom of my heart." She joined her palms together and bowed.

The two men placed a hand over their hearts and bowed in response. "We have been honoured to work alongside you. May God keep you safe in your travels, dear Maggie and we look forward to the day when you may return," said Yusuf with a smile. Abbas nodded in agreement and added, "We leave you in Ron's safe and loving care."

Ron stepped forward, "In my short time here, we have been through much together, my friends. I could not have asked for two better men to fight at my side. Thank you."

Ron embraced the two men briefly and then turned to Maggie, "Time to get our skates on, old girl. Let's get cracking."

"We will wait here until we know that you have been safely picked up. God be with you," said Yusuf with a final wave.

Ron and Maggie pulled the hoods of their djellabas over their heads and without looking back slowly picked their way over the rocks towards the water's edge.

There was no moon in the sky and the ocean looked pitch black. Then at exactly 23.00 hours, three quick flashes of light were visible from the darkness of the sea. Maggie had her torch at the ready and answered back with three flashes of light. A further three flashes returned from the sea.

"Right, they know we are here," whispered Maggie and Ron signalled his approval with a thumbs up.

Ten minutes later, they heard the gentle swish of oars in the water and from the gloom a dingy emerged. A rope was thrown onto the shore and Ron tugged on it, and pulled the dingy up onto the beach. Two sailors jumped out and Maggie moved to Ron's side to meet them.

"Flight Lieutenant Sen, I presume?" asked one of the sailors.

"Yes, and Flight Sergeant Yeomans too. Good to see you chaps," responded Ron.

One of the sailors took Maggie's bag and tossed it into the dingy. The sailor then turned and held out a hand to help Maggie climb aboard who, despite her strained ankle, had already nimbly vaulted onboard and was giving Ron a hand to scramble over the side.

The sailors settled into their seats, taking an oar apiece. The dingy moved away and out to the submarine waiting in the darkness.

As the dinghy moved smoothly across the water, Ron looked back to shore and imagined he could see two djellaba clad figures standing under a clump of casuarina trees raising their arms in a final gesture of farewell. Away in the distance, he saw the flickering lights of Casablanca.

A pint at the Hare and Hounds, Thursday 8th January 1942

The sun was just rising when Ron and Maggie arrived at Portsmouth harbour. After two nights at sea in a submarine, it was a relief to be back on dry land. They still had to find their sea legs as they caught a train to London.

As Ron and Maggie were now SOE operatives, they were no longer assigned to regular RAF bases and so Ron had suggested that Maggie come and stay with him at his little flat in West London. Maggie readily agreed to this offer as, apart from wanting to be with Ron, it would have been impractical for her to return to her family home which was in a village near Doncaster up in Yorkshire.

They reached Ron's flat in the afternoon and gratefully dived into bed for an afternoon snooze. They awoke a few hours later and made slow and passionate love. It was such a relief to finally know that they were now safe at home and were free from the constant underlying niggling anxiety that a knock at the door may be unfriendly.

Once they had showered and dressed in casual but warm clothing, Ron suggested going out to his local pub for a pint and something to eat.

At the Hare and Hounds, a few of the regulars recognised Ron. Clearly, he was a popular chap.

"Hey Ron, where have you been hiding, old mate?" asked one.

"Just in time to buy us a drink, Flight Lieutenant," joked another.

"And who is this lovely lass on your arm?" enquired a third.

Ron shook hands all round and introduced Maggie. He shouted out to the barman, "Drinks all round for this scruffy bunch. And I'll have a pint of your best bitter and a pink gin for my lovely lady."

The drinks arrived and after much clinking of glasses together, Ron and Maggie retired to armchairs in one corner of the pub. An open wood fire burned and crackled. cosily against the winter chill outside and as they stretched out their legs toward the fireplace they smiled at each other, luxuriating in the warmth of both the fire and their intimacy.

The atmosphere was just right for what Ron had in mind. Ever the romantic, Ron was not one to miss the opportunity to inject an element of extra theatre and so he stood up from his chair and then dropped down on one knee by Maggie's chair.

He looked deep into her eyes, "Maggie, you are the light of my life, my raison d'etre and I hope that you will agree to be my wife."

Maggie responded by reaching out, holding Ron's face between her hands and then covering every square inch of it with kisses. Still holding on she replied, "Of course, my darling, of course!" She then looked at him quizzically, "But what took you so long to ask?"

Ron's friends at the bar had spotted what was happening and as Ron stood up, the group burst into a spontaneous rendition of 'For they are jolly good fellows'! This was then followed by a loud round of applause as glasses were raised and toasts made to the newly engaged couple.

It was almost midnight when Ron and Maggie finally returned to the flat and collapsed into bed. It had been a long, tiring and very eventful day.

A meeting with the Headmaster, Thursday 8th January 1942

The next morning, Ron and Maggie made their way to Whitehall where they had an appointment with Greaves-Mortimer.

"Good to see you both. Capital work! Absolutely top notch!" said Greaves-Mortimer enthusiastically, as he greeted them.

"Thank you, sir," responded Ron and Maggie in unison.

"Do sit down and grab a cup of tea. By the way, this is my chief of staff, Major Smith."

Ron and Maggie sat down and took the offered cups of tea.

For the next few hours they then proceeded to provide a detailed account of all the events that had occurred in Morocco. Locations were marked on maps, and they were quizzed about many of the local aspects surrounding the mission.

When the debrief seemed complete, Ron added, "Sir, I'd like to mention something personal if I may?"

"Of course, Sen. Go ahead," said Greaves-Mortimer.

"Well, Flight Sergeant Yeomans and I have just become engaged to be married."

Greaves-Mortimer smiled and lifted an eyebrow, "My word! My congratulations to you both," he said with a smile. "So, the mission has had considerable fringe benefits for you both, shall we say." He reached his hand out to shake theirs, in turn.

"Thank you, sir," responded Ron. "And we have a request."

Greaves-Mortimer raised his eyebrow again and nodded for Ron to continue.

"In view of our new relationship, Maggie… err… Flight Sergeant Yeomans and I would understandably like to stay together, by which I mean work together, on our next mission, if that would be possible."

"Ah… I see, I see," responded Greaves-Mortimer thoughtfully. "Well actually there are plenty of opportunities for a couple of operatives to work together in France. A married couple sometimes provides quite a good cover." He paused, "Or there could be something else further afield, which has just landed on my desk. Given your background it may actually work well. How would you feel about returning to India, Sen? The situation in India and Burma is getting hotter especially with the Japs advancing. We could do with a small undercover team on the ground there."

"Thank you, sir. Would it be alright if we think it over and give you an answer within a couple of days?" asked Ron.

"Of course, you can," replied Greaves-Mortimer.

They shook hands and left. As they walked out into the cold winter's day Ron took Maggie's gloved hand in his and gave it a gentle squeeze.

An evening at the Savoy, London, Saturday 10th January 1942

To celebrate their engagement, and their safe return from Morocco Ron and Maggie had decided to spend an evening in style at the Savoy's American Bar.

Ron was dressed in a dark three-piece suit with a bright pink cravat around his neck while Maggie wore a dark green satin dress embellished by a matching feather fascinator and elbow length white gloves. As they entered the bar several heads turned in admiration.

They were ushered to a quiet table to one side of the American Bar which was kitted out in black and white in an art deco style. A jazz musician sat playing soft music at a white grand piano.

They ordered dry gin martinis - straight up with an olive and as they waited for their drinks the musician crooned the latest song from Hollywood:

"And when two lovers woo
They still say "I love you"
On that you can rely
No matter what the future brings
As time goes by."

Then, once their drinks had arrived, Maggie said. "Now, I have a proposition, Ronnie."

"I'm all ears, Mags."

"When we saw Greaves-Mortimer yesterday, he suggested that we may fancy a joint transfer to India as a team of two. You remember he said that the SOE urgently needed agents there especially as the Japanese are knocking on Burma and India's doors." She paused before continuing, "So how about taking that up and starting our next adventure there?"

"India, Burma, Timbuktu - as long as I'm with you, Mags, I'll go anywhere." Ron paused, "But you do realise that it's quite a different world in India though."

"Which is exactly why I'm suggesting it, darling!"

"Then, of course, I'm with you. India it will be!"

"Are you quite sure?"

"Mags, I could think of nothing I would love to do more, than travel to India with you. I could show you around the country of my birth and you could meet my family!"

Maggie smiled, "I'm already excited at the prospect, but let's double check that with Lady Luck. Shall we see what she thinks about all of this as well?"

She reached into her small handbag, rummaged around and pulled out a silver dollar coin. "Heads for India?" she asked.

Ron smiled and nodded, "Whatever you say."

Maggie tossed the coin and caught it expertly on the back of her gloved hand. Together they peered at the coin sparkling against the white of Maggie's glove. Heads!

"So, you see, fate also seconds our decision," said Ron.

"Aha! But before you put your trust in fate, Ronnie, I suggest you first examine my coin," said Maggie, handing him the silver dollar. Ron looked at the coin and turned it over. It had a head on both sides!

"In our lives, darling, remember that we shall always make our own destinies, together," said Maggie.

Ron lifted his Martini glass to his lips. He then looked straight into Maggie's eyes over the frosted rim and said, "Well, as they say in the states 'Here's looking at you, Mags'!" He smiled and gave her a wink before leaning over to kiss her.

Authors note: a postscript

Although the characters of Ron and Maggie and the Nazi poison plot are all fictional this book includes reference to many genuine and fascinating events which took place in Morocco during WW2.

When France fell to Nazi Germany, Morocco - one of France's colonies, came under indirect Nazi German control. As in the southern half of France, Morocco was administered by the Vichy French authorities. The Vichy administration of Morocco was headed by General Nogues who is referred to in this book. Sultan Mohammed V, who appears prominently in this book, also played a role in the country's governance especially as the local Moroccan population bore strong allegiance to him.

Sultan Mohammed is held in high esteem by historians for his principled position in attempting to protect Morocco's sizable Jewish population from Nazi and Vichy anti-Semitic laws. He is on record as announcing in public that regardless of their faith all Moroccans, Muslim and Jews alike, were all equally his citizens.

At Churchill's insistence the United States invaded Morocco in 1942. The invasion from the sea which began on the 8th of November 1942 was code named Operation Torch with amphibious landings made at various coastal locations and these included Safi and Fedala. Both these coastal towns appear in this book. Safi is one of the sites Ron and Maggie reconnoitred and recommended as a potential invasion site. In reality these and other landing sites were also identified by Allied spies based in Morocco.

The first few days of Operation Torch involved fierce fighting and there were many casualties. Then, with Allied troops at the gates of Casablanca, General Nogues, head of the Vichy administration in Morocco, agreed to a surrender. More than that, he also switched sides in support of the US and the Allies.

Sultan Mohammed, who had been in secret negotiations with the Americans well before Operation Torch, directed his regional governors and the troops under his authority to stand down and not resist the US invasion. In return for his support the Americans had promised to promote the Sultan's desire for Moroccan independence. Unfortunately, despite US pressure, when the war ended this promise was not honoured by the French. Moroccan independence finally only came in 1956 after a major armed insurrection by Moroccan Nationalists.

Casablanca in 1941 was heaving with European refugees desperately trying to flee to America in order to escape from Nazi persecution. The iconic Hollywood film Casablanca which was released in November 1942 immortalises their plight. In this book you will have noticed that we have made several nods to this classic film. Casablanca was a hotbed of spies during these early wartime years and so Ron and Maggie would not have been alone there, engaged in daring exploits!

Printed in Great Britain
by Amazon